NEVER
BEEN
BETTER

NEVER BEEN BETTER

A NOVEL

LEANNE TOSHIKO SIMPSON

G. P. Putnam's Sons
New York

PUTNAM
— EST. 1838 —

G. P. PUTNAM'S SONS
Publishers Since 1838
An imprint of Penguin Random House LLC
penguinrandomhouse.com

Library of Congress Cataloging-in-Publication Data

Names: Toshiko Simpson, Leanne, author.
Title: Never been better: a novel / Leanne Toshiko Simpson.
Description: New York: G. P. Putnam's Sons, 2024. |
Identifiers: LCCN 2023051721 |
ISBN 9780593714782 (trade paperback) | ISBN 9780593714799 (ebook)
Subjects: LCGFT: Novels.
Classification: LCC PR9199.4.T676 N48 2024 |
DDC 813/.6 — dc23/eng/20231103
LC record available at https://lccn.loc.gov/2023051721

Printed in the United States of America
1st Printing

Title page art: Ocean sunset © piixypeach / Shutterstock
Book design by Alison Cnockaert

To my obachan, who continues to visit me
on the days where I need it most.

NEVER
BEEN
BETTER

1

"CRAZY IN LOVE"
—BEYONCÉ FT. JAY-Z (3:56)

WHEN MY INVITATION for Matt and Misa's destination wedding arrived in the mail, Tilley pinned it to the dartboard in our kitchen.

"'Accept with pleasure or decline with regret,'" she snorted as she read. "Why is there never a check box for 'drain the open bar with relative apathy'? Especially if they're not even giving you a plus-one."

She yanked a couple of darts from the board and took five steps backward, bumping into the kitchen table. Narrowing her eyes, she whipped a single dart at the wall, then turned to me, noticing my pursed lips. "Are you okay?"

I surveyed the damage. My sister had punctured the palm tree crest, but the perfectly staged photo of Matt and Misa on the invitation remained intact. Burly in an ink-blue suit, Matt had his arms wrapped around Misa, who was beaming in a blush satin dress. She glanced over her shoulder at him with a warmth that made me think of breakfast in bed, shared bottles of dinner wine, joint bank accounts—all the things I could barely imagine for myself.

"He looks like he's going to absorb her," murmured Tilley, suddenly beside me. "Like a matrimonial sponge."

"It's fine," I said a little too loudly. "I'm fine. I knew this was coming. I have prepared myself for this moment for months. Actually, excuse me because I have to go do this thing in the bathroom."

I could feel the bad thoughts coming, so I panicked and deeply bowed at Tilley before speed-walking out of the kitchen and down the hall to our shared bathroom. *Keep your cool. Keep your cool.* I slammed the door just as I heard Tilley let out the largest sigh known to humankind. Ignoring her clomping footsteps coming toward me and the waterfalls building in my eyeballs, I scrounged through the medicine cabinet for a very old bottle of Listerine. Hands shaking, I poured a full serving into the lid, then scrunched my face as I tipped the shot of antiseptic into my mouth.

Tilley knocked on the door. "Dee, can I come in?"

"Nrghh," I said, swishing furiously. The mouthwash burned and my eyes teared up, but it felt good to control the discomfort. I spat into the sink, stuck my tongue out, and poured another capful.

"Okay, so I mostly asked if I could come in to be polite, but you know I had to take the lock off the door after the last incident," Tilley continued. "So, I'm going to come in now, and I want you to promise me that you're not doing anything . . . you know, suicide-y?"

I swished faster in defiance. "Nrghhh, nrghhh!"

Tilley swung the door open and bashed me with it as I stuck my arm out to hold it shut. I couldn't manage a mouthful of chemicals and a bruised elbow, so I turned and spat into the sink again. Tilley stared at the open bottle of Listerine, then back at me, and folded her arms.

"What?" I said. "Can't a girl value good dental hygiene?"

"Tell me you're not doing some weird self-punishment thing right now."

"I don't know," I said, sticking my head under the tap for a quick drink of water before elaborating. "I was trying to frame it like exposure therapy. Like maybe I'll handle the wedding better if I get really good at being uncomfortable."

"Dee, you met these people in a psych ward," she said into the mirror, examining her nose pores. "I think between the three of you, you've already got the uncomfortable thing covered."

I opened my mouth to retort but nothing came out. It had been many months since my discharge, and I still didn't know how to tell Tilley that I'd never been more at home than in the hospital with Matt and Misa.

She watched my shoulders droop in the reflection of the glass, then turned and threw her arms around me. "Hey. I'm not saying it's a bad thing," she mumbled into my shoulder. "You'd have killer small talk for cocktail hour."

"Who needs it?" I said, gently disentangling myself from her grasp. "I'm sure everyone will be busy gossiping about the whirl-wind engagement."

"I guess there's no established pipeline from involuntary commitment to marital commitment, especially in the span of a single year."

"Most of the guests only know half the story," I said. "Misa didn't even tell her family where they really met."

Tilley arched an eyebrow. "So you're just going to show up as a physical manifestation of their biggest secret?"

I gestured helplessly toward the bottle of mouthwash. "Like I could even make it through the flight without having a total breakdown. I want to be there for them. And, you know, be half-way normal. But I don't know if I have it in me."

"If you're not well enough, they'll understand better than anyone," she said, her voice softening just a touch.

"It's not that," I said, pouring one last cup of Listerine for good measure. "It's just that I'd rather shave off my eyebrows than watch Matt Costigan marry someone else."

As the final shot of noxious mint hit the underside of my tongue, I couldn't help but notice Tilley's pained expression in the mirror—as if she too was battling both gingivitis and certain heartbreak.

ℳ

HERE ARE FIVE good reasons why I—and not Misa—should have ended up with Matt:

1. Dibs.

Not to brag or anything, but I wound up in the psych ward first. On night one, Matt rolled into the hospital with bandages wound around his forearms and a crooked smile that lit up the ER. Ruggedly handsome and built like a teddy bear, he wore two hospital gowns tied together at the waist for comfort.

"I'm making a fashion statement," he said when he noticed me staring from the cafeteria. He was the first shiny thing I had seen in such a long time, and I wanted to scoop him up like a magpie, take him back to my depressing white hospital room.

2. We can laugh about anything . . .

"What are you in for?" I asked, like I was auditioning for *Prison Break.*

"I decided to play my last live show yesterday," he replied breezily. "Only problem is my band interpreted *last* as 'hang up your guitar' and not 'slice yourself open after the encore.' Bit of a miscommunication on my part, I guess."

I nodded emphatically. "Semantics, am I right?"

3. *But still get to the heart of a conversation.*

I told Matt how I threw myself—winter coat and all—into the swimming pool where I taught little kids how to blow bubbles just to see if I would sink. "I only did it because I thought I was immortal," I explained.

"Well, I don't know about that," he said, his eyes crinkling. "But you must be pretty tough to wind up here the first time and put a good spin on it. That's a different kind of endurance, if you ask me."

4. *We've always made a great team.*

"Lucie does the best bloodwork, but Marc does a mean Robert De Niro impression," Matt explained as we sprawled across the common room sofa. "So, it's all about what you want out of your tax dollars."

"You sure know your way around here," I said.

He grinned wryly. "I guess you could call me a repeat customer. The last few years haven't been the easiest." He scratched at one of his bandages. "You know, the first time I landed here, I thought this place would change my life. That it would be some symbolic turning point. But after this many failures, I guess it just feels like I need to shake it up somehow."

"Maybe now's your chance," I offered, and his eyes met mine.

"Why not?" he said. "We've got nothing left to lose."

5. *He can make me feel at home, anywhere.*

That first night, he walked me to my room and leaned against the doorway.

"So, you got any breakfast plans?" he asked.

I laughed. "I could squeeze you in before group therapy."

Matt surveyed the sterile decor of my dorm and gave a low whistle. "Nice place you've got here. The bars on the bed are a real homey touch."

"It's been a long time since I slept somewhere other than home," I admitted. "I'm a little nervous about it."

"Don't be," he said. "This is the best part of the whole day. No one's watching you or analyzing your next move. You just get to feel what you feel for a little while." He doubled-tapped the edge of my door, then shot me an encouraging grin before heading toward his own room. I watched him walk away, holding on to every snippet of our conversation. But the warmth that I felt that night, and every week we spent together after—it never quite seemed to fade, even when I needed it to.

∽

TILLEY AND I reconvened in the living room, sinking into the comfort of our couch. A few streets away, our parents were toting a Tupperware packed with cabbage rolls over to a harvest potluck with some of the neighbors. They didn't gather for the food, even though the Johnsons made the best sweetbread on the block and Mrs. Sato's chow mein was the stuff of legends. Everyone just liked to complain about how the neighborhood was changing—the bungalows getting knocked down for gray mini mansions, longtime families moving out at a record pace to districts you couldn't even get to without a car. I noticed it too—the last time Tilley and I climbed the roof of the local grocery store with a six-pack of beer, we discovered that someone had destroyed the couch that we had hauled up there to watch the sun set. It's a story I would have told the whole backyard congregation, had I been invited. But ever since my late-night sit-in on the highway overpass when Matt and Misa got engaged, my dad preferred that I steer clear of the neighbors. My sister and I were lucky to still be in the neighborhood at all—Tilley had nabbed this subleased bungalow through a friend of a friend, and she was letting me live here out of the goodness of her heart (and the steadiness of her waitressing paycheck).

With an impeccable sense of balance earned from years of serving patrons at Scarborough's favorite sketchy sports bar, Tilley carried bottles of cheap prosecco and Fanta plus two glasses to the TV table. She motioned for me to shove over and we settled in front of the screen, a reality show about drunk people on yachts filling the background. Outside, we could hear the kids across the street playing basketball, the murmurs of their trash talk punctuated by the occasional yell for a pass.

"I appreciate that you're trying," said Tilley, topping up my orange soda with prosecco. I glared at her and she tilted the bottle more, rolling her eyes. "But I don't think you can mouthwash away your problems. Even though I give you ten out of ten for creativity."

On-screen, a yacht honked its horn as it floated past a lush and empty island. "What else am I supposed to do?" I asked. "My doctor thinks I'm a drama queen. Mom and Dad are ashamed of my existence. I'm too broke to get a proper therapist—"

"Or to pay me back your half of Mom's birthday mani-pedi—"

"Exactly," I said, waiting for the fizzing to subside. "I've been trying my best, and the last thing I need is a calendar hold for the worst day of my life."

"At least you got an invite," said Tilley. "It's almost like they care about you or something."

I knew I was lucky to have an anchor of a friend in Matt, and in my better moments, I was grateful to be on the receiving end of Misa's protective nagging. But these days, that wasn't the kind of care I craved. Sure, having friends who understood your manic episodes and medication shakes and general malaise was great. It just didn't change the fact that at the end of the day, they also had this whole life together and I was stuck with Tilley, a sister with the gravitational pull of Jupiter. All I wanted was to find my own corner of the universe.

"I'm just saying, if I could have pegged anybody for a psychiatric meet-cute, it would have been Matt and me," I grumbled. "We were great, just the way we were."

"You mean deeply depressed?"

"I mean real as hell with each other," I said. "And then Misa showed up and everything changed."

The first time I saw Misa, she was standing in the ward hallway, swathed in a wrap dress that was definitely dry-clean only. I appreciated that she had put makeup on to come to a psychiatric hospital. Only the best for Scarborough's best-kept secret. Beside me on the couch, my ward neighbor Harsha sucked in her cheeks like a kid with a helium balloon. "That girl is so pretty. I bet she's a model too. Models just recognize other models sometimes, you know? It's like a sixth sense."

I didn't have much of a sixth sense, but even I could tell that the dynamic was about to shift as Matt rose to greet Misa. Her warm smile and quiet confidence made it suddenly feel like she was welcoming us into her home, even though we'd been there first. Harsha and Matt were immediately mesmerized, and I wondered if a few weeks alone with him was enough of a head start to make a lasting impression. The thing is, I think I wanted Misa to like me almost as much as I didn't want Matt to like her.

Tilley cleared her throat loudly, trying to keep me from drifting away. "If you'd like to be 'real as hell' for five seconds, can we just remember that this is the same 'great guy' who got you kicked out of the hospital in the first place?"

I tried to focus on the bubbles rising to the top of my glass, the sleek sounds of a perfume commercial flashing across the television, the angular tilt of Tilley's cheekbones—something to keep me fixed in this moment. But as usual, nothing could suspend that gnawing feeling in the pit of my stomach that accompanied the memory.

The day I got kicked out of the hospital, Matt sat with me in the common room while I waited for Tilley to pick me up. Down the hall, doctors cycled in and out of patient rooms with a briskness that matched the sterile decor. This was an ongoing theme—no one here wanted to touch us, but a few of us definitely wanted to touch each other. We heard the cafeteria window clank shut to announce the post-breakfast lull. The television was blaring a nature documentary on penguins, but the ward's longest-running patient, Jermaine, was fast asleep in his favorite armchair. He had been in and out of the hospital for years now. I wanted to wake him up to say goodbye, but he didn't need to be reminded that he wasn't getting out anytime soon.

I checked my hastily packed gym bag for any missing toiletries, the worn leather of the couch clinging to the backs of my thighs. In a final act of defiance, I had decided to keep my pajama shorts on for my grand exit, even though I could see muddy snow through the blinds, spattered across the parking lot below. The nurses exchanged snooty glances behind the protective glass of their surveillance station, but I kept my focus out the window, on the combination Tim Hortons–Wendy's restaurant across the street. Separated from us by keycard locks and suburban traffic, its neon sign shone like a beacon of hope for us psychiatric travellers. Matt and I had talked about it almost every day since our arrival, an obsession compounded by the terrible hospital food.

"When you get out of here," I said to him, leaving out that my departure—much like my arrival—was involuntary, "we're getting some goddamn Frostys."

I didn't want to think about Misa, or Jermaine, or Liz, or Harsha, my friends still trapped in hospital purgatory. I didn't want to think about the ward like a suburban bed-and-breakfast, where someone else would be lying miserably on my freshly bleached sheets, counting ceiling tiles until it was time for group therapy. I wanted it to be like the end of Die Hard, where the whole place becomes a bonfire and it's the best damn Christmas you ever had. Then I thought about how Die Hard had like seven sequels, so it's really not a bad analogy for psychiatric recovery as a whole.

"Sure thing, Shawshank," said Matt, his usual cheerfulness betrayed by the dark circles underneath his hazel eyes.

"Just don't forget about me now that you're a big shot who can wear your own clothes."

"Wouldn't dream of it," I said, and he flashed me his lopsided smile. My heart jumped and I tried to take it all in one more time—the antiseptic smell of the hospital, the view of the strip mall across the street, Matt's unshaven jawline looking wild and rusty under the fluorescent lights.

He scratched at his beard and I wondered if he was thinking about the night before. "If all goes well, I'll be out of here in a week or so," he added, and I wanted to believe him. But what he didn't say was that a week in ward time could somehow contain an eternity. How, here, relationships moved at light speed, built on the shared understanding that you were learning to survive a world that wasn't built with you in mind. I stared hard at the Wendy's, willing my body inside it. Matt noticed my uncommon silence and wrapped an arm around me. I breathed in a little too quickly, then sunk into the warmth of his thick shoulder.

"C'mon, Dee, you got this," he said. "You gotta stick it to those doctors and walk out of here with a shit-eating grin across your face. That's how you win today."

I blinked back tears. "It doesn't feel like I'm winning. It feels like I'm just as sick as I was when I got here, and now I'm going to be alone."

"You won't be alone," he promised, his voice low and hurried as a doctor stalked past. "Call me at the pay phone every day. Misa too. What else will we be doing? Macramé?"

I had told Misa I was leaving in the cramped quarters of our shared bathroom. At one point during our stay, we had swapped supplies to try to re-create that unfamiliar hotel toiletry feel, laughing at how L'Occitane and Dollarama soap were all just the same when you're depressed. She tried to keep her composure as she carefully packed up my shower gel and two-in-one shampoo, but I could tell that she was uncharacteristically shaken. "I'm going to miss you," she said, so quickly I could have missed it. We gazed at each other, saying nothing at all, and I wondered what her and Matt would be like without me here. We weren't allowed to come visit after discharge, although that wasn't usually an issue for most people. I wouldn't miss the bureaucracy, the surveillance, the feeling that we'd been contained for the protection of others. But maybe the craziest thing about me was that I didn't want to leave.

"You guys don't need to worry about me," I said to Matt, stifling a jab of anxiety in my chest.

He pulled me in closer. I could smell the cedarwood bodywash Tilley had brought him from the pharmacy downstairs. Jermaine snored and tossed in his chair, and I wished that we could say goodbye somewhere else, somewhere I might be braver. "Dee, I'm always going to worry about you," he said. "So you might as well get used to it."

My heart flickered but I couldn't find the words to carry the current forward. Instead, my playground instincts kicked in, and I punched him in the arm. "Matt, if I can adjust to antipsychotics, I can adjust to anything."

He snorted. "They should have quoted you instead of Wayne Gretzky on the hallway whiteboard."

"Yeah sure," I said. "That's when I'll know I've really made it in this world."

Matt stood up so abruptly that I fell into the arm of the couch. "Wait here," he said, then strolled out the door of the common room.

I've never been one to take instruction well, so I tossed my gym bag beside Jermaine's nap chair and followed Matt into the hall. When I turned the corner past the nurses' station, he was busy wiping the hallway whiteboard clean.

"Get out of here, lady!" he drawled like he was in some 1930s Western. "Save yourself! Don't come back for me!"

I gasped. "Is that a Sharpie? They're going to kill you!"

He uncapped the black marker and scribbled, If I can adjust to antipsychotics, I can adjust to anything, *as I watched in horror and admiration. He signed the addition with a single D, then stood back to admire his handiwork, beaming at me. "There," he said. "You've made your mark. Now it's time to get the hell out of here."*

"I don't know if I'm ready," I said into the floor.

Matt grabbed my hand and squeezed. "Do you trust me?"

"Always."

"Then believe me when I say that you have always been ready to face what's in front of you," he said roughly, and my heart lifted. "You're a goddamn survivor, Dee. Don't you forget it."

☙

HOW COULD I not love someone who believed in me that much? "It was my fault too," I said to Tilley, downing half my drink to numb the impact. "And of course, we can always give a little shout-out to the deeply flawed psychiatric system for their share of my trauma—"

"Amen."

"But you're right, when I left the hospital, that's when everything went wrong," I said. "That's how they ended up together."

"Uh," said Tilley, "are we not going to talk about the night you broke the rules so hard that your doctor didn't even put you in day treatment and your life basically became a Slip 'N Slide of bad decisions?"

I wouldn't have called it a Slip 'N Slide—maybe more like Snakes and Ladders. When Matt and Misa got engaged a few months ago and everything spun out of control, I decided to go cold turkey off my antipsychotics, Matt's whiteboard scribbling long forgotten. That night, I wound up contemplating life and death on a highway overpass, prompting unwanted visits from the cops like they were suitors calling on an eighteenth-century debutante. By the end of that month, I was receiving messages through my alarm clock, boiling twelve eggs at a time, and pulling petals from the flowers that Tilley brought home and pressing them between the pages of dictionaries for good luck. But even after Tilley convinced me to start taking my medication with a nightly banana and helped me get a part-time job that kept my brain from spiralling, one thing never changed: Ever since I met Matt, I felt like any path in the world would lead me back to him.

"There was something between us," I said. "There's no way he didn't feel it too. But all the time they spent in day treatment changed everything. After two months alone with Misa, he graduated the program with a laminate certificate and a five-year plan that suddenly didn't include me. It was the perfect crime!"

Tilley kicked her feet up on the couch as she watched two crew members make out in a lifeboat. "For someone who has actually done a bunch of sketchy stuff while manic, you do not seem to have a very good understanding of what a crime is."

She paused to pull a rogue lipstick out of a crack between the cushions, pulling the cap off to trace her puckered lips with a deep burgundy stain. "Also, I think it's hard to root for a relationship that has never seen the light of day because you're too scared to tell a giant man-child how you feel."

"It's not that easy," I said, snatching the lipstick from her fingers and applying it to my own chapped lips. I caught a glimpse of my tired face in the window's gleam. As expected, the color looked better on Tilley. Younger, blonder, and with 50 percent less regard for humanity, she was an upgraded version of me—Tilley would have thrived equally on *The Bachelor* or *Man vs. Wild*. "With the ward, everything existed between us in this safe, vacuum-sealed space. It's a big deal to let this kind of stuff spill over into the rest of your life."

Tilley put her glass down, leaned over, and wiped a smudge underneath my bottom lip. "Which is why Misa wants to keep the ward a secret, I guess."

"It's not the same," I argued. "I'm not ashamed of how we met. I think what the three of us have is really special and amazing, and if Misa can't acknowledge that, I don't think she's meant to be with him. That's all."

"So what are you going to do about it?"

"Nothing." I sighed. "Matt's going to marry Misa, who is an actual functioning human, and as usual, I'm falling behind. No need to add insult to injury and watch them tie the knot."

Tilley grinned at me. "That's a remarkably mature decision for someone who still orders Happy Meals regularly. Don't let this go to your head or anything, but I'm proud of you. For once, you're doing the right thing."

I thought about the worried crease that would form between Matt's thick eyebrows when I declined, the slight exhale he makes when he's trying to hide his disappointment. The pit in the bottom of my stomach opened up again, swallowing all the what-ifs that I'd finally be letting go.

"I think I might be becoming an adult or something," I said finally, raising my Fanta in salute.

Tilley grinned and clinked her empty glass against mine. "I'll believe it when you start paying rent."

2

"WATERFALLS" —TLC (4:40)

THE DAY AFTER my heart-to-heart with Tilley, the wedding
invitation took a premeditated fall into a garage sale shredder, but I
couldn't bring myself to tell Matt and Misa the bad news. Instead, I
directed all of their worried phone calls to my voicemail, convincing
myself that by the time I told them I'd be a no-show, they'd be too
busy with floral arrangements and cake tastings to care. I swallowed
my guilt and tried to carry on with the life that Tilley had helped me
scrape together—a dog-walking gig that let me dictate my own
hours and not interact with actual humans, monthly appointments
where my psychiatrist pretended to listen to me, the rare but perfect
evenings when Tilley didn't have to work and we could spend hours
rewatching nineties rom-coms. Sometimes on Sunday mornings,
she'd try to convince me to visit our parents, but even months after
I moved out, we never seemed to know what to say to each other. On
those days especially, it felt like I was spinning in place. Sure, Tilley
was pleased that I wasn't getting any worse under her watchful eye,
but if I wasn't getting better either, what did it matter?

Two months later, I found myself in the bathroom helping Tilley try on a black vintage corset for a date. She dug her thumbs into her sides and sucked in as I yanked at the laces just above her hips.

"Pull tighter! I'm trying to snag a future lawyer here."

I gave the laces one last heave with everything I had, which wasn't much since my diet is 30 percent off-brand Kraft Dinner. But I knew tying up my sister's weird lingerie was much lower on the scale of sibling martyrdom than visiting a psychiatric hospital every day.

"Will you be around when I get home?" she asked, watching herself toss her hair in the vanity mirror.

"I don't know, Til," I said, trying to maintain tension in the strings while tying an awkward bow. "I've just had so many social obligations lately."

"Maintaining perpetual victimhood must be so exhausting for you," said Tilley.

I tugged at the bottom of her corset and smirked back at her reflection. "It's the first full-time job I've been able to hold down."

On cue, Tilley's grimy Samsung sprung to life with a tinny rendition of "Call Me Maybe." I groaned, prepared to witness another transactional phone conversation between Tilley and her merry band of men from the pub, the grocery store checkout line, the run-down cemetery down the street. Honestly, she could pick up a man on the moon at this point.

"Helloooooo," sang Tilley. She glanced at me, listened for an uncharacteristically long time, then frowned. "Yep, hold on a second."

She thrust the cracked device in my face. "It's for you," she said. "Misa."

"Tell her she has the wrong number," I whispered, trying to wrap the phone in a bath towel. I thought I had taken every precaution to avoid contact, but I forgot that Tilley is the kind of person whose daily activities often hinge on calls from strangers.

"Oh, honey," said Tilley. "You think she wouldn't recognize this sultry voice?"

I made eye contact with myself in the mirror, hoping I could summon the strength to survive a conversation that would confirm that I was, in fact, a bad person. Instead, I noticed that my afternoon pajamas were misbuttoned, so I gave up and took the phone. "Hi, Misa."

"Hello, Dee," she said cheerfully. I could picture her sitting in her obachan's kitchen, a gleaming pen at hand in case she needed to take notes or start sketching to relieve the pressure in her brain. My ears yearned to hear the shuffling of her grandmother's slippers, a homey sound I'd grown accustomed to. "I've been meaning to talk to you."

"Good thing we're on the phone, then." I immediately wanted to walk off the edge of a cliff.

"We missed you at the fall fundraiser for the hospital," she said lightly. "I was hoping we'd be able to celebrate the six-month anniversary of our little support group, but I'm sure we'll get another chance soon."

My gut wrenched in guilt. "I didn't realize you'd want to remember that," I said. When we got out of the hospital, I left a bunch of bad Google reviews and Misa joined the junior fundraising board, carefully neglecting to mention the part where she had been a patient. I knew she was trying to make a difference, but on some level, it felt like a betrayal of what we had come to understand about the system.

"Of course I would," she said, then briskly pivoted to the elephant in the room. "Now, I know you've been extremely busy—"

I cringed. Most of my free time had been taken up by a surprise Neopets resurgence.

"But I hope you can join us for the wedding. I know you can get a bit overwhelmed by travel, so if you need help booking, I'm more than happy to assist." Misa lowered her voice like we were planning a heist. "I'd much rather use my frequent flyer points on you than on a discount air purifier."

"I can do it myself," I said, more loudly than intended. I shot a guilty look at my sister and mumbled into the phone. "I mean, if I can even come. I don't know yet."

"Excuse me?" Tilley flung a makeup sponge at my head from the corner of the bathroom. I ducked her and pressed the phone back up against my ear.

"I understand," Misa replied, then paused. I could hear the crinkle of a chip bag, a sure sign that the wedding planning was getting to her. When she was stressed, Misa could huff Doritos like it was nobody's business. I hoped she wasn't getting orange fingerprints all over her notebook, which could send her into a secondary spiral. "I know it's more difficult, especially given what I've told—or haven't told—my family. It's just . . . I don't know if this changes anything, but it really wouldn't be the same without you."

I wasn't used to Misa being direct about what she wanted. Usually the ask was well disguised, like deep-fried tofu. But this was a big one. We both knew that my presence would threaten the fairy-tale wedding that Misa had planned under her mother's watchful eye, that I was a living reminder of what she'd rather sweep under the rug. This ask wasn't just for my presence—it was also about my tactful silence. But in that moment, I realized that if the situations were reversed, I would have wanted her there too.

"Let me think about it." I sighed. "Things have been"—I chose my words carefully, not wanting to sound like I had been drowning for months—"exciting. You know, my work is picking up, I subscribed to this new astrology app, I might want to go back to college eventually . . ."

"That would be huge for you," Misa said eagerly, and my spiteful brain zoned in on that tiny, additive *for you*, like she knew we'd never find ourselves on the same footing. "Do you have to update your resume? If you do, I can help you with the design. We can make an afternoon of it."

Suddenly, the future I had been promising myself felt ten stories tall. Misa loved solving problems, and here I was, yet another problem to solve. The only casualty, as usual, was my own confidence.

"I can't," I said, my voice flattening by the second. "I have to go."

"Dee," she pleaded. "I didn't mean to put pressure on you. Can you please just hang on a second, I promise—"

"I have to go," I repeated before hanging up, my chest collapsing in on itself.

Tilley dropped the eyebrow pencil she was holding to wrap her lanky arms around me. "I mean, you didn't cry," she crooned into the top of my head. "It's basically an improvement."

"Don't be nice to me out of pity," I wailed.

"This isn't me being nice to you. That part comes after, when I ditch my date to take you for ice cream."

My phone buzzed, and I wriggled my way out of Tilley's grasp to check an incoming text message.

"Oh great," I said. "I hang up on Misa and suddenly Matt decides he's coming over. Can you believe they're tag-teaming me?"

Tilley frowned. "I can't believe Matt would dare show his face around here. Do you think it's too late to install a snake pit in the front lawn?"

We didn't end up having time for loose reptiles because, moments later, our neighbor's beagle howled at a heavy knock at our door. Running a brush through my hair and rebuttoning my pajamas properly, I strode down the front hall like I was on my way to the Met Gala.

"You're not even gonna change into anything hot for this?" groaned Tilley, who was peeking through the living room curtains.

"That's not what we're about," I shot back, then opened the door to Matt, who looked handsome and slightly sweaty in a flannel shirt and puffy vest.

"I was already on my way over," he admitted sheepishly. "I had a feeling you might require some backup." He held his arms out, and I hesitated, remembering all the missed messages piling up in my inbox.

Matt noticed the fangs of my insecurities beginning to dig in and kept talking, trying to soothe my overheated brain. "You know what I like about you?" he asked, barely pausing to take a breath. "You look great in pajamas, at all times of day."

Tilley gagged theatrically from the living room, so I stepped onto the concrete stoop and wrenched the door shut behind me, shivering in the cool air.

"Some people are bound to the ticking of the clock, and that is a terrible way to live," continued Matt, pretending that my sister didn't have her face pressed against the glass to watch us. "I always wish I was in pajamas. Why do you think I wear so much plaid?"

I threw myself at him and he picked me up in a bear hug, squeezing me so hard I almost lost my breath a second time. "I missed you," I yelled into his left shoulder. My next-door neighbor stopped sweeping his steps to glare at us, and I shooed him away with my free hand.

Matt dropped me to the ground. "I missed you too. Do you

know how hard it is to find someone who will let me play Name That Tune on their arm every day? I've got a whole repertoire going in your absence."

"Try me," I said, preparing for one of our favorite hospital games. We invented it after the nurses wouldn't let Matt borrow the ward's beat-up guitar on a Saturday night, citing "a lack of available supervision." I guess they figured there was high potential for a good old guitar smash outside the medication dispensary.

Matt and I fell into deep silence as he tapped a careful rhythm onto my upturned forearm. I don't know how many mornings we'd spent hunched over the cafeteria table, trading choruses back and forth. For a recovering musician and a mad girl who just wanted to be touched, it wasn't a bad way to pass the time. I felt the beats pulse through my body, in time with Matt's flawless internal metronome. I frowned. "Do I get a hint at least?"

"Saturday morning cartoons. Golden era."

"You're older than me, so your golden era is, like, ancient," I complained. Matt replayed it for me one last time and my eyes lit up. "Oh, you almost had me there. It's *The Flintstones* theme song!"

Matt grinned. "I knew you'd get it. Whenever I try this on Misa, she gets too ticklish. She's the toughest woman I know, but she has no tolerance for the taps."

I sat down on the steps, motioning toward the space beside me. Tilley had finally gotten bored of eavesdropping, so I figured it was a good time to feel things out. Matt nestled in between me and the railing, our thighs pressing against each other.

"I love that you're a professional musician and this is how you choose to apply your talents," I said, leaning my head against his shoulder.

"*Was* a professional musician," Matt mumbled, and I sat back upright.

"Whoa. Did you finally take that job with Misa's dad?"

"It's temporary," he said, a little too quickly. It was the exact same thing I'd said about my current gig to appease my parents. "Just until I figure things out."

I knew he didn't want any follow-up questions, so I didn't ask any. I just wallowed in that uncharacteristic gap between what he was telling me and what he was feeling. Maybe it had been a while, but I didn't like the extra space.

"Speaking of figuring things out," he said, changing the subject, "I wanted to come ask you about the trip to Turks and Caicos in person, since we hadn't been too successful using conventional forms of delivery, like the mail, cell phones, messenger pigeons—"

"Okay, okay, I get it—I'm an asshole."

"You're not," he said, offering me a sheepish grin. "You and I aren't the kind of people who can just fly to an island on a whim. I know this is a big, scary ask. But I want you there because you're one of the most important people in my life." He paused. "In both of our lives. You know that, right?"

"Of course."

Matt held out his elbow and I bumped it with mine, beaming like a loser. Misa thought it was silly to have a secret handshake to celebrate the fact that we were all institutionalized together. "What else did we have to do when we were locked up?" I'd asked her once. "I read historical fiction," she'd said.

I lowered my elbow and leaned my chin into my palm, trying to imagine a scenario in which I, Dee Foster, a person who hadn't left home for seven years except to hit an outlet mall in Buffalo once, somehow wound up at an all-inclusive resort in the Caribbean on a dog walker's wages.

Matt saw me struggling to put the pieces together and hastily interjected. "I know it sounds like a lot, but let me tell you about the perks." He threaded his arm through mine and leaned in close. "You know how Misa's family is super into real estate, right? Well, they actually part-own a chunk of the resort, so it's not like we're paying regular prices here. And I already spoke to her parents about arranging a room for you, so it's basically just the cost of the flight."

"I could never—" I started to protest, but Matt cut me off before I could get really dramatic about it.

"You always looked out for me in the hospital," he said, his tone suddenly more serious than I was used to. "This is the least I can do."

It was a small sentence that meant so much to me, but I couldn't shake the feeling that this was just another chance that would remain out of reach. "Thank you," I said softly, disentangling my arm. "I promise I'll think about it—but either way, I'm really glad you came by."

"I'm glad too," Matt replied, holding my gaze for just a second too long. A moment of silence stretched between us. I bit my lip, wondering if this was the chance I needed to get everything off my chest, surrounded by my nosy neighbor and the gentle puffing of a stalled bus in the distance. It had always felt like we deserved a moment bigger than what we had, but maybe if I kept waiting for that perfect opportunity, I'd miss my shot completely.

Before I could open my mouth, Tilley barrelled through the front door, a heavy coat thrown over her black corset. "I cancelled my date, you're welcome, let's get moving."

"Hey, Til," said Matt, swivelling around to greet her. "I was just—"

"Leaving?" She folded her arms over her very prominent boobs.

Matt and Tilley hadn't really gotten along since she picked me up from the hospital, blaming him for my unplanned discharge.

The whole Matt-choosing-Misa thing hadn't improved Tilley's opinion of him either, although she did once say that if he shaved, he would kind of look like a knockoff Archie Andrews.

"I don't want things to be like this," he said, putting up his hands in surrender. "We used to be buds! You kicked my ass at Scrabble on the regular, remember?"

"Hey, man," said Tilley with a shrug. "It's nothing personal. Just know that if you want Dee at your special day, you're gonna have to go through me."

"I get it—you're a package deal," Matt replied. His phone rang, and he threw me a final pleading glance before retreating down the porch stairs. "If it means getting you to this wedding, my offer stands for you *and* a plus-one, if you want it."

"Oh, Matthew," said Tilley as I nodded robotically, "if I had a dollar for every time you needed Dee's help, I could afford a vacation without your bullshit."

Matt already looked like he wanted to take back his invitation. "I gotta head back to work now, but I hope I see ya soon, Dee. I'm counting on you."

As Tilley and I watched Matt's rusting sedan speed down our street, she took one look at me and sighed. "Now we *really* need ice cream."

SOME FUN FACTS about Tilley's beat-up red Fiat include (a) it's basically a clown car so it's great on gas, (b) one time a guy went down on her while she was driving it, which is almost an ergonomic impossibility, and (c) since it only plays discs, Tilley has burned a truly enviable collection of homemade CDs. Today's playlist was titled *One-Hit Wonders*, and the sweet sounds of Sugar Ray filled every corner of the cramped vehicle.

We took a winding route along Kingston Road, rounding the corner at the decrepit pub where every underage girl in Scarborough managed to get served. We whipped by the golf club where my high school friends had worked during the summer, making sure to slow down as we passed the forested nook where the police liked to hide. As we approached the hospital where I'd spent a roller-coaster winter the year before, Tilley took a sharp left turn into the strip mall across the street, bouncing over speed bumps outside the discount grocer and the last Video 99 in the city. She pulled up in front of the Wendy's hybrid, and my heart started pounding in my chest.

For months after we'd been discharged, I had come to this location once a week with Matt and Misa for our informal support group, since I had been cut out of the hospital's regular programming. After our allotted time at Wendy's, Kei—Misa's cousin, home from school on the West Coast—would meet us at Kennedy Bowl, where their grandmother used to play on Tuesday nights. Kei would hop out of the driver's seat in combat boots up to their knees, racing to hug me with a ferocity I didn't expect as Matt and Misa glanced shyly at each other over the roof of the car. We lived between inflatable bowling lane bumpers, sharing nachos with liquid cheese and a friendship that felt infinite. I think about that beautiful span of time often, the good days before everything went downhill and I wound up on that highway overpass. The restaurant had begun to hold an almost biblical significance for me, for better or worse. It felt like the right place to make a big decision.

Tilley and I carried our chocolate Frostys to a four-seater by a window, looking down the dead-end road toward the hospital.

I counted up ten floors and wondered who was looking down at us right now, yearning for fast-food freedom. I sat there staring at the tray like I had once again forgotten how to eat without someone watching me.

Tilley swept a heaping spoonful of ice cream into her mouth and swallowed hard. "Well, what do you want to do?"

"He showed up for me, Til," I said into my Frosty. "No one ever shows up for me."

"Congratulations," she retorted, shooting me a look. "The guy met a basic standard of kindness by driving ten minutes to check in on your non-responsive ass. Do you also want me to send a thank-you note to every stop sign that prevents you from getting hit by a car?"

I didn't answer, just stayed hunched over my Frosty. I missed the tightly sealed ice cream tubs from the ward that came with wooden spoons and without the promise of seconds. At least you always knew when you were scraping the bottom. The ambient sounds of the restaurant began to rise around me, my breath hot and ragged. I tried to focus on my cold grip around the Frosty, but I felt naked under the track lighting and my head whipped from side to side, searching for an exit. I could feel everyone's eyes on me. They must have known that I was sick, so sick that this fast-food stop had been the cornerstone of my existence for weeks on end. I had made a mistake coming here without Matt and Misa. No one else would ever understand.

"Hey," said Tilley, balling up a napkin and throwing it at me. It hit me in the face, and I blinked twice, coming back down. "I didn't mean to be a jerk. Here's a little Kim K to brighten your evening." She slid her phone across the table, and I stared blankly at the screen.

To cheer me up, Tilley had started taking pictures of people eating at her restaurant and captioning them with Kim Kardashian quotes. This one featured a guy taking a hefty bite out of a fried chicken sandwich, red sauce spilling down his chin: *If I don't like something that's going on in my life, I change it. And I don't sit and complain about it for a year.*

"Thanks, Til," I said flatly, passing it back. Her face fell, and my ice cream began to pool around the edges. "It's just—when I was in the hospital, I thought by the time I made it to this Wendy's, I'd be better. I keep coming back here, but it feels like I'm still stuck—you know, up there." I motioned toward the looming shadow of the hospital.

Tilley frowned. "So what's going to get you unstuck?"

"Maybe this wedding? Anything's gotta be better than where I'm at. I'm tired of being left behind."

Tilley whistled. "Okay, so if you go, you have to watch the round man you love marry someone else," she mused, unbuttoning her coat to scratch at the hem of her corset. "But if you don't go, I lose my only valid excuse to take time off work for a discounted island vacation."

"Who says I'm bringing you?"

"Please," she said dryly, "even Matt gets that I'm the only one who knows how to call you on your shit anymore. Everyone else is too scared of sending you back to the ward." She pushed aside her Frosty and took a big gulp from her oversized Fanta. "Tough love, baby girl. That's what you need to make it through this wedding without messing up your entire life."

"I'm not going to mess up my life."

"Really? Because I don't know what you think you're going to get out of this."

I scrunched my face up and thought for a moment. "Part of being in the hospital means that your whole life is narrated by somebody else—at first, it's a doctor, but then it's every friend and family member who thinks you're too high risk to put away the steak knives after dinner." Tilley looked a little insulted, so I back-tracked a bit. "It's kind and all, but after a while you need to learn to take the wheel again. And I think now might be that time."

"I mean, I'm not going to be the one who discourages you from cleaning up the dishes for the first time in your life," she replied. "But is this really the right situation to jump back into?"

I considered all the secrets I'd have to keep, the financial bar-riers of getting to the island, the overwhelming pressure to be "on" in the presence of strangers. But more important, I thought about the deep friendship that tethered Matt and me together—and the nagging feeling if I didn't say something about what I'd always felt between us, we'd both end up making a huge mistake.

"I think that as a friend, I'm kind of morally obliged to go." An exasperated look crossed Tilley's face and I let out a short, desper-ate laugh. "Besides, what do I have to lose anyway?"

Tilley slammed her drink down on the laminate table and or-ange fizzy droplets splattered around her. "Can't you be even a little bit proud of how far you've come in the past few months? You're miles ahead of where you were, even if you can't see it. And if I'm being completely honest, I don't think it's worth it for you to go to this wedding and put yourself at risk. But I know you and I know you're going to go anyway, because they're your friends or whatever."

"You're right," I said slowly. "It's just that it's my last chance to—"

"—tell Matt how you feel about him? How very Julia Roberts of you," said Tilley.

"No," I said. "To tell him how I really feel about Misa."

3

"LOVE DON'T COST A THING" —JENNIFER LOPEZ (3:42)

A MONTH LATER, as we landed in Providenciales—the heart of the Turks and Caicos Islands—Tilley told me that some politician in Canada was trying to make it our eleventh province.

"Even people who are obsessed with Canada for a living want to get the heck out of there in the winter," she said, pressing her face against the plane window. Beneath us, turquoise waters rippled like marble, stretching infinitely into the distance. "I'm so glad we blew all my tip jar savings on this."

We walked off the plane right into the sunlight, thin ropes guiding us away from the aircraft and toward automatic doors that mashed open and shut like the jaws of a shark. The heat hit us hard—I shed my blue hoodie, tied it tightly around my waist. Tilley had been wearing shorts since we left home, much to the amusement of the bundled-up passengers on the Park'N Fly bus. Rhinestoned tote bag in her right hand, she suavely unfolded her sunglasses with her left and perched them on the tip of her nose. "So you're telling me Misa's family comes here all the time?"

I nodded, taking in the ring of palm trees around the airport hangar. A few hours away from home, and I already felt half-removed from my body. I tried to slow my breathing, stay on top of my stress.

"Girl," said Tilley, "you're going after the wrong half of this marriage."

Inside the airport, a three-piece band played a fast, pulsing island beat that seemed to falter whenever there was a pause in the incoming throng of tourists. The wall featured a large, lonely portrait of Queen Elizabeth II across from official headshots of the island's federal government and a coat of arms protected by a pair of flamingos. We slipped into the visitor line, which was dominated by well-off white families herding oversized suitcases while surrounded by ads for Canadian banks. I spotted mostly Canadian, American, and UK passports, plus several engagement rings the size of arcade knobs. All the purses were designer, and not the kind you could get on clearance at the department store. I gripped the worn strap of my mom's carry-on suitcase and gave Tilley a nudge.

"Did you see that fourteen-year-old girl with the Yves Saint Laurent backpack?"

"No," she said, whipping her head around. "Otherwise, I would have stolen it already."

I couldn't believe that this was Misa's second home. It almost didn't feel like a real place. The airport itself was so bare, but every person around us was dripping with excess. Beside our bulging crowd was a trim line labelled BELONGERS AND RETURNING RESIDENTS. A lone Black family walked through, the father high-fiving airport staff and the kids waving at the border agents stamping passports. Behind them, a large, freckled British family looked bored as they waited to pass through. At customs, I proudly handed over my query sheet—the purpose of my trip cleanly and dishonestly ticked *pleasure*.

Outside the airport, a muscular, bald man in a crisp uniform held up a sign with our names, his deep brown skin gleaming against the white linen of his dress shirt. He greeted us with a wide smile and threw our bulging suitcases in the trunk of his Land Rover like they were filled with marshmallows.

"I'm Washington," he said as we fastened our seat belts and mumbled our names. "You here for the big wedding?"

"Yes," I said, forcing enthusiasm into my vocal cords. "We're very excited for Matt and Misa."

"We're gonna do it up big for you this week," he said, matching my tone, presumably without the duplicity. "I love weddings. My friends make fun of me 'cause I'm a big romantic. I can't wait to get married. Gotta save up for that ring, you know?"

"How long have you been with your girlfriend?" asked Tilley.

His face split into a grin. "I don't have a girlfriend yet. You think that's gonna stop me? Nah. I'll be ready."

As Washington circled a cluster of ornamental palm trees and our luggage slumped over in the trunk, Tilley leaned into me and grabbed my hand with her griffin claws. She asked him if he could play her newest burned CD, which was titled *Disaster Mix 3000* in honor of our trip. When I asked Tilley why she added *3000* to the end, she said it was roughly the number of times she'd wished for swift death while I pined for Matt. The front cover of the plastic case was filled with a poorly sketched snail shell, executed with a thick and clumsy Sharpie. "This is what your brain looks like when it spirals," she'd explained, tracing the lines with a fake nail. Luckily for Washington, his car was too new to have a CD player.

When he heard we were from Toronto, he put "Nice for What"

on blast. We drove past tiny shops with dresses hanging over the railings, fried chicken shacks, a single sweet-tea joint with a line around the corner. Washington told us there weren't so many locals on the island because there was no naturally occurring fresh water here, so unless you were prepared to pay for a resort or a villa, it was a hard place to make a life (he said this cheerfully, but I froze up all the same). He saw us quietly observing the strip plazas and wooden houses gutted by the hurricane a few months earlier and told us how his family and many others had stayed inside the St. Monica Church, just along the Leeward Highway. He pointed it out as we drove past, but we could hardly see the building for all the scaffolding.

"Kept us safe during the big storm," he said, "but blew down in the next one, when we didn't need it anymore. Sometimes things work out, you know."

"That's a good way to look at it," said Tilley, but my gut jolted at the oversimplification.

He caught a glimpse of my face and smoothly changed the subject. I wondered how much of his life he had to erase for these short drives. "You might even spot a celebrity on island," he said, not breaking stride. "Drake golfs here all the time, and we had a couple of those Kardashians at fish fry a few weeks ago."

"That's amazing." Tilley gasped, the lure of reality TV outweighing any moral qualms. "Who else?"

"Well, most of 'em live all the way out on Parrot Cay, so you don't see too much." Washington thought for a moment. "But we got Prince's house with the purple driveway. Justin Bieber. Bruce Willis, if you like him."

"Well *that* explains why Matt agreed to get married here," I said, thinking of the countless times he had requested *Die Hard* for ward movie night.

"Does he also find bald men incredibly sexy?" preened Tilley. Washington grinned, his smooth head glistening in the sunlight.

The hotel driveway was a giant roundabout surrounded by palm trees and packed with cars. Washington pulled up to the front entrance, and a cheerful attendant in a turquoise tie opened the car door.

"Welcome to Breeze Bay," he said, helping us down from the Land Rover and handing us two tall glasses of crimson punch. As he hoisted our heavy bags out of the trunk, Tilley and I stared open-mouthed at stacks of sleek, white apartments with glass balconies, a massive outdoor chandelier hanging from a grandiose archway, and a glimpse of a long, clear infinity pool yawning out toward the beach. Lounge chair after lounge chair displayed bodies bronzing in the sun, separated by wide umbrellas. In the background, a blender whirred with the promise of cold piña coladas.

"Oh my god," said Tilley, taking a gulp of her rum punch. "Someone's totally gonna get murdered here, Agatha Christie style."

After we managed to snap our jaws shut long enough to finish our drinks, I dragged Tilley away from Washington so we could freshen up in our hotel room before the welcome party. Grace, the briskly efficient concierge, checked us in and gave us our itinerary for the week, printed on decadent turquoise stationery. Between the Nagasakas' welcome party, the stag and doe (a very Canadian addition), a bridal brunch hosted by Matt's mum, and the wedding itself, it looked like my nice-dress-to-bougie-soiree ratio had been slightly miscalculated. I was also surprised to see how many different places we'd be visiting around the island, courtesy of Washington and his Land Rover crew. I had heard that all-inclusive resorts were often gated off like weird luxury prisons, but after scanning the list of local bars and restaurants, I could tell this island had a whole social scene that I wasn't prepared for. I'd be lucky to get a tan between activities (minus the optional Jet Ski excursions that were definitely out of our price range). Tilley immediately folded her itinerary in half and shoved it inside her tote bag.

"Don't you think you might need that?" I said.

A uniformed waiter bowed as Tilley hurried past him, eager to get to our room. I watched him unload lunchtime cocktails at a nearby bistro table, his buoyant delivery flickering into fatigue as soon as he turned around.

"Schedules are just suggestions," she said, strolling through the grounds in her Old Navy shorts like she had been part of this world forever.

WITH A GENTLE nudge from Matt and Misa, the Nagasakas had very kindly booked us a cute studio suite from their block that made my childhood home look like a second-day yard sale. The room was bright and airy, with nautical-themed pillows arranged across an upholstered bed and wicker lamps sitting on wooden bedside tables. I kicked off my black Converse and collapsed onto the plush white duvet of our queen bed. After checking out our view of the pool from the side window, Tilley ran to the bathroom and, as usual, didn't shut the door while she peed.

When she emerged, she unzipped her suitcase and threw an overstuffed bag of makeup at me. I sighed and carried it to the bathroom counter, inspected my fading acne marks in the big round mirror. My eyes were sunken in my face, my skin mottled.

Tilley came up behind me, already half-naked. "What's wrong?"

"Nothing."

"You mean nothing a little bit of tinted moisturizer and some good old-fashioned sunshine can't fix." She reached into the bag, pulled out a depleted tube, and somehow managed to squeeze a few dregs onto my outstretched finger. "C'mon, I can practically hear your brain whirring. You'll be fine once you get to the welcome party. It's just the buildup that gets to you."

I smeared the moisturizer across my face in response. Tilley handed me a sponge with a pointed look before turning her attention to a stray hair just below the arch of her right eyebrow. We fussed over our various imperfections in silence for a few minutes. I knew no matter how much I blended, I wouldn't be able to cover up the awkwardness of seeing Misa for the first time in months. In a lot of ways, I'd missed her—not just since the wedding was announced, but before that, when she started dating Matt and I forgot how to be around her. I thought about her every time I met a dog with a food-inspired name (her favorite) or took the bus past her grandmother's street off Kennedy Road. Sometimes, in the middle of Tilley's well-intentioned ribbings, I longed for Misa's advice but knew I'd never be able to ask for it.

"Don't you dare abandon me at this party," I said, bashing my cheeks with a blush brush. "I need you to be a buffer between me and pretty much everything else."

"Didn't you say it was open bar?" she asked. She scooped up a powder brush from the bathroom counter and started expertly swiping across my cheekbones. "Don't worry—I'm not going anywhere."

"Til," I said after a moment. "What if they don't want me here?"

"Yeah," retorted Tilley. "I'm sure they showed up at everyone's house to make sure they were coming."

"Maybe that was just to be polite." This was just how my brain liked to operate: First, it prevented me from reaching out to people when I needed them. Then, once enough time had gone by, it would convince me that those people hated me, and that's why there was such distance between us. Finally, if they did reach out, I would feel guilty for being a burden and wouldn't respond. It was a cycle that had left me with few friends and a lot of unopened text messages. I could feel my body starting to ramp up, so I picked up the eyeliner pen. I felt like the best time to apply liquid liner was during a surge of adrenaline, so I didn't care if the line was squiggly.

"In your fucking dreams," growled Tilley, snatching the pen out of my hand and applying it for me.

I felt my skin getting hot as I thought about the way Misa always seemed to assess my comfort level in an instant, how quickly she would tune her frequency to mine so I could feel at ease. But beneath that comfort was a nagging resentment over her protection—a feeling that I was being managed, especially when there was an audience around.

⋮

When Misa first started volunteering on the hospital's junior board, I had hoped that we'd finally have something in common—we wanted to upend the system, even from the inside out. But that illusion disintegrated as soon as Misa met me at the door of her first fundraiser in an elegant black cocktail dress. The event was held in a hotel that most of our wardmates would never have been able to afford, far away from the reality of our care. Misa, I realized, didn't want her new colleagues to know she was one of us.

I shook the hands of countless board members who would teleport to private care in a millisecond if they ever got sick. If I was being honest, I knew Misa would have too, if it wouldn't have meant telling her parents that she was struggling. I asked what percentage of their council had lived experience of mental illness and grimaced when the suits looked taken aback, like no one had ever thought to ask that before. They loved that I was a patient. They asked what the food was like, if I had noticed the board-funded watercooler in the waiting room of the outpatient ward. I didn't know how to tell them that there was so much more to worry about, so much they could never imagine. Somehow, they were overwhelmingly white, representing a neighborhood best known for its diversity (and consequently, the best damn food in the city). Matt showed up late with tiger lilies for Misa and pride beaming from his eyes like highway headlights, and I walked out of the silent auction only slightly faster than they sold a $50,000 fishing trip.

Misa went on to run an entire golf tournament dedicated to bipolar disorder without happening to mention hers, which drove me (metaphorically) crazy. "Misa never makes it about her, you know?" said Matt when I subtly tried to point out her hypocrisy during her fundraising speech. "She's got a good heart," I replied truthfully. But what I really wanted was for her to spill her good heart all over that stage, be messy in her illness, like I was in mine. In the outside world, it felt like Misa was constantly wearing down her edges to make herself fit into surrounding terrain. But it was the jagged, messy parts of her that I loved best. They made me feel better about the fact that I had never been able to sand myself down in the same way—the exhaustion of trying to be normal always came for me in the end.

I blinked hard. "I think I need to take a nap."

Tilley handed me a tube of mascara. "Hard no to the depression nap. You're almost there, Dee. You got this."

Frozen with worry, I stared at the mascara in my hand and gripped it so tight my fingers hurt. Bad thoughts cycled rapidly through my head. I closed my eyes to try and banish them, but all I could see was Matt's face, disappointed at my inability to function in the real world. Misa standing beside him, the way she deserved to. Me, right there and a million miles away at the same time.

Tilley wrapped her arms around me and planted a brusque kiss on the top of my head. Her boobs squished into my shoulder. "Hey. I know this is tough for you."

"I shouldn't have come here." Dropping the mascara in defeat, I grabbed at a nearby hand towel to wipe off my face and gasped at the orange imprint my fingers left on the clean white cloth.

Tilley tugged it out of my hands and threw it behind the bathroom door, out of sight. "It's like a high school reunion, hospital style. I get it. All you have to do is make them think you have your shit together. That's what they're all pretending anyway."

Maybe that's what Misa wanted, but it wasn't the way we used to be. I considered my options—not showing up and having Misa know something was wrong or showing up and trying to fake it through—then mechanically picked up the tube of mascara again and began combing it through my lashes.

Tilley studied my face intently in the mirror. "Have I ever told you that you're a tough old bird?"

"I'm only three years older than you!"

"And yet somehow, I wound up with all the wisdom," she

mused, holding up a slinky black dress with a high slit. "Wanna trade closets for the night? You'd look killer in this."

I retreated to the bed, where my tried-and-true sage green maxi dress awaited me, only slightly wrinkled from the journey. "I'm good," I said. "I want to be comfortable."

"Comfortable, but never boring," she sang as I pulled the dress over my head and shimmied into place. She plucked a glittery bobby pin from the counter and pinned my hair back on one side, nodding in approval. "You're stunning. Let's go cause a scene, shall we?"

Ready or not, it was time to face Misa Nagasaka.

4

∾

"TIME TO PRETEND" —MGMT (4:19)

THE WELCOME PARTY was held under the largest gazebo I'd ever seen. It stretched from an ornate cocktail bar all the way toward the lip of the pool, shielding wedding guests in designer clothing from the beating sun. It didn't look like there were that many people our age in attendance, which didn't surprise me much. From what Matt had told me when we were arranging our accommodations, this wedding was more about impressing Misa's parents' business associates than anything else—which explained all the suits in this heat. Besides, most of our long-standing friendships had gone suspiciously MIA ever since the ward. Other than appearances from Matt's unsteady rotation of bandmates and a few classmates from Misa's design school, the party catered to an older crowd that demanded our best behavior, whatever that looked like these days.

Under the gazebo, white-clad waiters swooped in and out of social circles with the deftness of fighter-jet pilots. Trays of intricate hors d'oeuvres emerged from the kitchen doors, held high above the wolfish packs of hungry guests who had figured out the waiters' routes. Tilley managed to pluck a lone piece of tuna nigiri off a nearby platter and pop it into her mouth without smudging her lipstick.

"I think we've got a level-ten wasabi situation over here," she said, exhaling hard. One long leg protruded from the slit in her dress. "I'm gonna need to find a drink that tastes like jet fuel to combat it."

We were making our way toward the bar when I spotted Misa leaning up against it, sipping a watermelon smoothie and sporting a stylish floral jumper with an open back. I pulled at the damp fabric of my green dress, wishing it wouldn't cling so much. Misa's thick hair was upswept in a loose chignon, wavy tendrils falling toward her cheekbones tinted with a golden sheen. She wore her favorite Mikimoto earrings—a gift from her grandfather—and a swipe of coral across her lips. Her dark eyes shone as she spoke loudly to her obachan, who was wearing a pastel pink tracksuit without breaking a sweat. I watched them trade smiles, Obachan laughing so hard that she grabbed onto Misa's arm for support before spotting me and waving.

"Stay focused on the mission," hissed Tilley, trying to hail a waiter. "Just pretend you didn't see her."

"I can't—it's Obachan," I explained. I took a deep breath and walked toward Misa, my palms beginning to sweat. Tilley made a beeline for the bar, more out of mild alcohol dependency than respect for my privacy.

The last time I'd seen Misa, nearly six months ago, she'd been onstage as usual. The hospital was giving her some community service award that cemented her as a contributing member of society, while I had become an all-too-natural disaster since her relationship began. I clapped until my hands hurt and wondered how it felt to be up there, in the light, with all eyes on you. Misa had always been a good navigator—able to ebb and flow with her environment—but when Matt and I took her out for tonkatsu afterward, I could see that the demands were taking a toll. She mashed sesame seeds into dust as she explained why she was still living at her grandmother's house.

"I told my parents I'm helping Obachan," she said. "But it's kind of the opposite. When I'm with her, I feel like myself again."

I won't pretend it's not weird that I'm mildly obsessed with someone else's eighty-five-year-old Japanese grandmother. Maybe it's because I don't have any living grandparents, or maybe it's because my own parents would rather acknowledge Tilley's nipple piercing than talk about my mental illness. I remember how scared Misa was to tell Obachan about her bipolar diagnosis in the beginning. "She slept in horse stables during the war and never complained," Misa said, when she first found out Obachan was coming to visit her in the hospital. "How am I going to tell her I can't get out of bed?" I didn't know what to say. But in the end, Misa's trepidation didn't seem to matter. Every day, Obachan took the bus all the way to the ward, armed with senbei and green tea KitKat bars. I've lost track of how many afternoons we spent in the lunchroom, Obachan sharing memories from when her family was relocated to Toronto after World War II, Misa asking more questions than I'd ever heard before. That's the Misa I knew well—the one who didn't have all the answers.

"Hello, Dee," said Misa, approaching me cautiously, like I was a baby deer in the woods. I guessed she was still upset about my late RSVP. "So glad you could make it."

"Wouldn't miss it for the world." I gave her a panicked hug, inhaling the familiar scent of sunscreen on her skin, then turned to Obachan. "It's good to see you again."

"Oh, Dee," she said, her voice slow. I'd missed her petite frame, the endearing gaps before her words, the heavy pencilling of her eyebrows. "I haven't seen you in a long, long time." I bent over and hugged her, savoring the buzzing of her hearing aids.

When she let go, Obachan pointed at Misa and frowned. "Don't you think she needs a haircut?"

"You think everyone needs a haircut," said Misa. "I need some extra length to weigh my hair down in this heat!"

She gestured at the tiny curls around her face as Obachan strained to pick a stray leaf out of her hair. I tried not to let myself get drawn back into their easy rhythm. Things were different now. It was no longer us against the world—just me trying to fend for myself in yet another place where I'd never belong.

A waiter stooped to offer us a heaping pile of spring rolls. Obachan turned her chopsticks backward to pluck one from the top, while Misa studied the platter carefully. I knew that every food she chose had to "feel right," which really didn't fly with how food service worked. One time, I saw her take twenty minutes to choose between chocolate and vanilla pudding cups in the cafeteria.

Trying to buy Misa time, I grabbed a roll and flashed the waiter a smile. Tiny and impatient, Obachan placed her spring roll on top of a napkin and went back for seconds, waving the appetizer around with her chopsticks.

"Here," Obachan said, thrusting it toward Misa, "this is for you."

Misa reluctantly accepted the slightly squished spring roll, wrapping it in a napkin offered by the waiter. As the waiter walked away and Obachan took a hearty bite out of her roll, I leaned toward Misa and spoke softly. "Let me know if you want me to get rid of that."

"Thank you," she whispered, covertly passing me the bulging napkin. I understood the guilt of destroying the evidence of your own weirdness. Misa gazed over the top of Obachan's head to beam at me, and it was suddenly like we had teleported to equal footing.

In moments like these, we were an indestructible team—we recognized each other's truest forms and didn't ask for anything else. But these moments had become few and far between as Misa acclimatized to the outside world, which, in her case, meant fitting in with a circle of people that definitely didn't include me and all my mess.

* * *

I had already felt the ground shifting the moment I told Misa I had been discharged. After we said our goodbyes, she chased me down the hall, her urgent footsteps echoing down the empty hallway.

"Let me help you," she panted, finally catching up to me by the medication dispensary.

"Don't worry about it," I said. "My bags barely weigh anything."

"No, I mean . . . with the hospital," she said, her voice sharpening slightly. "I can ask my uncle to speak to someone. Maybe he can change their minds."

Misa's uncle was a hotshot doctor and a fairy godfather of sorts, having gotten Misa into a hospital catchment area far away from her well-off neighborhood by using Obachan's Scarborough address. Dr. Koyanagi already spent time at our hospital, working mainly with newcomer families. Although her parents could certainly have afforded private care, Misa's need for secrecy outweighed everything else. She had chosen our neglected healthcare system because she knew she wouldn't run into anyone from her world. And with Dr. Koyanagi and Obachan covering for her, Misa was able to keep her parents completely in the dark about her hospitalization. And now, it seemed like she was trying to control mine.

"I think I'll be fine," I said, disentangling myself. I felt like all the air was suddenly getting sucked out of the hallway.

"You're not fine," Misa said. "I want you to be able to take the time that you need. It's important."

What she was saying made sense, but somehow her words hit me like a gut punch. I exhaled all at once, barely realizing that I had been holding my breath. Maybe she knew something I didn't, something that everyone else in my life had been too afraid to tell me—that this hospital was my last shot. And like everything else in my life, I had blown it.

My fingers clenched around the handle of my duffel bag. "I'm good, Misa," I said flatly. "Not everyone needs special treatment."

I saw hurt flash across her face, but she composed herself too quickly for me to take it back, to apologize and thank her for caring. As always, there was no room for mistakes with her, and if I was good at anything, it was making mistakes.

⋮

The acoustic guitarist launched into a sparkling version of "Red Red Wine," pulling me back to the present. I heard Matt's voice rise over the small talk behind me, which meant the conversation was leaping from the Rangers-Celtic soccer rivalry to homemade pickles to which way toilets flushed in Australia in a matter of minutes. The last debate ended with Matt clapping some bewildered guy on the back and roaring, "Find me later, and I'll buy you a beer!" He spotted Misa, Obachan, and me and pushed his way through the crowd in our direction.

As he approached, bouncing his head along to the reggae beat, I searched frantically for Tilley. Across the patio, she was chugging a glass of wine like it was Power Hour at the sports bar. I was all on my own.

"My three favorite girls," boomed Matt, sliding into our circle and planting a kiss on top of Misa's head. He looked handsome and familiar in a Tragically Hip T-shirt and scuffed-up deck shoes, interrupting the sea of button-downs that surrounded us. "Dee, you look great," he said, despite the fact that I didn't.

"You look the same," I said, by which I meant *great*, but it came out wrong.

Matt slung his arms around me, and I tried not to enjoy it too much or breathe in too deeply. I once went on a date with a guy who accused me of smelling him when we hugged, so I am now overly conscious of any extracurricular nose activity, especially with soon-to-be married men. I counted beats in my head, anticipating and dreading the moment when I had to let go.

"What happened to the nice shirt you were wearing?" asked Misa, tugging at his left sleeve.

"There's a perfectly reasonable explanation for that," he replied, releasing me from his grasp. "It had long sleeves and we're in a tropical climate, my dear. It just wasn't meant to be."

She poked him in the chest playfully. "Just remember, we're here a whole week and you can only use that excuse so many times."

"I'd marry you in the hospital gown I met you in," he said softly.

Misa laughed under her breath, and I tried my best not to hurl. "But of course, it wouldn't match my bow tie."

"And your mom spent weeks finding one with your family tartan," she replied. "She would never forgive you."

"Don't pin this one on her," he retorted. "You're the lady with the high standards. God knows how you wound up with me."

I could have broken it down for them, if they'd asked me, diagrams and all:

Indisputable Fact #1: Matt Costigan always made you feel safe. This was especially alluring for folks like me and Misa, who had the home-life stability of the San Andreas Fault.

Indisputable Fact #2: Misa Nagasaka loved a project. Figure 1? Me, obviously. Figure 2? Her weird soapmaking phase. Figure 3? Matt and Misa's entire relationship. Misa was always pushing Matt to dress nicer, work harder (ew), and strive to be more than the music-loving weirdo that he truly was. Can you gentrify a person? I don't know, but she might be halfway there.

Which brings us to Indisputable Fact #3: Matt Costigan was born to perform, and that's how he wound up in his current role, playing the part of Misa's picture-perfect groom in a family that would never accept the way their story began. Except I knew he wouldn't be able to keep up the pretense *forever*, which is apparently an important part of wedding vows.

Misa smiled and leaned into him a little. "I'll think you look great no matter what, but I'm trying to save my spoons for the big stuff. Can you try to work with me on this one?"

When Misa brought up her spoons, it was serious business. We'd first learned about Spoon Theory from Harsha, on a gray afternoon in group therapy. She'd leaned back in her plastic chair and explained that healthy people expect you to have a certain supply of energy to get things done—that's what she called our "spoons." But when you have chronic pain, or mental illness, or other disabilities, you can't predict how many spoons you start out with, and it's almost always fewer than you need. Simple tasks, which may take a single spoon from most people, can clean you right out. And as someone who prided herself on always getting things done, Misa held on to Spoon Theory as a way of tracking her limits.

Matt grinned. "I love you and your giant drawer of cutlery," he said. "And I'll make sure to change before dinner. But in the meantime—Obachan, do you like my shirt?"

Obachan pursed her lips and walked in a circle around Matt, tugging at his shirt hem as she passed. Once she returned to her place, she patted Matt on the arm with so much enthusiasm it probably bruised. "This is a nice shirt, you know," she announced. "Good material."

Misa rolled her eyes. "You've got to be kidding."

"See? It's Obachan-approved!"

"I know," she said, the hint of a smile creeping across her face. "And she's a seamstress. She's not easy to please."

As a waiter passed by, Misa traded her finished smoothie for a brimming glass of lemon water, and we all exchanged pleasantries like Rock 'Em Sock 'Em Robots. Except Obachan. She was more interested in the appetizers passing by, but too short to get a good view of the spread. She ambled away mid-conversation, her white sneakers gleaming against the pavement. Meanwhile, I tried to avoid watching Misa's hand snaking its way into Matt's.

"I feel like I haven't seen you in ages," said Misa casually. "What have you been doing lately?" We both knew that she kept monogrammed Moleskine agendas for each passing year, and therefore could tell me exactly how many days I had been MIA from their lives. Luckily for me, she was also terribly polite.

I tried to think about the last worthwhile thing I had accomplished. It was a toss-up between discovering that I could use my waffle maker as a panini press and riding the bus through Scarborough without having a panic attack. So I told them about my day job.

"I've been walking dogs."

After the swimming-pool disaster, my old place of employment was fairly unenthusiastic about hiring me back. "We have to think about the children," they'd said when I called from the hospital pay phone to see if I still had a job. I didn't blame them, really. But I also felt like the children would have understood that, sometimes, all you could do was sink.

Instead, Tilley set me up with this wealthy lady who liked to drink at her bar and had a mini Goldendoodle named Jack Sparrow. One day I came home with Jack during her book club to a room full of rich white women who were reading books by other rich white women and suddenly I had a full schedule—if you count full capacity as one dog per day, which at that point in my recovery, I most certainly did.

The area they all lived in was Scarborough's easternmost hold on Lake Ontario, past the Bluffs, past Galloway, separated from the headlines of my neighborhood by two thick concrete bridges. We called it the Island and had dreamt of moving there before even the bungalows cost upwards of $500K. I'd walk along the waterfront and lock eyes with rival dog walkers steering Shih Tzus and golden retrievers and the occasional Irish setter, knowing that the real enemy was the obvious gap between the twenty dollars per walk we were paid and the waterfront houses our dogs lived in. It didn't surprise me one bit to find out that Matt and Misa had plans to move there as well, after things were official.

"It's a really fun area," said Matt earnestly, like Toronto real estate was a thing normal people could do. "There's a local pub that does great brunch and Scottish breakfast on weekends. Black pudding and everything. You should come with us sometime."

I scrunched up my face. "Why would I get out of bed and wait in line to eat one meal instead of two? Especially when that meal is basically 90 percent sausage."

Misa released a musical laugh, and thousands of fairies were born in Iceland. "Oh, Dee," she said. "I can't wait until you see the bridal brunch Matt's mom has planned on Thursday morning."

I knew this was the part where I was supposed to laugh and ask her what she'd been up to, but I didn't know if my patchwork recovery could withstand another cycle of comparison. Even though I harbored all these opinions about the psychiatric system, I wasn't exactly out there moving mountains for mental health. And from creeping Misa's social media before my flight, I knew she had been busy with fundraisers and freelance designing and stupid hot yoga. So busy, in fact, that I sometimes wondered how she was doing with so much on her plate.

Instead, I retreated to common ground, asking if they had incorporated the hospital's potpie tradition into their wedding menu and whether we'd have to use plastic utensils, until we were laughing at the improbable place we had come from while catching stray sand in the bottoms of our dress shoes.

"It's funny how nothing's changed and everything's changed at the same time," said Misa, dropping her slice of lemon into the bottom of her empty glass and scanning the room for potential eavesdroppers. "This morning, Matt had to come get me because I was having leg tremors and walking laps around the pool!"

Matt raised her arm in the air like he was declaring a knockout. "My little Olympian. Gonna speed-walk her way to the top of the podium."

I groaned, both at the display of affection and at the traumatic memory. "They never did let us use that track. Where did they think we'd go? It was a closed circle!"

"If we're going to start a list of all the things that didn't make sense in the hospital, I'm going to need a refill," said Misa slyly.

"You're drinking water!" said Matt.

"Exactly!" replied Misa. "My throat will get dry!"

He laughed and grabbed the glass from her hands. "I get the hint. I'll be back in a sec." He eyed my half-full drink and headed toward the bar, trying to avoid getting pulled aside by other guests along the way.

I was suddenly conscious of being completely alone with Misa for the first time in ages. The thin wings of her liquid liner disappeared into the creases of her eyes as she smiled expectantly at me. I didn't know what to say. Feeling the heat, I ground the heel of my cork wedge into the patio floor.

"So," she said, "is it as bad as you imagined?"

"Worse," I said. "There's a guy in an unironic Hawaiian shirt over there!"

Misa snickered but didn't lose her line of inquiry. "Seriously, Dee," she said. "Anything I can do to make this easier, let me know. I appreciate you being here for us."

I briefly considered if there was an appropriate way to ask if she would call off her own wedding, then decided against it. Instead, I nodded toward the elaborate trays of champagne and tiny appetizers being circulated. "Do you ever get used to this?"

Misa tilted her head softly. "This is one part of my life that's expected of me. My fundraising work is another. It's not always easy, but as long as I have my own space, it's manageable."

I felt a twinge of jealousy at the thought of managing, well, anything more than dog-walking. "You're lucky."

Misa gazed toward the bar, where Matt was waiting in line and becoming fast friends with an older woman in an elaborate sun hat. "I am," she replied. "For a long time, my life was more possible when I kept things in different places. With Matt, it feels like I can be all these things, or none of them, and it's enough."

"That's good stuff," I mumbled, shielding my eyes from the sun. I knew the feeling she described all too well, and I wanted to be happy for her—I really did. But a twisted part of my brain felt like Misa had taken something meant for me. My nervous stomach grumbled, and I snagged a piece of inari off a passing platter.

As I took a hefty chunk out of it, a suited man with perfect stubble and a slightly orange glow materialized between Misa and me. His pointy teeth gleamed in the sunlight, and he didn't look at me even once. I watched Misa's body straighten, as if she were tethered to the ceiling by invisible strings. Her movements became calculated and choreographed as he praised her parents for hosting such a beautiful event. I did my best not to spit out the rice in my mouth.

"My apologies," he said, only remembering I had a heartbeat once he had run out of elaborate adjectives. "I didn't catch your name."

Misa pounced before I could even finish chewing. "This is Dee Foster," she said, her voice suddenly taut. "We volunteer together at the hospital."

I choked on my last bite of inari as the man lit up like a gaudy Christmas display. "That's wonderful," he boomed. "Such a valuable way to spend your time." I had no doubt that he stuffed a fistful of cash into a Salvation Army tin every year and called it a day.

I stared directly at Misa and offered a wide smile that ripped my guts out. I don't know why I had expected things to go any differently. I thought about how she'd subsidized my trip here, not to mention our entire friendship. I thought about this wedding and how I'd hoped she had finally come to appreciate all that we had gained in the hospital. This was what I needed to explain to Matt—that Misa would never truly be on our side because of the constant reminders that she was better than us. There was a part of her that always wanted to *be* better than us. And in my opinion, it was her damn loss.

I swallowed my anger and chose my words carefully. "There's nothing like charity, am I right?"

In that moment, something was lost between us, but something familiar also crystallized in the pit of my stomach, jagged and striking and sharp with pride.

The man looked uncomfortable, took a step back. "Well, I suppose I should—"

"I need another drink," I said robotically, beating him to the punch. "Nice meeting you." And I guess, in a way, I could have said the same to Misa.

5

"TRY AGAIN" —AALIYAH FT. TIMBALAND (4:49)

I ONLY GOT Matt alone after the welcome toast, while Misa was busy being someone impenetrable in front of family friends and business sharks. Swallowing my hurt pride, I sunk a whole glass of champagne and grabbed another before pushing my way through the crowd to get to him. Matt's wedding contingent was much smaller, and his best man, Vik, hadn't even arrived yet due to a work conflict. From what I could tell, Matt had spent most of his time trying to make a good impression after an unexpected engagement, and even for a former barkeep who knew how to make small talk with eternally disappointed Leafs fans, this was a tall order. I could tell from his forced smile that he was starting to get frazzled from the whole show.

When I finally got to Matt, Misa's great-aunt was in the middle of showing him how to jitterbug, which was great, except she was closing in on ninety and had thrown her cane aside for dramatic effect. I caught her outside arm and helped him dance her back to the family section of the party, where she immediately sank into a patio chair to recover. "When my song comes on, you come back and find me, okay?" she called after him.

I took one look at Matt's face and realized he was almost out of gas. "Wanna get out of here?" I asked.

He nodded, and I pulled him into the shade since his skin was already starting to redden. We found a wicker couch hidden at the side of the patio and fell into it like we had been away at sea for months. I hugged my knees into my chest, then handed him my fresh glass of bubbly.

"It's all yours," I said, but he had already drained half of it. "You're doing great, by the way. I don't know how you manage."

"I like talking to people," said Matt. "I just don't like talking to people when it feels like an evaluation, you know? Makes me weird and sweaty."

I laughed, and he gestured regally toward his shirt. "Exhibit A."

"What good is a concert T-shirt if it's not in its natural environment?" I replied.

"I'll be honest with ya, Dee," he said, leaning his head over the back of the couch. "It's kind of like I need a vacation from the vacation already."

It was the exact same way I felt, and I had only been here for an afternoon. I couldn't imagine looking into the wealthy abyss and trying to picture myself a permanent part of it. I looked at Matt in his rumpled shirt and wanted to curl up next to him, tell him that he was more than just good enough. But I knew I wouldn't be able to keep the longing out of my voice—for him, of course, but also to hear those words repeated right back to me. I felt a pang of guilt as I thought about Misa, who was probably the logical person to provide this kind of support.

"Have you talked to Misa about it?" I asked carefully. "Maybe she can, like, tone things back? Maybe lose the ice sculpture of the goose or something?"

Matt snorted. "I don't know—that seems pretty essential."

"How else would they keep the vodka cool? Use ice cubes like commoners?"

"Right? It can be really weird being around, you know, all this." He pointed vaguely at the white silk tablecloths, the three types of fruit-infused water, the extremely high percentage of people who sailed for fun. "I don't want Misa to feel bad about it, but it's definitely not where I thought I'd end up."

Me neither. I pictured pre-hospital Matt, playing weeknight sets all over the city, taking late shifts at the bar, pushing himself closer and closer to mania just to keep his basement apartment by the mall. I thought about Matt in the psych ward common room, absentmindedly strumming my favorite song as we waited for the recreational therapist to arrive. I tried to imagine Matt now, working nine to five at Misa's dad's real estate company, crisp dress shirt tight across his shoulders and eyes bright from a good night's sleep. Even though the earlier versions had come with their baggage, I missed that authenticity.

"I don't mean to sound ungrateful," he said quickly. "The flip side is that a lot of the stuff that was hanging over my head is gone now. I finally have stable hours and health benefits—it makes a difference, you know."

"That's really great," I said, suddenly quiet.

"I'm sorry, this is all coming out wrong," he replied, shaking his head. "I'm just so fucking happy to see you, Dee. You have no idea how much I missed you."

"Me too," I replied, and I didn't mean it like I was bitter or sad or helplessly in love with him, even if I was all of the above. I just liked that he kept me in the picture.

Tilley once told me that if I had met Matt literally anywhere else on this earth—in the grocery store, on the bus, at the top of the Eiffel Tower—he wouldn't have this ridiculous hold on me. But I think she's wrong. I think I would still crave his bear hugs and sly sarcasm. His everyday stories that take up twice as much time as necessary in their telling, but always feel perfectly complete. How when he talks to you, his voice cuts through all the noise and makes you feel like you're the only person on the planet.

Something cold pressed against the back of my neck, breaking through the roar of the welcome party. "The bartender laughed at me when I asked for a splash of Sprite in your rosé." Tilley pouted, handing me a brimming glass of wine. "It might be time for you to find a signature drink that doesn't make me feel like I'm aiding and abetting a minor." She levelled her gaze at Matt. "I'm sorry, have we met before? Maybe behind an Olive Garden dumpster, or in hell?"

I nudged her. "Can you be reasonable for, like, five seconds, please?"

"I'm glad you used your plus-one so wisely," said Matt thinly.

Tilley rolled her eyes. "Relax, psychiatric Cinderella," she said, nestling her ample butt between us on the couch. "I'm just here to enjoy your ball."

Matt eyed Tilley suspiciously, then sighed and turned back to me. "Dee, my mum is dying to meet you. Got enough spoons for a parental introduction?"

"For you? Anytime."

"Great," he said. "Don't move—I'll be right back with the goods."

I watched him walk away, and Tilley smirked. "Wanna play a drinking game?"

"No."

"The name of the game is 'Suck It Up, Sister,'" she said, holding her wineglass to her mouth like a microphone. "Every time you stare longingly into Matt's big hazel eyes or check out his concave booty when he leaves to go talk to—oh, that's right—*his fiancée*, I finish my drink."

I snuck a glance, and yes, Matt was talking to Misa. I watched him pull her in for a kiss as a nearby camera flashed. "To be fair," I said, pretending I wasn't crawling with jealousy, "you were being a bit of a jerk."

"To be fair," snapped Tilley, "I can't think of a single person who has derailed your recovery more than that sack of potatoes."

"Uh, my psychiatrist?"

Tilley clinked her glass against mine. "I'll drink to that."

By the time Matt returned, Tilley had spotted someone drinking straight out of a pineapple and had scurried to the bar to obtain an alcoholic fruit for herself. I hung back on the couch and nursed my spritzer, trying to look classy as Matt led his mother toward me.

"Mum, this is Dee," he said. I stood up and he gestured toward a broad-shouldered woman in a navy shift dress. Her face was nearly lost in a sea of box-blonde curls, but when she smiled, her gums peeked out a bit more on the right side than the left, just like Matt. I loved her immediately.

"The famous Dee!" she said with just a hint of a Scottish brogue and threw her arms around me. I craned my neck, trying not to get Tilley's highlighter on her outfit.

"The one and only," said Matt, and when he looked at me, I felt something shift in the bottom of my stomach, not enough to register on the Richter scale but enough to remember that I was not standing on steady ground. Across the patio, Tilley locked eyes with me. I had to do better.

"I know we've never met, but I've got to tell you, I'm so grateful for what you did in the hospital," she continued. "I was just a wreck when he disappeared. I had no idea where he was or how long he'd be gone or if he was even alive, for god's sake."

"C'mon, Mum." Matt sighed. "It only took Dee, like, two weeks to get me to call you."

"Oh, it was terrible," she said, rolling out the adjective like a dusty carpet. "I was worried sick." She plucked a stray fluff from the shoulder of Matt's shirt. "He's always been a wee chancer, but I could've killed him that time. I really could've."

Matt grinned. "I mean, I could have too, but I guess that's how I ended up in the hospital in the first place, isn't it?"

You could have fit a seven-layer chocolate cake into her open mouth. "Well, that's just a horrible thing to say," she said. "You can't just *joke* about these types of things. They're not funny, Matt. They're just not."

I didn't want to put off someone who appeared to like me immediately, but secretly I knew if Matt and I didn't package our suicide attempts into neat little joke boxes, they would expand and expand in the backs of our skulls until the only thing we could see was our darkness. So I tried honesty instead. "I'll be real with you, Mrs. Costigan," I said. "I think Matt's bad jokes are what got me through the hospital. It helped, being able to laugh about some of the hard stuff."

"Call me Elinor, hon," she said warmly. "Now, your generation is so different than mine, and I'm glad for it. Back home, you'd sooner fall into a pit than let anyone know there was something out of the ordinary happening."

"That's how my parents grew up too," I said. "So they're not exactly thrilled with my recent track record."

"Well, that's a loss for them, isn't it? They're missing out on all you have to offer." Elinor pulled me in for a second hug, and I was struck by the warmth of the gesture, something that I had long missed in my own home. Matt watched us with a wide smile as she whispered, "You're a good friend and a very brave soul."

While compressed in Elinor's arms, I wished there were more words to describe me than *brave*. One day, I'd like to be called *successful*. *Responsible*, even. Something boring that didn't take into account all the holes I had fallen into along the way. But for now, I wore *brave* the way that Misa wore *resilient* (with a heavy eye roll), and Matt lugged around *optimistic* (like his life depended on it). All the same, it was nice to be seen as something other than a burden.

A waiter came by, and Elinor refused a glass of champagne with a cool smile. I knew part of the reason Matt hadn't called his mom when he was committed was her complicated history with alcohol, the worry that his illness could potentially unbalance the scales of her recovery. The last time she'd relapsed, it was because his absent dad had made an unwelcome reappearance, leaving Matt and Elinor to spend most of his high school years piecing things back together. Matt never talked about it like he missed out or anything—he always just said he was lucky to spend so much time with her when she needed it. I wondered if perhaps Elinor would understand—in a way my own parents never seemed to—how it felt to carry around the potential to harm the people you loved best, just by nature of your being. Every year that I moved toward the fictional stability of adulthood, I learned again and again that growing up didn't always mean outgrowing your worst tendencies. Yet here was someone who had lived through all this, someone who didn't shy away from our history in the ward or her own demons. Maybe there was some hope for me after all.

Instead of dumping my deepest existential questions on top of her, I told Elinor about the breeds of dogs I walked, and she told me about the time Matt and Vik held her neighbor's cat for ransom, complete with demands made out of newspaper clippings and an empty school bag for the payoff. Elinor's eyes sparkled as she told the story, stopping occasionally to pinch Matt's arm or protest his contributions to the narrative. I watched the way she looked at him—like he was the New York City of her America—and thought that if I was on the receiving end of that much love and couldn't absorb it, I would have felt ungrateful too. I'm much more comfortable being the Omaha, Nebraska, of people's worlds.

After a while, Misa gravitated toward us and hovered at Matt's elbow with a half-eaten gyoza in her hand. The social output of the party was clearly starting to get to her too. Her smile faltered between faces, and her gaze was hard. I was still nursing a healthy bit of rage over the "volunteering" incident, but I felt for her. It was a night where she was expected to take care of everyone, and I wasn't sure that anyone was doing the same for her.

"I've run into about ten people who tell me you've offered to buy them a drink tonight," said Misa. "At an open bar."

"Bartender's habit," he said ruefully.

"Everyone loves you," Misa replied gently. "You can relax a little bit."

Matt threw an arm around her, and she nestled into his shoulder. "This one's always looking out for me," he said to Elinor, and she beamed.

"If I was really on top of my game, I would have told you to reapply your sunscreen already," said Misa. With Matt by her side, she looked like she was catching a second wind. She pressed a finger into his cheek and watched the skin turn white, then back to red.

"Don't worry," I said to Matt. "I've heard that lobsters mate for life."

Elinor sighed. "All my years of Coppertone, gone to waste."

"That's why I'm marrying Misa," joked Matt. "She's going to stamp out the ginger gene for future generations of Costigans."

Misa's smile dimmed slightly.

"I can't wait," gushed Elinor. "Soon you'll be all settled in your new home and ready to start a family. And once I finally cut ties with my landlord, I'll be right around the corner too!"

I may have a hit-or-miss relationship with Misa, but I can pick out her discomfort like a good pair of jeans at Value Village. Elinor leaned over to grab her hand, offering the same warmth I had clung to earlier, but it seemed to have the opposite effect. Misa's entire body stiffened—it was as if her brain had skipped a beat, leaving her mired in Elinor's words. It was such a strange reaction to a passing comment, especially for someone who was so skilled at smoothing over rumples in conversation. My veins buzzed with a kind of optimism I hadn't felt since we booked our flights here. Something was wrong in paradise, and in that case, maybe my interference in this wedding wasn't uncalled for after all. Maybe—and I leaned real hard into that maybe—I would be doing everyone involved a favor.

Elinor picked up on the tension and backtracked quickly, trying to take the pressure off Misa. "Of course, I'm sure you'll be very busy with your own schedules. I didn't mean to imply that I'd be around all the time—"

"No, it's fine," said Misa, suddenly regaining her words. "I think the heat just hit me, all at once. I've got a bit of a headache." She glanced toward Matt, who was watching in dismay as his mom's face crumpled.

"We'll have a great time hanging out together in normal

weather," he chimed in, slapping a comforting hand on Elinor's back. "Hey, Mum—do you think you could, uh, pop up to your room and grab Misa an Advil? It would really help her out."

Elinor leapt into action. "Anything for the bride-to-be." She strode toward the elevators like she was joining a top-secret NASA mission. Beside me, Misa whispered into Matt's ear and he nodded, tension etched into his forehead.

"Well, isn't this fun?" bellowed Tilley as she barged into our little circle of secrets. Booze sloshed over the lip of her hollowed-out pineapple. "The psych ward Scooby-Doo gang is back together again!"

You could almost read the error script running behind Misa's eyes at the unwelcome intrusion. Matt reached for her hand. "Hey, Misa," he said softly, "wanna go for a walk? There's a quiet corner over there that has your name on it."

She nodded, and they shifted away from the party hand in hand, Misa's shoulders jerking occasionally. Dodging well-meaning guests and hotel staff along the path, Matt led her toward a concrete stairwell at the back of the resort.

Tilley shoved her drink into my hands. "Hold my damn pineapple," she grumbled, then took off down the path to offer an uncharacteristic apology, exhaling like a fighter bull.

I didn't want to be left standing alone, so I followed my sister. I caught her just outside the stairwell, poking her head around the corner. She turned back toward me and put a finger to her lips.

Matt and Misa were slow dancing in the silent stairwell. One hand in hers and another on her waist, Matt rocked them back and forth to a rhythm that we couldn't hear. Misa's face was pressed into his shoulder, and her breath rose and fell steadily in his embrace. I couldn't stop looking at them, even though it hurt, so Tilley grabbed my hand and tried to yank me away. But it was Misa who put a stop to the scene—she placed a hand on Matt's chest and shook her head slowly before exiting through the back door. Matt remained stationary after she left, staring at the ceiling like it might hold the answers he was looking for.

Tilley hauled me around the corner and snatched her drink out of my hands, taking a long swig. "Your friends are weird, Dee."

"Matt learned that one from his mom," I said slowly. "She thinks it's impossible to be upset with someone when you're dancing with them. But I guess Misa found a way." My mind replayed the transition from the party to the stairwell, searching for clues. "Something's going on with them, something she's trying to hide."

I tried to sneak another look back at the stairwell, and Tilley smacked me upside the head.

"Dee. Dee! Are you seriously checking out his Timbit ass right now?" She drained the remainder of her drink and sighed dramatically. "I hope you remember this moment when I throw up in our bathtub tonight."

And just for the record, I did.

6

"DON'T SPEAK" —NO DOUBT (4:23)

WE MISSED THE complimentary breakfast because Tilley was up painting our bathroom like Jackson Pollock until four A.M., but we made it out of our hotel room just in time for lunch. I watched teams of servers take away the remains of this morning's buffet, marvelling at the excess and worrying about the waste. The very concept of all-inclusive resorts was staggering to me, even as I sprawled out in the middle of one.

Tilley didn't seem to mind. She had bounced back after a few extra-strength Tylenols and a little hair of the dog and was happily lounging by the infinity pool in a bright blue swimsuit that had a highly questionable fabric-to-holes ratio.

"You look like a mermaid who got caught in a net on purpose," I said, glancing down at my understated black one-piece.

"I told the golf instructor to meet me at the pool at three so I can emerge from the water like a Bond girl," Tilley replied. "It's been a recurring dream of mine. That, and running over catcallers with my tricked-out red Fiat."

"Even in your dreams, you own a red Fiat?"

"Yes, but the dream one has air-conditioning," she said. She took a long sip of something that looked like orange juice but probably wasn't, then pulled her beach towel over her face.

"What are you—"

"Not now," she whispered as an expressionless man with bleach-blond hair walked behind our part of the pool deck and disappeared up a flight of concrete stairs.

"Who the hell is that?"

"I don't want to call him the flavor of the week because this trip is only a week long," she said, emerging from behind the colorful fabric. "But he was definitely on the menu yesterday."

"I don't even know when you would have had time for that," I said, but then remembered the chunk of time when I wrapped myself in our hotel duvet, heavy with the guilt that on some level, I had always been rooting for my friends' relationship to fail. I had tried to quiet my brain by repeating a fragment of my favorite No Doubt song, but the trick wasn't working. My brain still wound itself up and refused to release until Tilley returned with a bowl of soft-serve ice cream from the kitchen and a suspicious mark on her neck.

As we sat by the pool, Tilley looked me dead in the eyes. "It's amazing how much you can accomplish when you're not tied to something that is never going to happen," she said, then paused. "That's actually pretty good. Maybe I should use that line on that guy."

"You don't want to see him again?"

She rolled her eyes. "He reminded me too much of that dude I dated from my mental health first-aid course. Like okay, it happened four times," she said. "Doesn't mean we have to complete the hand."

Eventually we sat down at a shady table with mimosas and watermelon goat cheese salads. I plunged into mine, savoring the rich taste and wondering just how far I could stretch my tax refund this year. Being a dog walker wasn't the most lucrative gig on the planet and definitely didn't provide health benefits, but Tilley shouldering our rent had allowed me to scrape together the resources for one big spend—which ended up being this trip.

The original plan was to save up for the next time I got sick, a last-resort resort kind of thing: private mental health care, the kind I googled at night when I was feeling mechanical and hopeless. I started planning my hypothetical collapses like vacations— would I soothe my overheated brain in a quaint country manor that offered culinary workshops with a Red Seal chef, or would I find sweet, sweet recovery at a four-acre mental health resort nestled in the depths of a rainforest? Would I even have time for therapy between posh tennis lessons and ten-pin bowling? I tried not to focus on the fact that a month of treatment would cost upwards of twenty grand, but I knew that this time, I would not be a mere psychiatric tourist. I wanted to stay long enough to pick up the intricacies of the local language, become a regular at the coffee shop, start a book club with my new best friends, beat a recreational therapist at Scrabble. My doctor looked at me very strangely when I named off these options like a grocery list, but trust me, there are worse things than having an institutionalization bucket list. For instance, there's having no bucket list at all.

"So did you figure out what you're going to say to Matt?" asked Tilley.

"No," I said between mouthfuls.

"Good," said Tilley brightly, "because he's heading this way and looks more dishevelled than usual. I know how you like that."

She was right. Apart from the rumpled hair, I could tell Matt was stressed because he was wearing his green Zelda Triforce T-shirt, the soft cotton gently wrapped around his sides. It's Misa's favorite so he sometimes wears it when she's sick. I didn't hope she was sick or anything, but part of me hoped that if she was, she was quite unattractively sick. And not just because I wanted her to be unattractive, but because I often feel that ugly-sick is the most genuine iteration of myself. Sometimes I am delicately depressed, like a wet tissue-paper flower, and then there are times when I am in my terry-cloth bathrobe screaming at my parents for telling me I'm not well enough to drive and it feels like I have shed my skin like a snake and I'm burning up in the sun, thinking in sharp cardiovascular spikes, *This is who I really am, this is why I deserve nothing, this is why you should leave me.* I have rarely seen Misa like this, but I like to think there is a side of her that only Matt knows—and loves anyway. I think this also might be why I'm so obsessed with him.

"Hey," I said to Matt (in a completely non-obsessive way).

"Hey," Matt said back, but his eyes were scanning the patio like he was on the run from a mall cop. He plunked down into an empty chair at our table and glanced at Tilley. "Can we talk? Maybe somewhere else?"

"Hello, Matthew," said Tilley, furiously stabbing a chunk of watermelon. "Did you know that Dee and I are reincarnated twins? It's very rude of you to try and get us to keep secrets from each other. I didn't take any bullshit in my past life and I'm not about to start now."

Matt stared at her. "Do you know how to have a normal conversation?"

"It's called having a personality, Matt," purred Tilley. "I'm sorry you haven't had a chance to develop one yet."

"I just—I wanted Dee to help me with my vows," he sputtered. "I'm having trouble finding the right words for the beginning, you know?"

I coughed up my mimosa, and Tilley leaned over to whack me on the back. Once I had regained the ability to breathe, Tilley stopped to survey me and briskly assessed the longing in my eyes. "She'd love to," she said cheerfully. She wanted time to seduce the golf instructor anyway.

I choked down the tail end of my salad, then Matt and I made our way to the beach. Deck chairs were everywhere, but I sat down in the sand to avoid making the hotel workers carry one over for us. I hadn't realized it when I boarded the flight, but coming to this island meant setting off a chain reaction of consequences for other people that I wasn't entirely comfortable with, all in the name of "getting away from it all." I had asked Matt if he felt as weird about it as I did, since we both (had, in his case) made our living in hospitality back home, but he just said that us being here was good for the island's economy and left it at that. I hoped he wouldn't turn into the kind of guy who didn't make eye contact with waiters.

"Every good love story has this great genesis moment, right?" said Matt, kicking off his sandals. "But with Misa not willing to talk much about the ward, and with so much changing over the past year, it's hard to get back into that headspace and remember how it all started."

"Well, that's what everyone tells you, right?" I said, trying to keep the bitterness out of my voice. "To look forward, not back?"

⋮

They told all of us not to keep in touch after we were discharged, that we would drag each other down. I wonder if Matt might have listened to them if I hadn't pushed, hadn't told him that I needed him more than ever. The first day I got out, I called the ward in tears from my parents' bungalow.

Jermaine picked up the phone since he had taken on the responsibility of hallway phone secretary.

"Who's this?" I could picture him snarling into the grimy plastic mouthpiece.

"Jermaine, this is Dee. I was three rooms down from you, like, four hours ago. Can you go get Matt?"

"What's the password?"

"What?"

"The password," he repeated, breathing heavily.

"What are you talking about? There is no password!"

"You're right," he said slowly. "Only one of us would know that."

I heard a loud clunk as Jermaine dropped the phone, then the soft patter of his ward shoes against the tile floor as he went off to find Matt. My old neighbor Harsha must have been on the pay phone beside Jermaine's because I could hear snippets of a tirade about her cuticles, and how she wasn't sure she could be a model with nails this short. When Matt finally got to the phone, he sounded flustered and out of breath. Ward hallways are longer than you'd think.

"Dee, you alright?" he heaved into the mouthpiece.

"You have to promise not to make fun of me, okay? Promise me," I said in one breath. "You don't know what it's like yet because you're still in the bubble and outside seems like the dream, but it's not the dream, Matt, it's not the dream at all."

"I promise, Dee. I promise."

"Okay," I said, and took a deep breath. "I need to take a shower because I smell like hospital, but Tilley had to go to work and I haven't taken a shower without someone timing it in weeks and I just feel like, I don't know, lost? I don't have a schedule anymore. I don't know how long I should be in there or when I should eat, there's just this huge expanse of time in front of me and I'm just watching it go by and it's fucking overwhelming and I feel like a failure because all I wanted when I was in there was to get out, and now I want back in, Matt. I want back in."

There was silence on the other end of the line. Then: "Put the phone down on the floor."

"What?"

"Put the phone down on the floor," he repeated, "but leave it on speakerphone. I'm going to time you from here, okay? I'll let you know when your time is up. I'll be with you the whole way."

"Okay."

I placed the phone close enough to the shower so I could step away from the water and hear it, but far away enough to avoid collateral damage. Stepping into the tub, I let the warmth cascade from the showerhead over my shoulders and back, running down the parts of me that felt clinical and detached. I closed my eyes and thought about the little tubs of applesauce that I wouldn't have to eat, the metallic clank of the lunch window opening and closing, the sticky pads of the EKG. Tried to replace these with new and familiar impressions—lingering wafts of Tilley's favorite apple cinnamon candle, the soft edges of our blue gingham shower curtain, a stray Gillette razor sitting on the snarled lip of the tub. Picked up the razor and put it down, decided it was too brash an addition to my fresh routine, and besides, I was kind of enjoying the dark hedges of my underarms.

"*How are you doing?*" Matt's tinny voice echoed from my bathroom floor.

"*It's weird but okay,*" I shouted back, unsure of the shower acoustics. "*Just gotta wash my hair.*"

I hurried through the rest of my shower routine, wrapped myself in a worn towel, and picked Matt up off the cold white tile. "*Did it,*" I said, shivering in the breeze from the open window.

"*Proud,*" he said, then paused. "*Wanna hang out for a bit?*"

I curled up on the bath mat and Matt told me how Jermaine had confiscated Liz's second juice at lunch, which had caused a bit of a shouting match over the cafeteria table. I tried to think of something equally funny about my return home but ended up telling him how my dad refused to take the day off to make sure I was okay, even though Tilley had already maxed out her employer's kindness to visit me at the hospital. We talked until my butt went numb on the bath mat, my hair dried from window breezes, and Jermaine came by and informed Matt he was hogging the phone, and that while he had tried to make a small exception for an ex-patient, we were really taking advantage of his goodwill. I hung up with a grin longer than string licorice and decided I would hold on to this warmth any way I could.

❧

"I GUESS THERE'S not much use in looking too far backward," Matt said. "We've got enough to think about just getting to tomorrow."

In some ways, I envied his ability to brush the memory off, but deep down, I craved the comfort of that psychic return to the ward. I had come to appreciate how rock bottom had made me brave, while Matt and Misa had come to fear it now that they had something to lose. I wondered if that was part of the reason why he couldn't find the words to capture their beginning—because it had become nearly unimaginable. I couldn't bear to stand on the sidelines while this wedding erased everything that made him the kind of person I'd be lucky to love.

"But if you want to get back into the headspace of when you and Misa first met, you have to think about the gap," I said carefully.

Matt's brow crinkled. "What do you mean?"

"Think about it—in the ward, no one listened to us," I said, wishing I could stand on some sort of shoreline soapbox. "Care looked like locked doors and checkboxes. It wasn't exactly a hopeful place."

He nodded furiously, and I continued, swept up in the story. "And despite all that, look at what we found together. Friendship. Community. The will to make macaroni art when we could barely find a reason to stay on this planet."

Matt threw his head back and laughed, a deep throaty sound.

"That's what you need to remember," I said, looking him straight in the eyes. "That finding love where you did wasn't just unlikely—it was damn near impossible. Now that's something to write a speech about."

His smile faltered. "I wish I could, Dee, really. But Misa would never go for it." A terse bark crawled out from the back of his throat. "I don't know why I thought things would change when she started volunteering at the hospital. It's like I'm living in a full-time PR agency—you know, don't let the board find out why she volunteers, don't get help from her uncle when things get bad, don't tell her friends where we really met."

"Doesn't it bother you that she wants you to lie?" I asked, wondering if this was a contributing factor behind last night's dancing.

Matt paused. "It's not lying, really. It's just making sure she's comfortable with what we share with others. Not everyone has to treat their diagnosis like a manifesto."

"What's that supposed to mean?" I thought about the uneven scrawls of Tilley's burned CD and started using the back end of Matt's pen to carve a giant snail in the sand. I wouldn't say they're my favorite animal, but they take their sweet time getting places, and I respect that. Kind of in the same way I respect Snoop Dogg.

"It means that we're out here cracking jokes about our depression," he said. "And Misa's muddling through in her own way. Actually, that's one of the things I like most about our relationship—it's a balance, you know?"

"Yeah," I replied, still sculpting the surface of the beach. I wanted to push him to say it, that he thought she was beautiful but disingenuous, and give me a tiny crack that I could squeeze my heart into, let it expand. "I get why you'd see it like that."

"I just see her," he said, and I didn't let my smile waver, not even for a second. "She's right sometimes. People have to move on."

I dug a trench in the sand with my heels and tried to bury the twinge of guilt in my stomach. "But is it really moving on," I said stubbornly, "or is it pretending that it never happened?"

"I think if Misa really wanted to pretend it never happened," said Matt softly, "she wouldn't be marrying me."

We sat in silence and watched a blue catamaran launch from the shore. I thought about the way Matt had proposed to Misa—with his mother's ring on a good day and with a Ring Pop on a bad one, just to remind her that he'd be there no matter how she was feeling. I wanted him to have that same unwavering support, but I worried that Misa would falter in front of an audience. Because more often than not, it was our bad days that attracted attention.

"Sometimes it feels like she's miles ahead of me, recovery-wise," he said after a while. "It's like having Donovan Bailey as a running partner."

I could tell he was rooting around for the next punch line, something that would fill the empty space. "Have you considered going back to therapy?" I asked.

"I don't need therapy," he said roughly. "I just need to start writing music again. I haven't been able to get anything down since I joined her dad's company. I know it makes everything easier for us in the long run, but it does feel sometimes like I'm giving up a part of myself."

It was Matt's dad who taught him how to play the guitar, during that brief appearance in his teens, but it was Elinor who stopped him from abandoning it after he left. She put holes in their living room wall to hang his instruments, watched him perform every chance she could, and even tolerated the year he spent learning the banjo. "What's for you will not go by you," she'd say firmly every time he'd think about quitting. "It's only a matter of time." I wondered how she felt about the redirection he was taking, whether she also worried that Matt couldn't stay grounded without that familiar refrain. She knew better than anyone that when the words left him, there was a higher chance that he would leave too.

"You don't have to give it all up, you know," I said. "Being part of Misa's family doesn't mean being exactly like them."

He shook his head. "You don't understand, Dee. When you're with someone, you do what you need to do to secure the best possible tomorrow with them."

His words stung more than I'd anticipated. Maybe he was

right, and I couldn't understand. After all, I had been on my own—besides Tilley—for as long as I could remember. I also knew that after growing up with a dad who only stopped by when he needed something, Matt's idea of love was constancy—the one thing we all struggled to attain. But even so, I didn't think that falling in love should mean sacrificing who you really were.

I balled my hands into tight fists. "Everything is different now, and I hate it."

Matt paused. "You mean I'm different, don't you?"

I didn't know what else to say, so I pulled away, kept drawing sand spirals for the biggest shell I could imagine.

He let out a sigh that was barely audible above the waves. "Sometimes I feel that too. But you know what brings me back?"

I levelled my gaze at him, but I couldn't hold on to the bitterness when he looked at me like I was the only person on this entire island.

"It's us," Matt said simply, not waiting a moment for me to respond. "The one thing that matters is that we don't give up on each other." He started to say something else but then spotted Misa's family walking toward us.

"Just—hold on a second," he muttered. "I don't want to leave things like this."

I bit my tongue and stabbed his pen into the center of my ballooning snail, wondering why it always felt like we were leaving something unsaid. At home, in paradise, or anywhere in between, I could always find the words to tear myself down. But where the hell did they go when I wanted to be brave?

7

"MAPS" —YEAH YEAH YEAHS (3:40)

KEN AND JULIE Nagasaka moved toward us at a sloth's pace, with Obachan sandwiched between them. She wore a wide sun hat and her white sneakers even on the beach, taking careful sinking steps around sandcastles and discarded towels. She let go of Ken's arm briefly to wave at me, and I waved back, momentarily forgetting about my desire to burrow deep into the sand.

With the sun beating down on our backs, Matt introduced me to Ken and Julie without mentioning where we'd met. Whenever these conversations arose, it felt like we were living in some alternate universe where we couldn't be fiercely proud of how we'd come together. It was strange to know Misa so well and yet have to hold her at arm's length. What she was afraid of, I wasn't entirely sure, but I was curious to find out.

I hastily stood up, brushed the sand off my ass, and said hello, sticking a reluctant hand out to Ken. His vigorous handshake nearly pulled me over in the sand, a big smile splitting his face in two. He had a wiry build and thick, wavy hair that framed his angular face—definitely a combination that Misa had inherited.

He was all decked out in tennis clothes, a curious contrast to his wife, who might have had more rings than fingers. Julie was short with sparkling eyes and heavy bangs. Despite the wind, her pale blue linen dress stayed perfectly unwrinkled as she gave Matt a warm hug. She eyed my scraggly black one-piece and neatly remarked, "Sorry to interrupt you."

When we first got the wedding invitation, Tilley had been surprised by Ken and Julie's names, written in flowing script across the top. "How does someone with parents named Ken and Julie wind up with a name like Misa?"

I had asked Misa about it once, after I found out Obachan had a Japanese name that she never used. *Mitsu.* I only knew her as Obachan, but her friends called her Martha. Misa told me her grandparents had stopped giving their children Japanese names after the internment, to avoid drawing extra attention to their race. They wanted Julie and her brother to fit in with the white neighborhood they resettled in after the war, so visits to the cultural center or Japanese language school were rare. After Mitsu's mother passed, there was no one left to speak to in Japanese anyway. But when Misa was born, Julie saw a chance to reconnect with her heritage, raising her daughter in between presiding over Japanese Canadian festivals and fundraisers. Everyone in their community knew the Koyanagi and Nagasaka families, and everyone lived to please Julie in particular.

As soon as sufficient greetings had been exchanged, Ken pulled a pair of binoculars out from an orange satchel to watch a flock of birds overhead. Misa had once told me orange was his favorite color, but her mom thought it was too gaudy for the house, so all of their garden equipment—shovels, watering cans, wheelbarrows—was orange in a domestic protest.

Julie looked apologetically at her husband. "Ken," she said

softly, as Obachan leaned on her arm. He didn't budge. She sighed and nodded conspiratorially at me. I smiled uncertainly, hoping she didn't think I was here to make trouble, even if I was.

"He likes animals better than people," she said. "We went to Hawaii last year and you'd think we'd be hiking volcanos, but all he liked to do was watch sea turtles swim in circles. I wanted to see things explode."

Obachan laughed heartily and Matt grinned. "So any words of wisdom for me as I finish up my wedding vows?"

In all honesty, I had completely forgotten that's what we were supposed to be doing. *Selfish*, screamed my brain. I swallowed hard and tried to focus on the words emerging from Julie's thin lips.

"Did Misa ever tell you that I once threw my engagement ring on the lawn?"

Matt lit up. "How has this stayed in the Nagasaka family vault for so long? Ken, you're keeping the good stuff from me." Ken nodded cheerfully and aimed a camera over Matt's head, toward a circling sandpiper. As it swept down the shoreline past an anchored party boat, he muttered his apologies and strode after it.

"He was very late for our engagement party," said Julie, undeterred. "I was so angry that I took my ring off and threw it into the grass. So, he spent the rest of the night crawling around looking for it. But he knew I was right, and he didn't give up, and we're still together—thirty years now."

"So you're saying I should be on time for the ceremony?" Matt grinned.

"I'm saying that when Misa is stubborn, she's also probably right." Julie patted Matt's shoulder brusquely. "Now, we're going to look for more birds. But I hope you find the words you're looking for."

Julie tugged on Obachan's arm, but she didn't move. A mere observer might think that she had lost most of the conversation to the crashing of the waves, but I knew Obachan's selective hearing was often strategic.

"Dee," said Obachan. She lifted the brim of her sun hat and beckoned me closer, her arthritic fingers curling. "Do you know where Misa is?"

"I'm not sure, Obachan," I said, leaving out that I was actively avoiding her out of guilt. "Do you want me to find her for you?" Julie looked at me, her lips pursed.

"I want to give her my pearls," Obachan said, pointing at her neck.

"Mom, you can give them to her on her wedding day," said Julie firmly. I could tell they'd had this conversation before, and Julie wasn't thrilled about a repeat episode, especially in the presence of non-family.

"I want her to have them," she repeated. She grabbed my hand. "Dee, tell Misa to come see me after lunch."

"I will," I said, even though it was the second-last thing I wanted to do on this earth. My current vow-writing situation edged it out by just an inch.

"I didn't know you knew my mother so well," said Julie lightly. "How did you and Misa meet again?"

I could feel Matt starting to sweat beside me. "I—uh—I volunteer at the hospital with her," I said, hating that I was now part of this weird network of deception. I glanced at Obachan, but she was busy watching kids from the hotel next door wreak havoc on a water trampoline. "In Scarborough. You grew up there too, didn't you?"

I tried to picture Julie—young, free-spirited, and just a little bit imposing—riding her bike past redbrick bungalows with metal awnings and creaky screen doors, squeezing into the tiny neighborhood ice cream shop tucked between strip malls. But she seemed eager to distance herself from the sprawl of Scarborough. Instead,

Julie examined me closely, as if she could pick out a reason why I'd be so comfortable at a neglected suburban hospital. "Why do you spend your time there? It doesn't seem like a place anyone would want to stay long," she said.

I wasn't quite sure if she was talking about the hospital or Scarborough itself, but either way, it wasn't an unfamiliar sentiment. My neighborhood had long been a landing place for people who dreamed of going elsewhere, and the ward was a revolving door of folks who just couldn't find their footing. The people I grew up with, the friends I grew alongside in the hospital—we were always caught in transition. But I think it was the natural movement of these communities that allowed me to plant the sprawling roots I needed to sustain myself in the outside world, where people feared the places I had so proudly come from. Between Scarborough and the ward, our communities thrived on one person caring for the next, ad infinitum, when no one else ever looked our way. The fact that Julie couldn't appreciate this helped explain why Misa hadn't told her parents about us either.

"Misa and Dee do great work," interjected Matt, noticing my freeze-frame expression. "I think you'd be surprised by what goes on there." He winked at me, and I felt myself slowly returning to my body.

Julie nodded quickly. "Of course," she said. "I just wish Misa would spend more time helping me out at the cultural center. Although I'm sure the poor souls who end up at the hospital need her more than I do."

I gritted my teeth. This poor soul was starting to run out of patience with this conversation.

"I never go to the cultural center," said Obachan, wagging a stern finger at Julie. "The people there, they like to talk too much. Even though the food is good, I don't go."

Julie looked so deflated that I almost forgave her for her previous comment.

"Mom, we're trying to make sure that no one forgets what happened to you during the war," she said. "It's important for us to remember."

"The war? That was a long time ago, before you were even born! I learned how to sew then, you know."

"I know, Mom," said Julie, giving up. She looked down the beach, toward a distant speck of orange. "We'd better go find Ken."

Obachan took a few steps forward, unsteady in the sand. She turned to me and pointed again. "I'll talk to you later, Dee. Don't forget."

When they were safely out of earshot, Matt turned to me and grimaced.

"Sorry about that," he said. "Julie's an expert in internment history but hasn't quite figured out how to mention psychiatric hospitals without looking like she swallowed a lemon."

"Yeah," I replied. "I can tell."

He offered me a lopsided grin and held out his arm for a secret handshake. I half-heartedly bumped elbows with him.

"Almost makes you grateful for Tilley, doesn't it?" he said. "Almost, but not quite."

I laughed, trying to brush it off. But it didn't matter how many times I'd been hit by pitying words like Julie's. The sting was always the same. I scrunched my toes into the sand and exhaled. "I suppose we should get brainstorming."

We found our imprints in the sand, nestled back into their comfortable grooves, and started from the beginning.

"So what did you think the first time you saw her?" I asked, tucking a wayward strand of hair behind my ear.

"What did I think," repeated Matt slowly. "Well, to be honest, it wasn't a right-away kind of thing. I mean, I had just tried to kill myself, so I wasn't exactly looking for—Wait, am I even allowed to say that?"

Yes, screamed my brain. "No," I said aloud. "Let's not lead with attempted suicide. But what *are* you supposed to say about how you met?"

"Dunno. Misa just said to leave the ward out of it."

"Then tell them you met online," I said. "It's so boring now that no one will ask any questions."

"That's not going to fly with Julie, I'll tell you that much. The whole six-month engagement thing is already hard enough to swallow."

"So try honesty," I said, determined to make this work. Part of me was firmly convinced that I loved Matt enough to help him figure this out—that if he came up with an answer that proved he would be happy with Misa, I could walk away with my heart intact. But the other half of me was busy absorbing his broad, rounded shoulders, wondering how I could get closer to him. "Can you remember the moment when you really fell in love with her?"

Matt shook his head. "I just don't think it's realistic to have one moment that changes everything."

Lord help me, I was in love with the least romantic person in the world.

Matt saw my unimpressed face and tried to compensate. "I mean, Misa is my baseline. No matter how far I stray from where I want to be, I can always find my way back. Because of her. Or is that a compass? I think I'm mixing metaphors here."

"Just a little bit," I said, taking a deep breath. "Okay, is she your best friend?"

Silence.

"Matt?"

"That'd be more like you or Vik, I guess," he allowed, and my heart did a roundoff triple back handspring. If I had to fight a jacked British Indian guy for first place, I'd still jump into the ring. "I don't know who made that best friend rule, but I don't think you should depend on one person for everything. It's just bad news bears, Dee."

* * *

I remember the exact moment I fell in love with Matt, even if he doesn't believe in that kind of thing. I hadn't been able to keep down my new dosage of medication the night before, and I was struggling with the morning after, crumpled up in a corner of the rec room couch. Matt slid into the seat beside me, his hospital gown catching slightly on a torn piece of leather. I tried to wipe away my operatic tears before he took a good look at me.

"How are you holding up?" he asked, offering me a contraband banana from the breakfast I'd missed.

I straightened up, ashamed to be spotted in my natural puddle form. "It's fine. It's just—sometimes when my meds kick my ass, I wake up knowing that I'm going to have a terrible day, and there's nothing I can do about it." My voice broke, and I shoved my head into my hands. "I just want to fast-forward and try again tomorrow."

"I know the feeling," he said. We sat in silence a moment, listening to the early spring rain fall against the window.

"I'm sorry I'm not my best today," I mumbled into my palms, wishing that I could be beautiful and sad like a Lana Del Rey song.

Matt cocked an eyebrow. "Dee, you're at your best every

day you get up and try. You never have to apologize when some days are harder than others."

He said it so casually, like he was reading the back of a cereal box, but his words hit me deep in the gut. From what I'd picked up from the few relationships I'd run into the ground, I thought that to be cared for, I'd need to bury all the weepy, irritable, deeply embarrassing parts of myself. My longest-serving suitor, as he was packing up his things, had thrown one last dagger over his shoulder: Do you honestly think anyone else could put up with this? *Huddled up in my trademark blanket burrito, I didn't bother responding because I knew the answer all too well. But here, years later, was a guy who was happy just to sit with me, even on my worst days.*

"You know my family's originally from Scotland, right?" Matt said. I nodded. "Well, I don't know if you've ever been there, but there are tons of hills, it's cloudy on a good day, and more often than not, it rains like a mother. But I'll be damned if it's not a beautiful place to be." He placed his hand on top of mine—which was still clutching the stolen banana—and raised an eyebrow at me. "And so is your brain, even when it doesn't feel like it sometimes. Okay?"

"Okay," I whispered, then paused. "Is it really that great in Scotland?"

Matt grinned. "Maybe I'll get to show you around someday."

⁓

SITTING NEXT TO Matt, I wondered what I'd say if I ever struck up the nerve to turn both our worlds upside down. "What if you tried something like this," I said. "What if you tell her that you fell in love with her in sickness, and that love has led you back to health. What if you tell her that you'll love her on her good days and bad days and days without descriptors, because every day you get with her is one that's worth living, and that's a feeling you thought you'd never have again."

"That's beautiful, Dee," he said, looking at me like he had just noticed I had a face. My cheeks flushed. "But don't you think that's kind of dangerous? You can't equate being in love with being healthy. That's not how it works."

It was easy for him to say that because he had both love and health, when I had nothing to hold on to at night but nausea from antipsychotics and the overripe bananas that kept them down. It just wasn't fair. I knew if I had the chance to be happy with Matt, I could never fall into the same pit of hopelessness I'd come to call home. When we traded laughs, brushed hands, dreamt of a world outside of the limits of normal—in those moments, I'd never been better. And yet here he was, taking it all for granted. Resentment crawled up the back of my throat. I spiralled, and I spiralled fast.

"I don't remember asking you for therapy, Matt," I snapped. "Although now that I think about it, I might have actually gotten some in day treatment if it wasn't for you."

His brows flattened in an instant. "I'm sorry, Dee. I didn't mean to patronize you."

"But you did," I said, furiously scratching out my sand snail. "You and Misa are always acting like I'm some sort of charity case and I'm fucking tired of it."

Matt threw his hands up in the air. "Why does there always have to be a bad guy with you? Things never seem to just be hard because they're hard—it's always you against your parents, or you against your doctors, and now you're acting like I haven't been on your team this whole time?" He turned away from me and muttered under his breath. "If you spent less time fighting the people around you and more time listening to them—"

I stared at him, hard. "Did I not just spend the last hour listening to your bullshit and running a goddamn paint-by-numbers class so you could find one good reason why you're getting married this weekend?"

Matt stood up and brushed the sand off his shorts. "That's a pretty shit thing to say, Dee. Even for you."

He walked back toward the resort, leaving me sitting alone on the beach with an empty notepad and a sinking heart.

8

"GOT 'TIL IT'S GONE" —JANET JACKSON FT. Q-TIP & JONI MITCHELL (4:01)

IT WAS LUCKY that I had managed to piss off the groom before Misa's itinerary really got out of hand. With any luck, Matt and I would both have some time to decompress before we ran into each other at the stag and doe festivities later that evening. When I got back to our hotel room, Tilley was also taking advantage of the calm before the storm—she was sprawled out on our unmade bed in a see-through gold cover-up, chowing down on a family-sized bag of salt and vinegar Kettle chips.

"Hey," I said, kicking aside a damp towel she had left on the floor. True to form, Tilley had immediately hung a DO NOT DISTURB sign on our door to prevent anyone else from having to clean up our bullshit. Because of her moral stance, her entire wardrobe was sprawled across our tiny suite. "Would you say that I'm a self-destructive person?"

"On a scale of velour tracksuits to the *Hindenburg*, I would say you're clocking in around a first date at Medieval Times."

"Thanks," I said, snatching a chip and collapsing on the

bed beside her. Tilley has a running theory that people who buy individual-sized bags of chips are deeply disturbed. I don't know if there's any empirical proof to back this up, but our mom sometimes buys tiny bags of Hickory Sticks, and she once forgot us in a dollar store. "How was your golf lesson?"

"Well, it's a game with negative points that requires patience," Tilley said. "And the way he treated the staff reminded me of the assholes I deal with on bottomless wing night. Dude had the hair and the attitude of a John Hughes bad guy." She nudged the chip bag in my direction. "Do you wanna tell me what happened?" she asked.

I took another chip, letting the salt sting my lips. "Sometimes I don't know if I actually have a mental illness or if I'm just a bad person," I said finally.

"Why not both?" snorted Tilley, then processed my expression. "Okay, what makes you think that?"

"It feels like I don't react to stuff properly," I said. "It's like when you're watching TV and the commercials always come on louder than the actual show. If you turn it down, you lose the plot, and if you turn it up, it feels like the room is screaming at you. I spend all my time adjusting because I want to be the right volume for people, you know? And it's been years now, and I still don't have it right."

"That doesn't mean you're bad. It means you're trying your fucking guts out."

I knew that was what it felt like, but I couldn't help but notice people like Misa clicking with the first antipsychotic they tried, while I turned the medicine cabinet into a goddamn Bulk Barn. "It's just . . . sometimes it feels like everything would have been different if I had been the first one to get better."

My old therapist used to always tell me, "You can't love anyone else until you love yourself." (This is partly why I ghosted him.) But what he didn't say was that if you spent years trying to love *yourself* and your broken brain kept sabotaging you, then you might miss out on the *anyone else* too.

"Hold up," said Tilley. She rolled over on the cushy bed so she could stare directly into my soul. "Do you think Matt is with Misa because he sees her as being less sick than you?"

I didn't say anything.

"I'm sorry, but did I miss the part where your life became *The Amazing Race: Psychiatric Edition*?" Tilley crammed a handful of chips into her mouth and chewed furiously. "I refuse to live in a world where the hypothetical opinion of the Pillsbury Dopamine Boy matters more than your actual recovery."

I wasn't even sure if I had a recovery to speak of. Every self-help book I had ever read promised some sort of happy ending, not the dull grind of my wheels spinning in place for years.

Tilley poked around the bottom of the chip bag for any remaining survivors, then crumpled it up and threw it in the general direction of the garbage.

"Look, I want you to get back on your feet more than anything in the world," she said after a moment, "but I'll be damned if you're going to do it for a boy. Have you ever considered that your fixation on getting better for him is a reason why he didn't date you in the first place? That's a lot of pressure to put on a guy who thinks individual therapy still has too many people involved."

"It would just make everything I've gone through worth it, you know, if we wound up together," I said in a voice so small it could have curled up inside an espresso cup. "I need something good to come out of this."

"Yeah, so," she replied, staring up at the ceiling, "who says it needs to be him?"

I HADN'T FORGOTTEN about Obachan's pearls. I decided to take a stroll through the resort, and if I didn't run into Misa, at least I could tell myself I had tried to pass on the message. It was the kind of moral loophole that was becoming increasingly familiar in my day-to-day life.

Tilley announced that it was time for a siesta, so I softly closed the door to our hotel room and headed toward the lobby. I passed the neatly trimmed hedge path that led to the spa and dodged a rolling tray of fruit platters clanking toward the dining area. Underneath the dazzling lobby chandelier, incoming tourists sat cheerfully in wicker chairs, sipping rum punch with their feet kicked up on glossy suitcases. The concierge bustled around behind the front desk, dealing out room keys and restaurant reservations before helping a frazzled young honeymooner organize a champagne surprise for his new husband. A lanky Black man around my age noticed me watching her and grinned.

"Grace is amazing, isn't she?"

He wasn't wearing the trademark turquoise tie worn by most of the resort staff. Instead, he wore a crisp white dress shirt with a name tag. "I'm Marco," he said, before I could even read it. He offered me the kind of handshake that told me he was a real adult, despite being around my age. "I'm the recreation coordinator at Breeze Bay. Is it your first time on island?"

"Yep," I said, and his eyes lit up.

"That's exciting! Let me tell you about some of our activities," he began, and I shook my head sheepishly.

"I'm really sorry," I said. "I'm not, like, a good person for you to spend your time on. I could barely afford to fly here and I'm still not used to the all-you-can-eat thing, so I keep choosing cereal from the breakfast bar even though there's self-serve waffles, and yeah. I'm sorry. You seem really nice and I don't want to let you down."

He smiled at me with a kindness that crinkled the edges of his eyes. "Well, you seem really nice too!" He lowered his voice and shot me a conspiratorial grin. "We don't have to talk about activities. I'll be honest with you—you couldn't pay me to go parasailing anyway. Too high for me. What's your name?"

"I'm Dee," I said, holding out my hand. He shook it enthusiastically.

"Nice to meet you, Miss Dee. So what kind of cereal have you been enjoying?"

"Froot Loops," I said, only slightly embarrassed.

"Excellent choice," he said. "I'm a Wheaties man myself, but sometimes I feel like I should be a bit less practical and live a little, you know?"

A woman with blinding blonde hair and scalpel shoulders pushed past me and stood in front of Marco, arms crossed. A string of chunky diamonds dangled from her left wrist—just casual travel wear, I guessed. "Our bags aren't in our room yet," she said. "Just wanted to let you know that we're still waiting. Twenty minutes later."

The tiny hairs on my forearms raised in discomfort. Marco straightened his posture slightly and nodded, his smile not moving an inch. "Thank you so much for letting us know," he said. "I'll make sure one of our attendants is right with you."

The woman huffed and returned to the shady corner that she had emerged from, watching us out of the corner of her eye.

"Yikes," I said under my breath.

"I'd better go," said Marco, then beamed. "I'll see you around, Miss Dee!"

He strode off toward reception and playfully drummed on Grace's desk. She laughed and swiped at him as he fetched a bellhop for the irritated woman. On the other side of the lobby, I looked around at all the Tommy Bahama polos and Ted Baker beach bags and suddenly felt alone. I backed away from the throng and headed toward the deck.

The avoidance gods were not smiling down on me that day. As soon as I stepped out onto the pool deck, I saw Misa was floating inside a giant engagement ring. She was wearing a nautical striped bikini that looked fresh off a yacht. I wondered if Matt had told her about our fight on the beach, then decided it didn't matter. If she was mad, she wouldn't talk to me anyway. Problem solved.

"Hey, Misa," I yelled.

"Dee!" Misa sat bolt upright in her floaty and toppled over in the pool, her tanned arms flailing. I heard snickers beside me and turned to see Kei, Misa's cousin, heaving with laughter.

"She's going to kill you," Kei said, collapsing into their lounger. My cheeks flushed, knowing that this was another friendship I had let languish, even though they had moved back to the city months ago. Their messy brown space buns shook with every breath, and they were wearing a roomy crop top that proclaimed OUTTA HERE alongside cartoon spaceships and neon planets. "Do you know how long it takes her to straighten her hair in this heat?"

I had always pegged Misa for a classic only child—until I met Kei. If Tilley was the match to my dynamite, Kei was the moral compass to Misa's private boat. Kei showed up to family entanglements and doomsday anxiety attacks armed with reasonable solutions and the occasional one-liner to knock Misa off her high horse. Come to think of it, we could have used their calming presence at the welcome party.

"We missed you yesterday," I blurted out.

"My flight got in late," they explained. "I barely caught the end of everything. Besides, I missed you first—I haven't seen you in ages! I'm damp but come give me a hug anyway." They held out their arms and pulled me in.

"Sorry I've been out of touch," I said, glad that my unreliability hadn't claimed another casualty.

"No worries, Dee," Kei replied. "Friendship-wise, I'm kind of like a succulent. I thrive on neglect. Misa, on the other hand—"

"What am I?" asked Misa, surfacing and pushing her dripping black tresses out of her face. "Besides extremely wet at an inconvenient time, that is." She didn't seem to be mad at me, which was kind of a plus.

Kei threw Misa a towel as she climbed out of the pool. "As your official bridesmate, I've decided that you're a prickly pear. Because you appreciate a good floral, but you also can be spiky."

"So I'm an attack plant?"

"Or," said Kei, "a plant with strong defenses."

I was too afraid to ask Kei what kind of plant I'd be.

"I think you need to spend less time in the garden and more time with actual people," said Misa.

Kei pointed at a palm tree, and then me. "Check it out—I'm halfway there!"

Misa sighed and started wringing out her hair as Kei smirked and leaned back in their lounger. "So, Dee," they said, "how's vacationing with the one percent?"

"Very weird," I said, then turned toward Misa. "By the way, Obachan asked me to find you. She wants to give you her pearls."

"Big surprise," said Kei wryly. "Obachan wants to give Misa everything."

"Kei," said Misa, sounding eerily like her mom.

"All I do around here is tell the truth. And pick people up from the airport." They checked their watch. "Actually, can you go get changed so we can grab Vik? I know he's a guest of honor or whatever, but I still think he would have been fine dealing with the hotel shuttle like a mere mortal."

My ears perked up. I was more than a little excited to meet Matt's best man. I knew the basics — that he was the son of Elinor's long-distance best friend, had already been married and divorced by thirty-two, and was (in Matt's words) obnoxiously fit. But I also imagined that he would be just like Matt in all the best possible ways: funny, caring, lover of puns and pineapple on pizza.

"Matt said he would do it, but he needed more time with his vows, and Elinor's already catching up with Vik's mother over lunch," replied Misa. "And you know our family — once you offer something, there's no take-backs."

"Our most endearing and annoying quality." Kei sighed.

Misa checked the time before throwing her hair into a truly gigantic bun and slipping into a pair of sandals. "Okay, so I'll meet you in the lobby at three for Uber duty. Don't be late!"

"You sound like the Nag," Kei called after her. Misa turned and vaguely apologized with her hands before disappearing behind a jubilant South Asian family heading to the pool.

"I forgot you called Julie that," I said.

"Are you kidding?" screeched Kei. "That running gag is basically my claim to fame in our family." They looked around before continuing. "And the lead-up to this trip has really amped up the Nag's tricks. At New Year's, she swapped out all the shoyu in the cupboard for the low-sodium kind. She wanted us all on a health kick."

"How . . . dare she?"

"Exactly," said Kei. "I think it drives her up the wall that soy sauce is the Japanese Canadian hill I've chosen to die on. But even if we did hang out at the cultural center more, it's not like Aunt Julie would trust us with any real responsibility. It's the same with this wedding—all about appearances."

"Huh." I sat down on the edge of their lounger and mentally re-engaged sabotage mode, feeling slightly shady. "So do you think this thing's gonna go off without a hitch?"

Kei shrugged. "It depends on whether Misa can hold it together. She's under a lot of pressure from the Nag, and they don't have the easiest relationship to begin with."

"Come on," I said. "There's no way Misa won't pull it off. She's too good."

"I don't know," said Kei. "Sometimes goodness is just a defense against being swallowed up or pushed down. You're pretty close with Misa—don't you worry that she's going to extend herself just a bit too far?"

I reddened a little, and not just from the sun. "I guess because she's always come through, I've never thought much about the alternative."

"Well," said Kei, "you've seen the alternative."

We ordered a pair of Coronas from the poolside bar, and I got caught up on all the family gossip—the Nag's slipping stronghold at the cultural center, Obachan's disapproval of Dr. Koyanagi's divorce from Kei's French Canadian mom, Kei's own vehement opposition to their family's vacation spot. "If this isn't neo-colonialism, I'll eat that guy's bucket hat," spat Kei between sips of beer. "But I'm here to support Misa, even though I'm low-key hoping they'll sell their shares in this place after the wedding wraps up."

Outside of lobbying their family, Kei had landed a sweet gig working as an animator for a kids' dinosaur show, which had made it a bit harder to travel. With Misa firmly in the family spotlight,

Kei had shifted between Toronto and Vancouver for years, acting as a bridge between the different branches of their relatives.

"The thing you've gotta know about Misa is that she grew up with the whole Japanese Canadian community watching her—a community that spends half its time worrying that it'll disappear because our parents' generation intermarried at warp speed after resettling," said Kei.

"Are Ken and Julie upset that Matt's not Japanese?"

"Nah, most of our families are already mixed," said Kei. "It's more about the fact that Julie can't seem to get Misa involved in the cultural legacy stuff she loves so much. But I don't really blame her. Julie casts a long shadow, and it sometimes feels like she's looking for a certain kind of representation that I'm not sure either of us fits. But it's harder on Misa, you know, because that's her family's whole world."

"She's never really talked about that with me," I said slowly. "I wish I could do something more to help her out."

I remembered the birthday card that Misa had made me a few months ago—a delicate wiener dog that unfolded across my kitchen table like an accordion, just like the therapy pup that had visited us on my second-last day in the ward. I had pinned it to the dartboard in my kitchen, wishing she had come over instead to interrupt the silence.

Kei looked me up and down carefully. "Well, this weekend might be your chance. Help me make sure Misa gets down the aisle."

I opened my mouth, searching for a way to avoid making a promise I couldn't keep. Luckily, a middle-aged Japanese woman with a pixie cut and sparkling teeth came up behind us and tapped Kei on the shoulder.

"Kei! How was your flight in? I hope you and your partner had a good trip." She drew out the word *partner* like she had just invented it. "I have to tell you—it was so nice seeing Ana again at Auntie Yoshi's funeral. Of course, it was a funeral, so it could have been nicer, but still. Such a pretty girl. Very well educated. Tak and I, we are so happy for you." She leaned in very close to Kei's face. "Perhaps you'll be the next Koyanagi to tie the knot!"

She gently breathed in Kei's face, waiting expectantly.

"Uh," said Kei. "Thanks, Auntie Amy. If I decide to make a lifelong commitment, you'll be the first to know."

Auntie Amy looked a little crestfallen. She withdrew and placed a manicured hand on her hip. "Well, I'm going to go watch sea turtles at the reef—we'll chat again later, Kei."

"I bet we will," replied Kei, grinning. "See ya, Auntie." They waved as Amy took off in a hurry, stumbling over a loose sandal. They turned to me once she was out of earshot. "She's going to be so disappointed."

"I mean, even if you don't want to get married, it's nice that your family assumes that you'll end up with someone," I offered. "My parents are mentally preparing for me to get eaten by my own cats."

"No, I mean Ana and I broke up two weeks ago," said Kei. They lowered their voice a little. "It was mutual, but I don't want to deal with it right now. I'm supposed to be on vacation."

Ken and Dr. Koyanagi walked by us, the latter carrying a bulging bag and squeaky-clean tennis shoes. Dr. Koyanagi waved at us but Ken maintained a brisk pace toward the tennis courts, forcing Kei's dad to catch up apologetically. I waved back half-heartedly but Kei ignored them both, wrapped up in their confession.

"I don't have the heart to tell the family, especially at Misa's wedding. They'll be devastated," said Kei. "Ana's much more likable than me. I'm always ruining people's favorite brands by telling them which evil conglomerate they belong to."

"I'm always having psychotic breaks on people's birthdays," I offered, remembering Tilley's horrendous drunk tobogganing rager. I stretched my legs out on my lounger and realized I hadn't put sunscreen on the backs. As usual.

"Nice."

I turned over and let the sun take me. "Sorry you have to deal with so many questions about your ex."

"It's cool. For the most part, I've just been telling them to go ask her. You can usually find Ana by the pool."

Kei waved across the water at a Latinx woman in pert pigtails. She waved back, then returned to scribbling in her notebook.

My jaw hit the floor. "She's here? At the wedding?"

Kei shrugged. "Have you ever tried to get a refund two weeks before a flight? We didn't want to eat the cost, so we decided to go as friends."

"And that's just . . . working out?"

"We're giving each other some space, but yeah, it's totally cool. I love Ana." They looked at me pointedly. "Plus, she'll make sure I'm on my best behavior through all the bullshit."

I glanced back at Ana. She wasn't trying to eavesdrop on us at all, even though we were clearly talking about her. It was incredible. What self-control, what poise! Was this what a fully functioning breakup looked like? I didn't have much experience in that department, but from what I'd learned pining over Matt, I knew that close proximity could be a real challenge.

A shadow suddenly loomed over my chair. I turned around and found Misa exhaling loudly. Her hair was back under its usual restraint. "Guess what time it is," she said.

"Goddammit," said Kei. They opened up their backpack and started tossing debris inside—sunglasses, books, sunscreen. I threw on my cover-up while trying to absorb the merit badges affixed to Kei's bag. RUNS WITH SCISSORS, read the one on the left strap.

Across the pool, the Nag strode past unfinished daiquiris and palm trees wrapped in string lights, waving in our direction. I watched Misa's jaw set as she approached us.

"Hi, Mom," she said.

"There you are," Julie replied, then gave me a once-over. "Are you enjoying yourself, Dee? How's the food been? What do you think of the gardens?"

I looked around, not sure which question to answer first. "It's wonderful," I said, hoping that could work as a catchall. Kei tittered at me from their lounger. "This is the most beautiful place I've ever been."

And it was. It was a place so beautiful, I wasn't sure I belonged. I was much more at home with the splendor of Scarborough, from bonfires at the Bluffs, to evening skates at the Civic Centre, to the bursting stacks of the Malvern Library.

"Good," Julie said, then turned to Misa. "Did you hear about the pearls?"

"Yes," said Misa. She looked like she was going to say something else, then stopped. I was starting to get a weird vibe from this conversation. It was like a tennis match where no one could return a serve.

"How long have you been coming here?" I said, dying to fill the silence.

"It must be ten years now," replied Julie, straightening a stack of rings on her finger. "It's a good place to get away. Very private."

Kei rolled their eyes. "You know, Aunt Julie, if you gave up your board position at the cultural center, you could get the same level of privacy at home. Look at how relaxed my dad is these days. He's thinking about buying a Vespa."

Julie looked horrified. I couldn't tell if it was over the idea of resigning or the notion of Italian scooters. "We have a legacy to look after. Important work to be done," she said, then offered a tentative smile to Misa. "You know, Mrs. Uda was just saying that we could really use your help with the spring festival. It's something we could do together."

Misa paused and Julie's face fell, as if she already knew what was coming. "I'd like to. But I'm working on a bunch of projects for the hospital right now and—"

"I understand you want to carve your own path," said Julie, recovering her composure in an instant. "But does it have to be there? Don't you want to do something for your family?"

For a second, I thought Misa would let her two worlds collide. That she would explain how her history and her health were tied up into one big knot she was always trying to untangle. But she took a deep breath and simply said, "I just don't think the time is right."

"The time never seems to be right," Julie said, unable to keep the regret out of her voice. The air temperature around us dropped several degrees. She pulled Misa aside and murmured into her ear, her voice just audible above the bustle of the patio. "Just remember— this work we are doing with survivors, it has a time limit. Perhaps you should think about that when you're wearing Obachan's pearls."

Kei coughed dramatically and Julie's eyes flitted toward my face. She nodded to Misa. "Anyway, we can talk about this later."

"Sure," said Misa into the ground. "Kei and I should get going."

It was the second crack I'd seen in Misa's veneer in two days. Her eyes weren't focusing, her shoulders were taut, and I could tell she'd give anything for an escape. The way she was collapsing in on herself felt a little too familiar. I thought about my parents back home, whether they were not-so-secretly celebrating a week without the burden of my body nearby.

"Hey." Kei put a hand on Misa's shoulder once Julie had excused herself. "Shake it off. You're doing everything you need to right now."

"I just—" Misa's voice broke. "If I told her the truth, she wouldn't understand. It feels like I'm not Japanese enough, and at the same time, I'm too sick, and I'll keep having to choose between the things I care about. I'll always be letting people down."

"No, you won't," said Kei, pulling Misa in for a hug while inhaling a piece of her hair. "You're always bringing who you are to the work that you do. And even if mental health doesn't have the Japanese street cred of taiko right now, it's going to make a difference for us."

Misa laughed and blinked back her tears, and I figured it was safe for me to chime in again. I might not understand these exact tensions, but I sure knew how to make a mentally ill person feel better: offering the immediate cancellation of stuff they were supposed to do. "Why don't Kei and I go pick up Vik for you? That way you can get some rest before the stag and doe tonight."

"Again, terrible name for a party," said Kei. "But yes, we're happy to do that. You look like you could sleep through the Santa Claus parade."

"I'm fine," Misa said, wiping her smudged eyeliner and putting her game face back on. She took a look at Kei's expression and tried again. "Really, I'm completely fine. Everything is fine."

"Well, that's the right number of fines," I said, deadpan. "One more and I would have been concerned."

Misa cracked the smallest of smiles. "Sometimes I forget how well you know me."

9

∽

"BACK IN YOUR HEAD"
—TEGAN AND SARA (3:00)

Before Matt and Misa got engaged, back when I could still scrape together some semblance of normalcy in front of them, I once ran into Misa in a Walmart. I had cut through the entrance to snag half-price, end-of-day sushi from the mall's food court but got tripped up by the sight of Misa, carrying so many shopping bags that the plastic handles were cutting into her wrists. She was standing alone in a marked-down seasonal aisle, looking up at stacks and stacks of twinkle lights.

"Hey, Misa," I said, trying to sound casual and not desperately lonely.

"Dee!" she said, like I was the greatest invention since astronaut mac and cheese. She grabbed my arm, and everything around her crinkled. "I can't believe I'm running into you today! It was meant to be!"

It was nice to hear that someone wanted me around, even if it was the person who was dating my one true love. "Are you stocking an apocalypse bunker or something?"

Misa laughed for a few seconds too long. "It's Obachan's birthday this weekend!"

When we last caught up, Matt had mentioned that they were taking Obachan to see Stars on Ice, a tradition that had begun with her obsession with Kristi Yamaguchi in the nineties and led to mandatory figure-skating lessons for Misa when she was growing up. But it sounded like Misa was taking their celebration to a whole new level. One bag was exploding with pastel streamers, while another held enough baking supplies to wipe out Martha Stewart. The remaining bags held boxes of snowflake stationery, plus a few unidentifiable glittery objects that were tracking dust all over Misa's slim black jeans.

"Do you need some help?" I asked, gesturing toward her bulging cargo.

Her hands clenched around the handles of her bags. "I'm good, thanks. Really good, actually. Just have one more thing to do."

But by the time I picked up a green dragon roll and strolled back through the Walmart, that one more thing had left Misa sitting in a ball on the floor. Her plastic bags were splayed out around her and a dozen boxes of half-opened lights lay to her right, the strands dangling out of place. Part of me wanted to take off in a cartoon puff of smoke, but I found myself walking toward her again.

"I can't close the boxes," she said without looking up.

I crouched down beside her, my quarter-life-crisis knees cracking in protest. "That doesn't sound so bad." I pulled a strand out of its container and started folding it into smaller sections.

Misa shook her head. "You don't understand," she said, as Sheryl Crow belted "If It Makes You Happy" over the store's sound system. "I needed this to go well, and everything is going wrong."

I tried to shove my tightly wound bundle back into its cardboard container, cursing as the box tore open at the back. Giving up, I pushed the entire mess underneath the metal shelving, destroying any evidence of my involvement. "How long have you been here, exactly?"

"I don't know," she said, her voice breaking. She whipped out her phone and clapped a hand to her mouth. "Oh my god. It's been five hours! I've been in this mall for five hours!"

I wouldn't have wished that fate on even my worst enemy. Misa looked like she wanted the ground to swallow her up whole. "Can I . . . take you home?" I asked. "And by that, I mean call my sister to take both of us home. Because I can't drive anymore for insurance reasons."

"No!" Her voice rose in pitch, attracting sideways glances from the teens riding toddler bikes down the aisle from us. "I can't leave until I'm done. I need the right kind of twinkle lights for Obachan. I have to get the right ones." She scratched her nails along one forearm, leaving red rakes of anxiety embedded in her skin.

"I get it," I said, because I kind of did. I put my hand over her scratches. "Just let me help you."

"You can't help me," she said, jerking away. "No one can help me."

"You're probably right," I said, scooting my butt closer to hers and offering her my take-out sushi. "But I can keep you company."

AS KEI DROVE us toward the airport in the Nagasaka family's vacation car (complete with a personalized license plate missing a single *A* from their last name), I stared out the window at an osprey nest perched high atop a telephone pole, the palm trees around it bowing slightly in the wind.

"Thanks for convincing Misa to take a break for once in her life," said Kei, rolling down all four windows and cranking the AC. "This could be a turning point for her—like the next thing you know, she'll be super into jade rollers and making sourdough."

"Sounds like my nightmare," I said. We drove past a bustling cabana bar and a boarded-up Kingdom Hall for Jehovah's Witnesses on the same block and I had to double-take. "This island is really full of surprises."

"It's definitely a weird space to occupy as a tourist," said Kei. "A lot of people just want to come here without acknowledging the roots of the island. I mean, there's a whole historic plantation site with multiple bad online reviews because it's 'too run-down.' What the heck do they expect?"

"People have too much time on their hands," I said, ashamed that I hadn't even thought of visiting any cultural sites while I was here.

We drove through the tourist district of Providenciales, a completely different world from the local downtown I had seen just a few days before. The line outside that sweet-tea joint would have looked out of place here. Instead, the main road was lined with Italian restaurants and jewelry shops, tiny cafés with colorful umbrellas, and a patio bar showing a soccer game on a big screen. The people were, like me, mostly visitors.

"Can I ask you something?" said Kei, as we passed two kids

getting hauled down the sidewalk by an energetic puppy. They didn't wait for an answer. "It's about your medication."

"I've been on as many medications as there are seasons of *American Idol*," I replied. "You'll have to be more specific."

"Okay," said Kei, then paused. "Do you ever think about going off them?"

"All the damn time. But I also know that every time I've done it, I've also tried to off myself—" I backtracked. "Sorry, that's a lot. I'm a lot."

"No, no, it's okay," said Kei. They swerved around some chickens that were spilling out onto the road from someone's front yard. "You're the right amount, always."

I grinned, relieved that they could handle the truth. "Okay, so I usually get into trouble when I convince myself to stop my medication cold turkey—"

"Where did 'cold turkey' even come from?" interrupted Kei. "Wait, sorry, not my turn. Please continue."

"Right. So, my doctor told me once that it's like playing piano. If you practice a song for ten thousand hours, your fingers will be trained to play that song," I explained. "I guess the more your brain practices being manic, the more often it will happen, the stronger it will be, and the less effect your medication will have."

I thought about how after the shock of Matt and Misa's engagement, it had been so easy to lean into that heightened frequency again. But I also remembered Tilley staying up with me all night to make sure I didn't leave, the lingering feeling that I was walking along a razor-thin edge of survival.

"So it seems like a bad idea, then."

"I mean, some people live great lives off medication. And the beginning is always awesome—it feels like everything you touch glows just a little bit," I said. "So you convince yourself you don't need the meds, that you'd be better off without them. But for me, there's always a fall after the rise. It's the comedown that gets me."

When we pulled up to the front of the airport, we came to a grinding halt in a long line of cars waiting for passengers to arrive. Men in brightly colored linens waved taxi signs at tourists who huddled under the shade of the roof's overhang. A woman with long braids and an orange vest directed us to the curbside and Kei put the car into park, their eyes glued to the crowded scene in front of them. Whenever the airport doors squelched open, I could hear the faintest traces of the welcome band.

Kei drummed their fingers against the faux leather of the steering wheel, the steady pattern building into a final two-handed tap. "Well, not to disrupt your vacation or anything, but I think there might be a problem with the wedding. Remember when I asked you to help me get Misa through this wedding? I think that goes double for Matt."

My pulse started racing, but I kept my face neutral. Maybe Kei could see what I had started to suspect—that Matt and Misa had hit more than a few speed bumps on their race to the altar. Maybe, just maybe, there was a chance for me after all.

"My priority here is to spare Misa from as much drama as possible, right? She's already dealing with the Nag, and that's enough for anyone," continued Kei. "That's why I could use your help. You're the closest to Matt—I mean, except for his mom, but honestly, I have a really hard time understanding Scottish slang. I spent most of our Christmas dinner together politely laughing at the wrong time. If I hear one more crack about my fringe—"

"I love you, Kei," I said. "But I need you to focus. What's wrong with Matt?"

Kei took a deep breath. "So, last night I arrived at the hotel just as the welcome party was wrapping up." They paused, then reached into the back seat to pull an ombre bundle of yarn out of their bag. "Do you mind if I crochet while I tell you this? I'm getting all worked up."

"Go for it."

"Okay, so I'm minding my own business, trying to get my hands on some leftover inari, when I catch sight of Matt sipping whiskey alone in the stairwell. Weird vibes for your own wedding week, if you ask me," said Kei, winding yarn around the hook. "So I went over to make sure he was okay."

"And how was he?"

"Well, I guess he'd had one too many fancy whiskeys, because suddenly he was talking about you and my dad and the hospital," said Kei, not noticing my sharp inhale. "Then out of nowhere, he blurts out that he's gone off his meds without telling Misa. That seems bad, right? Like, that's information she definitely needs to hear from him. But I couldn't convince him to come clean."

"Shit," I said. "I need to talk to Matt."

It wasn't the kind of problem I had hoped for, not in the slightest. I knew how long it had taken for Matt to adhere to any semblance of a treatment routine—and even when he started dating Misa, she basically had to hold him at gunpoint to get him to commit to the care plan she drew up for them. I could only imagine what would cause him to disrupt that routine. But before I could say anything else, a brown fist rapped on the driver's side window.

We looked over and saw a very handsome man waving at us, his black hair effortlessly caught in the breeze. In a tucked-in button-down and slacks, he was oddly dressed up for an island airport, but he somehow pulled it off, even in the sweltering heat. I looked down at my wrinkled cover-up and flip-flops and sighed. First impressions had never been my strong suit.

Kei looked at me pointedly. "I can see we've lost our window, so I guess we'll come back to this later. Just—if you see an opening for a conversation with Matt, take it. Please." They popped the trunk, and Vik chucked his bulging luggage inside before sliding into the back seat.

"Thanks so much for picking me up!" he said, pushing a few strands of hair out of his face. "Thank goodness for the Nagasakas' penchant for vanity license plates, because it's been a day. Heathrow was in shambles this morning, and I think the vegetarian dinner they served on the plane was supposed to kill us. It's good to finally see some non-murderous faces." He squinted in the hazy sunlight. "You must be . . ."

"I'm Kei. Nice to meet you, Vik." They carefully packed away their yarn before putting the car back in drive.

"I'm Dee," I said, waving with too many fingers from the passenger seat. "And sorry I'm a bit underdressed for the occasion."

Vik looked slightly abashed. "I know, dressing up to fly is terribly old-fashioned. But there's something about it that I enjoy. Makes the trip feel more special, I suppose." He paused for a moment, then grinned. "Although this is Matt's wedding, so I can hardly imagine a more memorable adventure. I can't believe he's finally found someone willing to sit through his play-by-play rugby match recaps."

"Forget that," I said. "Misa doesn't even think it's that weird that he eats tomatoes like apples. She says it kind of makes sense because they're both technically fruits!"

"Does he still leave the cupboard doors open all the time? I can't remember how many times I came home from class thinking we'd been robbed," Vik mused.

"It's nice that you've stayed friends with such a monster," I said. "There must be something terribly wrong with you as well."

He thought for a moment. "I'm in finance."

"That'll do it," I said.

Kei released the tiniest of smiles as Vik studied me like a Sunday crossword. I wondered what Matt had told him about me, if he had described my face in a way that would launch a thousand ships from the shores of Grace Bay. Then I remembered that we had once done the chubby bunny marshmallow challenge together and I figured I might as well let my dreams be dreams.

"It seems we have quite a bit in common," said Vik, leaning forward in his seat. I couldn't tell whether his tone was, in fact, very flirtatious, or if it was just the effect his posh accent was having on me. "We'll have to spend a lot of time together this week, you and me. We've got tons of catching up to do."

"Can't wait," I said, but secretly planned on excusing myself for a giant nap as soon as we got back. Maybe I could sleep right through this revelation about Matt's medication, or the next damn party, or the next week if I really needed to. There was something too intense about the way Vik looked at me, like he could see through my insecurities immediately.

As we drove back to the resort, Vik told us how he and Matt first became friends. He explained how both his mom and Elinor had immigrated to Canada from the UK, but only one of them could handle Halifax. "It had all of London's rain without the Tube!" he said, and I laughed harder than I needed to. After Elinor resettled in Toronto and his mom returned to the UK, Vik spent a few summer vacations running through the Bluffs with Matt at his side. He had even bunked with Matt and Elinor in Toronto during a semester abroad in his final year of undergrad, where he and Matt had commandeered the kitchen table for a makeshift Ping-Pong tournament, set to the soundtrack of all the "old man bands" that Matt loved best.

"Matt helped me survive the toughest internship of my life

that year," said Vik. "But I was working so much that I didn't even realize he was struggling himself. I had just gone back to England the first time he got really sick."

"I think he wasn't in the hospital for long that time," Kei said. "Just a week or so."

"Sure," said Vik. "But I didn't find out until months later. He didn't want to tell me. But I really should have known that all those last-call bartending shifts were taking a toll. Even his sense of humor had become, I don't know, *sharper*, if that makes sense."

"Spiky is what I like to call it," I said. "But it's hard to recognize if you're not familiar."

"Being a long-distance best friend means I've never become as familiar as I'd like to be," admitted Vik. "That's why I really want to nail this best man gig. I want to come through for him this time."

Kei looked at me and I could tell they were debating whether to bring Vik in on our little secret. But I shook my head softly.

"I'm sure your speech will be great," I offered gently.

He slapped a hand to his forehead. "The bloody speech! Would you believe I left my notes in London?"

After assuring Vik that he'd be able to recall all his best lines, we pulled into the parking lot at Breeze Bay without incident—unless you count Vik having to get out of the car and direct Kei. After the successful maneuver, Vik and Kei discovered their shared love for running and planned a quick jog before the evening's festivities, chatting eagerly about possible shoreline routes as Vik gathered his bags from the trunk. I tuned them out as Tilley waddled over to the car in a butt-skimming golf skirt and hot pink, bejewelled flip-flops.

"There you are!" she said, peering over the tops of her oversized sunglasses. "I thought you were off moping on the beach somewhere."

"We were picking up the best man from the airport," I said, gesturing toward Vik. He poked his head out of the trunk and waved cheerily, and I turned his way. "I would just like to take this opportunity to apologize in advance for the fact that my sister may pretend she's British when she's drunk and/or talking to you."

"Oh my god, Vikesh?" squealed Tilley at a pitch only audible to dolphins and irritated big sisters. She teleported over to where he was standing and clutched at his hand, gazing at him adoringly.

"Have you two met before?" asked Kei.

"No," said Vik wearily. "I don't think we have."

"But I feel like I know you already," swooned Tilley. Exasperated, I walked over and punched her in the arm. She scowled and swatted at me. "What was that for? Can't I get a little excited over a celebrity?"

"I'm not a celebrity," said Vik, trying to wrench his hand out of her viselike grip. "Please, can we just not talk about this?"

"Talk about what?" Kei asked.

"About that time he married a complete stranger on reality TV!" screeched Tilley, and we all turned to look at Vik.

He sighed. "I really quite hate the internet."

10

"WHENEVER, WHEREVER"
—SHAKIRA (3:16)

TILLEY WAS LOCKED in on Vik like he was the last Boston cream doughnut at a truck-stop Tim Horton's.

"You know," said Vik, walking a very thin line between polite and exasperated, "I probably would have thought twice about the whole television-wedding thing if I had realized that anyone still watched those shows."

She flashed him a saccharine smile. "When I ran out of North American content, I started streaming *Instant Marriage* after Twitter blew up over reports a contestant was selling a wedding sari straight from the set. How much did Amira end up getting for it anyway?"

Vik's clenched eyebrows could have sheltered a small nest of baby birds. "How is it humanly possible to run out of reality television?"

"I am a woman of many talents," Tilley replied, fluttering her eyelash extensions at Vik. I picked up his garment bag from the edge of the trunk, dreading Tilley's next question.

Kei cleared their throat. "Well, if we're just going to hold a

parking lot staring contest for the rest of the day, I'm heading in."
They heaved Vik's suitcase out of the trunk and slammed the door
shut. I was torn between chasing after them to talk about Matt
and staying put so I could witness the standoff of the century. The
part of me that lived for the dramatic won.

"Thanks for the ride," I called out as Kei walked back toward
the hotel. The relative civility seemed to snap Vik out of his funk,
and he blinked furiously before picking his bag up off the ground.

"I'm terribly sorry," he said to me, scratching the back of his
head. "I just really didn't expect anyone here to know about that
part of my life. I tend to get a bit touchy over it."

"I knew you had been married," I said. "But Matt clearly left
out a lot of details." The three of us started off after Kei, Vik's suitcase jerking over ruts in the concrete.

"You know," said Vik. "He's my only friend who didn't watch
the show and make fun of me mercilessly. I hid out with him and
Elinor for weeks while it aired in Britain."

"That's really sweet," I said, and Tilley let out a theatrical
cough, like she had suddenly been stricken by the black lung.

"At any rate," said Vik, firmly ignoring her, "I'd really prefer
we didn't talk about my miserable divorce this week. I want to keep
the focus on Matt and Misa." He turned and looked pointedly at
Tilley. "I trust you can restrain yourself in front of the other
guests?"

She cocked a perfectly threaded brow. "Only if you give us the
scoop beforehand."

"If you've watched the show, you must already know how it
turned out," said Vik.

"What I really want to know," said Tilley, "is how you saw the
first season and still managed to sign yourself up for this car fire of
a life experience."

Vik looked at her curiously. "I mean, you watch enough reality TV that you must understand to some degree. Isn't love what everyone is chasing? And wouldn't you try almost anything to find the person you're supposed to be with, even if it seems a bit daft to everyone else?"

My heart thudded. I knew I needed to talk to Matt—about his meds, first of all, but also about what I'd always felt between us. No matter what the fallout might be, I owed it to myself to try.

"Sure," said Tilley, oblivious to my emotional breakthrough. "That's what Tinder's for."

WE HAD BARELY made it through the door to our studio before Tilley started texting all her friends about Vik. "I can't believe Matt finally had something interesting to talk about and he never said anything," she huffed, typing furiously from the bathroom.

I kicked my flip-flops at the wall and collapsed on top of our unmade queen. "He was being a good friend," I said, then wondered if I'd be able to come through for Matt in the same way this week. My brain started whirring as Tilley picked up her creased itinerary and studied it with a frown.

"Bold move on Misa's part to schedule the stag and doe the night before her bridal brunch. With any luck, I'll find someone at the party willing to serve me breakfast tomorrow morning." She caught my look of disapproval and rolled her eyes at me. "Look, I appreciate your concern about my sexual history and all, but it also kind of makes you a killjoy."

I didn't say anything, just counted the pot lights in the ceiling and waited for my uneasiness to wash away.

After I got kicked out of the hospital, Tilley and I both went through questionable phases at the same time. Tilley started bringing home guys from the bar even on weeknights, while I stole my dad's old copy of *The Beach Boys Greatest Hits* and started spending mornings blasting "Wouldn't It Be Nice" on repeat, meticulously scrubbing the kitchen baseboards on my hands and knees until my forearms throbbed. Our paths would cross around ten A.M., when Tilley would screech, "Can't you be obsessed with a song that isn't trying to brainwash me with shitty 1950s values?" as she pushed a scruffy random out the door. I cycled through classics by Alanis Morissette and Paul Simon, but Tilley hadn't changed her tune. Every time I tried to talk to her about it, she'd laugh it off—but as someone who had once escaped reality through a string of manic one-night stands, I worried that we were more alike than she was willing to admit.

Tilley put her hands on her hips. "Are you showering first or am I?"

"I don't really feel like being wet," I mumbled, rolling over to face her. I thought about my secret and Matt's secret and all the talking I'd need to do to resolve anything at all, and my mouth went dry.

"Don't you dare pull a depression shower strike on me in the middle of the damn Caribbean."

"I'm not depressed," I said, staring at the ceiling. "I'm just flat."

"Tell that to your D-cups," said Tilley with a wink. I didn't crack a smile, so she grabbed the end of the bed's duvet and folded it over me, then over again. "Come on, my sad little blanket burrito. I'll give you ten minutes to puddle but then you're drinking a full glass of water and jumping in the shower. It'll help clear your head."

Tears dripped down my cheeks and pooled on the soft blanket

like a Rorschach test for the cleaning staff. "You don't have to wait for me. I'll just make you late. And if we're late, everyone will look at us and know I'm sick, and then I won't be able to talk to anyone."

"First of all, being fashionably late is the dream," said Tilley. "Secondly, I already budgeted depression time into our makeup schedule. We'll be just fine."

I sniffled. "Aren't you tired of this? Isn't this exhausting for you?"

She plucked a blue wrap dress from my suitcase and laid it over a plump chair. "It's kind of like playing a board game, except it's always my turn."

I pushed myself upright and layers of blanket slid off my shoulders. "I wish we had our freezer spoons." Tilley kept a rotation of dessert cutlery in our freezer for de-puffing on my waterfall days. "My eyes are going to be total marshmallows."

Tilley crawled under the blankets with me and set her timer for seven minutes. "Don't worry—we can just tell everyone I punched you in the face twice, and they'll believe it."

"You're the best, Til," I said, and meant it.

❧

ONLY AN HOUR and a half behind schedule, we slid into Washington's shuttle with that lustrous glow Scarborough girls get when we move through spaces we were told we'd never occupy—metal hoops brushing against the soft skin of our necks, back flesh gently carved by the underwire of our prom-era strapless bras, drugstore lipstick clinging to our mouths. The stag and doe was taking place at a sister resort that couldn't wait to host the Nagasakas' guests, and judging by the dress code, it was even more exclusive than ours. As we drove through the unlit roads that hugged the shore of Grace Bay, it felt like Tilley and I were crash-landing on another planet.

"I swear to god everyone has their high beams on," said Tilley, peering out the windows of the Land Rover. "How do you even drive like this?"

"I could drive these roads blindfolded," boasted Washington as our headlights illuminated a scattered group of stray dogs chilling by the side of the road. "I've lived here my whole life, so nothing surprises me anymore." He turned to shoot my sister a playful look. "Not even you."

While waiting for Tilley to shower, I had quickly searched the island's history and discovered a lot of important details you'd never read about in a tourist guide—communities destroyed by competing European powers, enslaved people abandoned on failed plantations, a brief takeover by Britain only a few years ago. I wondered if the sprawl of tourists seemed less surprising when your airport was funded by a hotel chain, if Washington himself minded our intrusion.

"Can I ask you something?" I ventured, and Washington nodded cheerily. "Why does everyone call the locals 'belongers'?"

"Depends who you ask," he replied, his voice unusually earnest. "Me, I think islanders don't 'belong' to anybody. But I like to think that this land is where I'm meant to be."

We drove in silence for a few moments. I noticed that the hotels were all immaculate but many local homes still bore signs of the hurricane. Looking out the window, I could see lights illuminating a stretch of paradise that could be purchased by the square foot. I wondered if the people who lived in those exclusive villas felt like they belonged here too, or if they carried their discomfort in neatly packed suitcases like I did.

We pulled up to yet another roundabout driveway, this one bordered with spotlights, lush hedges, and blooming bougainvillea. Washington slipped out of the front seat to open the door for our first wobbly steps out of the car.

"You ladies have a wonderful night, okay?" he said. "And you call me for a pickup if your boyfriends give you any trouble."

"What boyfriend?" said Tilley with a wink, and Washington chuckled as he hopped back into the driver's seat.

I looked at Tilley, who was now fixated on the arched entryway before us. "You ready?" I asked, feeling a familiar churning in my stomach. She grabbed my hand and squeezed tightly.

ℓℓℓ

WHEN TILLEY AND I walked in, the stag and doe was already in full swing. We stood awestruck beneath layers of thick nautical ropes cascading over the sleek circular bar, the skeletons of shattered houses still hovering in the back of my mind. Bright lights caged in by suspended baskets glowed like hollow planets above our heads, while women in cocktail dresses sipped thin glasses of champagne. Outside the covered patio, palm trees wrapped in twinkle lights towered over an open fire, with a trail of torches leading from plush couches to the dark shores of Grace Bay. Overlooking the crowd was a lone DJ blasting David Guetta and pulsing his crotch gently with the trade winds. It was one predictable bass line away from being the most magical party I had ever seen.

"I'm glad I wore my push-up," said Tilley, eyeing the DJ.

"I'm glad depression gives me the sex drive of a ham sandwich," I replied, scanning the mass of people for Matt and finding Elinor instead. She was beside the fire pit talking to a tall, angular South

Asian woman who I figured was Vik's mom. "I'm going to ask Elinor if she knows where Matt is, if that's cool with you."

"Goes to a glamorous party, hangs out with the moms," Tilley said with a sigh, already making a beeline for the DJ booth. "You do you, baby girl."

A few yards ahead, Elinor caught sight of me and waved me over. I exhaled all my insecurities and plastered a smile across my face, ready to make small talk with the best of them.

"Dee!" Elinor threw her arms around me and shouted over the music. "It was getting so late that I wasn't sure you'd make it out for this one."

She was blunt as always, though I couldn't help but hear the kindness behind her words. Shifting my weight, I offered my best explanation. "Sometimes it just takes me a bit longer to get going, you know?"

Elinor gave me a knowing nod. "Better bend than break, I always say." She spun around and grabbed her companion. "Anila, this is the girl I was telling you about."

Anila offered me a warm smile. She was wearing a gold dress with delicately stitched scaling down to the hemline, and between her lean build and thick hair, I could definitely see the resemblance to Vik. "It's fantastic to meet you," she said. "Vikesh said he had such a nice ride back with you from the airport."

I blushed, partly because I too had enjoyed the ride. "Right," I said. "It was fun to hear about all the trouble he and Matt used to get into."

"For two boys who lived thousands of miles away from each other, they still seemed to find ways to cause us stress," complained Elinor.

Anila laughed. "But look how far they've come! Now we get

to celebrate Matt's beautiful wedding together—no camera crews, no reality television girls. I feel as if I'm getting a second chance at it all."

"Ah, well," said Elinor. "Love can make you impulsive. Even Matt and Misa have only been together a year!" She glanced toward me. "I wish I had more time to get to know Misa like you do. I've always wanted a daughter."

"And now you'll have one!" crowed Anila, but Elinor didn't seem to register it.

"I just want her to be happy in our family," she said slowly. "And while I know for certain that Matt is what she wants—I'm just not sure that me and my big mouth are what she imagined for a mother-in-law."

As a fellow oversharer who didn't always pick up on personal boundaries, my heart broke for her. "Anyone would be lucky to call you family, Elinor. Just give her some time to get comfortable. You'll be happy you did."

"Bless you, sweet girl," she said, giving my arm a squeeze. "I'm hoping this week, Misa and I will find our way. We've got too much in common not to."

I followed her gaze across the crowd and spotted Matt, looking burly and handsome in a parrot-print shirt he definitely hadn't ironed himself. He was sharing a pint with Vik, at the outer edge of the party's fray. "I've actually been looking for the man of the hour myself," I said. "Would you mind if I went over and paid my dues?"

"Of course," said Elinor, giving me one last hug. "And thanks for the wee chat."

I made my way toward Matt and Vik, pushing through throngs of people drinking and dancing the night away. As I approached, I tried to telepathically apologize to Matt for my outburst on the beach. He lifted his eyebrows in response, and I knew he wanted to talk when Vik wasn't around, which was certainly fine by me. This psychic connection had emerged from many hours sitting around a circle in group therapy, keeping our mouths shut but trading elaborate glances over other people's misfortunes. Group therapy was like the Oscars without a host. You'd get halfway through an acceptance speech for strolling down a highway on-ramp and suddenly the camera would jump to someone else's greatest cinematic moment. It was the only form of talk therapy available for inpatients, so everyone really tried to get their tax money's worth—except Matt, who silently protested.

"You made it!" roared Matt, slinging an arm around me and nearly spilling his beer on me in the process. I didn't mind one bit—he always knew how to make me feel like being around was worth it. "I can always count on you, Dee Foster. Let's drink to that."

Vik shot me a mischievous look as he took a long sip of his beer. "Someone is celebrating a little too hard tonight."

"You can't blame a guy for wanting to appreciate his two best friends," protested Matt, and I couldn't help but smile.

"I wasn't aware I had competition," said Vik, looking me up and down. I grinned but lowered my eyes, all too aware of the muscles carved into his arms. "Would you like a drink, Dee? I'm due for another round and can grab you a lager." Matt raised his hand, and Vik laughed. "I think you're doing just fine with what you have."

"Thanks." I saluted Vik, and he slipped between two coffee-colored couches, heading back toward the covered bar. I watched him walk away a little longer than was necessary.

As soon as we were alone, Matt plunked his beer down onto the crowded table and looked at me apologetically. "I hate to be a downer, but we should probably talk about earlier today."

All of my regrets tumbled out in a single breath. "I didn't mean to make it sound like you don't love Misa, or aren't on my side, or anything like that—sometimes I just react before I can regulate, and it never seems to come out right."

"I've got you, Dee," he said. "I know you're trying your best, and I'm doing the same over here. It's just—I see how great you are and I want to support you, so much that I can sometimes put my foot in it."

"Misa is rubbing off on you," I teased.

"Or I just really, really want you to be happy," he replied.

Locking eyes with Matt, it was like the rest of the party ceased to exist. It was addictive to be understood like this, to know that even the worst parts of myself could be held with love. We sunk into one of the couches and I grabbed his hand and squeezed it. I longed to feel the electricity between us, but my nerves were dulled by quetiapine.

"I want the same for you," I said instead, then paused. "I guess I assumed that doing adult things like getting married meant that you were way past what we went through together. And I'm starting to think that was a lousy hypothesis."

"I'm fine, Dee," said Matt gruffly. "Honestly."

I didn't believe him for a second. I let go of his hand, disappointed that he was still holding back.

He sensed my frustration and tried to muster up the right words. "It's mostly just the wedding," he said, waving aimlessly at the crowd. "I could get married in a parking lot and find the magic in it. But Julie really wanted to host the wedding at the resort, and Misa really wanted to make Julie happy, and I really wanted to make Misa happy, so we're here. I'd be lying if I said it didn't make me uncomfortable, especially for my mum."

"Because of the money?"

He nodded. "The money, and because she's already so fixated on what she has or hasn't given me over the years. I think she feels like I missed out when she was struggling, and she wants to make all that time up now. That's part of the reason she wants grandkids so badly—it's a chance for her to try again."

"And how do you feel about it?" I asked.

"I want to be the kind of dad that I never had," he said quietly. "But I don't want my mum putting that kind of pressure on herself, if or when it happens. I already know that she's amazing. She has nothing left to prove." He threw his arm around me and the surface of my skin lit up piece by piece—like a pinball machine—leaving gaping chasms in between. I knew I still wanted him, but my body couldn't compute the sensation.

"I get where she's coming from, though," I said, trying to think of additional ways to touch him. I wanted to smooth out the fading scars on his forearms, rub the webbing between his forefinger and his thumb. "When you go through something that hard, of course you want a redemption arc."

"That's the problem with stories like ours," Matt replied. "Everyone expects a fairy-tale ending or it's like everything we went through was a waste."

"Well, what's the alternative? We just hang out in psychiatric purgatory?"

"I just don't see why it has to be so linear," he said. "Bad things happen, like the hospital. Good things happen, like falling for a courageous and kindhearted woman who snores like a buzz saw. Misa chose me, despite everything. I should consider myself lucky."

I let his words hang in the air just long enough to swallow the lump in my throat. Matt looked over at me and sighed. "She chose me, and she's pouring her heart into this wedding, and I'm still struggling, Dee. I have everything I've ever wanted but I can't make it work. There's something wrong with me, even now."

He averted his eyes, looking out toward the shoreline, and I wondered how many times you could tell someone that they didn't have to suffer alone.

While we were locked up, I got to know Matt best in the moments when he was hiding from everyone else. He'd joke around at the medication dispensary, run his doctors in circles, and rarely reveal anything but a crooked smile during group therapy. Only afterward, when it was just me and him, would he let his guard down a little bit. Part of me worried that this reliance was holding him back, but the intimacy felt too good to disrupt. For once in my life, it kind of felt like I was special.

When Misa showed up, I felt things shift in more ways than one. Suddenly, we didn't have those private moments of decompression. But more significantly for Matt, Misa was too protective to let him half-ass his way through the few resources we had.

I strolled into the common room one morning when Matt was doing a puzzle with Obachan, who was visiting for the third time that week. Her arthritic fingers carefully pressed the border pieces into place, while Matt worked on a rustic barn in the corner of the scene. I plopped down beside him and he barely reacted, just kept connecting piece to piece like his life depended on it.

"You good?" I asked quietly, hoping Obachan wouldn't hear.

"Misa's mad at me," he replied under his breath.

"What did you do?"

Misa stalked around the corner. "He's quitting group therapy. There are only three available activities in this entire place, and he can't be bothered to show up anymore."

I glanced back at Matt, and he shrugged his shoulders. "I just don't see the point of going. The only person who's going to get me out of this mess is me. I don't need the extra noise."

"You can be so dense sometimes, you know that?" huffed Misa. Obachan smiled and passed Matt a segment of the barn door. "It feels like you're just passing the time until you wind up back here. Is that what you want?"

Matt, taken aback at her uncharacteristic candor, put down his puzzle pieces. "Of course not," he said, then cracked a wry smile. "In terms of my psychiatric career, I'm pretty sure getting to hang out with you guys is the peak. It's all downhill from here."

"I care about you, okay?" said Misa, ignoring the wisecrack. "So I'm not going to sit back and watch you make the same choices over and over again and wonder why nothing is changing."

Deep in my stomach, the fleeting idea that I could be special was swallowed up by a rising wave of guilt.

"Sometimes, even when things feel hopeless, you have to throw absolutely everything at the wall until something sticks," Misa continued. "That means trying to be vulnerable—and if it's not going to happen with them, you could at least try it with us."

Matt sighed. "I don't want to weigh you down with my stuff."

"Have you ever wondered if maybe you're so weighed down because you never let anything out properly?" she replied, and Obachan put a gentle hand on Matt's arm.

"You guys are teaming up on me," he said softly.

Misa threw her head back and laughed, and he looked at her so intently that my heart hurt. "Well, is it working?" she said.

Misa knew how to push Matt in a way that I could never bring myself to do. Being a pusher came naturally to her—usually for the benefit of others, and often at a significant cost to herself. That day in group, Matt talked about how he was afraid to call his mom after so many days of silence, that it reminded him of when his dad used to disappear on her too.

But I was the one he asked to sit by the pay phone with him, knowing that I'd let him take his time, say less than perhaps the occasion called for. He knew that sometimes Misa cared so much, she didn't know how to leave any space.

෧൫

NESTLED IN A spot away from the crowd, I leaned into Matt gently. He smelled like campfire and Irish Spring. "There's nothing wrong with you. You're allowed to be overwhelmed."

He exhaled heavily. "It's more than just being overwhelmed. I can feel myself doing exactly what he did. My dad, I mean."

"You're nothing like your dad, Matt."

"Yeah, except I'm disengaging and I don't know how to stop it," he said, gazing out over the uproar. "Sometimes, I don't know if I can keep up with her. We're so different."

Despite the twinge of pain I felt for Misa, I couldn't see past the glimmer of hope I had been waiting for. Without any sabotage on my part, Matt's doubts had floated to the surface. I didn't say anything, just let it pour out of him the way he needed it to. The way it used to.

"If I told her how I really felt about the hospital, about this wedding, I'd just be dragging her down in a way she would never do to me," he continued. "And the more she tries to help me, the less I feel like I deserve it. Or want it, even. I don't know what to do. Lately there have been more bad days than good."

"But are they bad days because your brain is messing with you, or bad days because you don't want this anymore?" I asked, readying myself to ask about his medication.

"Well, isn't that the classic bipolar conundrum? She's always so sure about everything, Dee, and when you asked me this morning what made me fall in love with her, I could barely tell you. That's not fair to her, is it?" Worry lines etched themselves into his forehead. "You've seen me at my worst. You know everything. Do you think we're making a mistake by jumping into this so quickly?"

Medication completely forgotten, I opened my mouth to tell him the truth—that he deserved the kind of love that lit up his darkest days, that it wasn't his fault that things weren't working if they weren't meant to be—but Vik swooped in with an entire tray of drinks, Misa a few steps behind him. "The wait was so bloody long that I figured we'd best stock up for the next hour." He looked at Matt, and then at me, and then back at Matt. "You alright?"

I think we were all waiting for Matt to break the silence, to come back at Vik with a signature quip, but as I watched his glazed eyes and tight grip on the armrest, I realized nothing was coming. The silence stretched around the entire coastline of the island, and Vik and Misa looked worriedly at me.

"I've been feeling depressed," I said, the half-truth fizzing between my teeth. "Matt was just giving me advice. Kind of a bummer conversation to have at a stag and doe, to be honest."

I watched Misa's face relax, because, of course, Matt pulling me out of a pit was nothing out of the ordinary. It was just another part of the job description. She walked over to his side of the couch and ruffled his hair the way I always wanted to, then turned to me. "How's your appetite been? Are you having trouble sleeping?" she asked. Matt looked at me apologetically, but I didn't mind. I was relieved to see the color returning to his face.

"Honestly, things aren't great," I said, thinking about my pre-party blanket burrito. "When I try and move my body, it feels heavy and slow, but when I lie still, it feels like my limbs are buzzing. You know, the depression catch-22."

"I get the buzzing too," said Misa softly, and Matt nodded. "And terrible nausea. I brought some ginger Gravol, if you'd like me to drop some by your room."

Vik, who was still carrying his full tray of drinks, finally got tired and put them down on the cocktail table. "You know, it's really quite amazing that the three of you found each other. The support you can offer—it's all so natural."

"I think when a lot of regular people ask how I'm doing, they're really wondering if I've overcome my illness yet," I replied. "But it's different with us. There's no expectation to be better than the way we wake up that day."

But maybe I spoke too soon, because the next thing I knew, Misa was roping me into her pre-bridal-brunch workout class to help battle my brain zaps. If I were to list the top five things I'd rather not do, morning barre with Misa was right up there with burying a dead body and Tilley's taxes. My wheels spun in place as I tried to think up an excuse for being busy while on vacation.

"Just let her do her own thing, Misa," said Matt quietly, breaking my awkward silence. I guessed he was still thinking about our earlier conversation, how sometimes sympathy was better than solutions.

She shot him a familiar look. "Sometimes trying something new—"

"Can stress out someone who's already at their max capacity," he finished firmly, raising his eyebrows at her. I appreciated that he was trying to help out, but I also felt like the conversation wasn't really about me anymore.

Misa sighed and then turned to look at me, eyes wide with apology. "I didn't mean to put you on the spot, Dee."

"I know. Maybe I'll give it a try, though," I offered, eager to cut the tension. "It might be good to change things up."

Matt and Misa continued to eye each other as Vik handed me a drink. "That sounds fantastic," he said. He put an arm on my shoulder and I stared at his bracelet of wooden beads. "And if you're up to it, you're welcome to join Kei and me for a run later on."

Matt, still hunched in his corner of the couch, slid his foot over to rest against mine in a show of camaraderie in the face of unwanted physical exercise. Despite the stretch of leather between us, I felt warmth spread from my metatarsals to my rib cage. It was Matt and me against everyone, the way it was always supposed to be.

"Let's see if I survive the morning," I said, mustering up a smile. "Maybe I'll even rope in Tilley."

❧

I FOUND MY sister camped out in a nearby cabana, guarding a metal bucket that held two bottles of Moët—an upgrade from our usual $10 prosecco. "Do you want a drink?" she asked.

"Are you offering me an entire champagne bottle as 'a drink'?"

"You're the one who complained your whole damn childhood that I didn't know how to share."

I sighed and plopped down at the foot of her chair. Tilley peeled the glittery tinfoil from the top of the bottle and released the cork into the blinking night. She handed me the opened bottle, its intoxicating buzz holding me close as she unfastened her own. I took a long sip off the top, bubbles settling at the back of my throat. I could feel my heart beating through the curves of my eardrums, picking up pace with every swallow. My lips spread into an easy smile.

"Why are you doing that with your face?" asked Tilley, leaning back in her lounger and peering down her nose at me. "Where have you been?"

"Take a wild guess."

"If you were smart, you would have been sidling up to Vik. That man is unreasonably attractive," she said, pressing the cool condensation from her bottle against her chest. "You should have seen him talking to Misa's grandma. He asked about her pickled daikon! How many men have time to be that hot and care about Japanese radishes?"

"Why didn't you talk to him, then?"

"He's not interested in me," she said wistfully. "Now, you, on the other hand, might actually have a shot if you pulled your head out of your ass."

It was tempting, sure, but I couldn't shake the feeling that I was finally getting somewhere with Matt. I told Tilley about the doubts he was harboring, the noticeable tension with Misa, and the moment he pressed his foot against mine and it felt like we were an unstoppable team, just like we used to be.

"He loves her, obviously, but maybe not in the same way he

used to," I said. "And I think the more I help him understand this, the more he's going to realize that I'm the one he can depend on. I don't even have to do anything backstabby. I just have to be a good friend."

"I see where you're going with this," said Tilley slowly. "But I also see huge potential for this to turn into a garbage fire in terms of your own recovery, even if things go the way you want. Do you think you can handle the weight of another person right now?"

"But maybe this is the motivation I need to get better," I explained. "I don't have anyone to get better for right now."

"Excuse me?" Tilley's eyebrows blasted off into the stratosphere.

I backtracked quickly. "I mean, of course I have you—"

"What about yourself, though?" she said, abruptly putting down her bottle of Moët. "Don't you think you're important?"

As I opened my mouth to answer, Tilley's phone started beeping. She dug through the bottom of her purse to shut off the daily alarm, then pulled out a lone banana. "Alright, party's over—if we're going to make it to the barre class from hell, you've got to start prepping for your meds at least somewhat on time."

I accepted the slightly bruised fruit and started peeling it mechanically. "You really came prepared."

"That's my job," Tilley replied, stumbling to her feet. "Now what time is this class at?"

"How do you feel about waking up with the sun?"

Tilley kicked over her empty bottle of champagne. "Just tell me I can't do it, and I'll be there."

11

"MS. JACKSON" —OUTKAST (4:30)

"YOU. FUCKING. ASSHOLE," said Tilley, whacking me in the head with a lumpy hotel pillow. "I'm hungover as shit and now I have to wake your zombie ass up at the crack of dawn."

"Brrghf," I mumbled, fighting off the fire snakes. Tilley's voice buzzed in and out of earshot like a pirated radio station. It felt like my arms were jerking erratically but from her reaction, I was guessing I hadn't moved an inch. Good morning, medication.

"I understand that you're on more drugs than the later-years Beatles, but you set like twenty alarms and your ringtone is 'Take a Chance on Me.' Weren't you afraid someone would catch on to your ABBA-fuelled desperation?"

"I s'need . . . help now," I said, words tumbling over each other. I had already had a dream where I did wake up and go to barre class, so this was a little too *Groundhog Day* for my liking.

"After this many years of living in the same house, I should have earned a damn black belt in helping you wake up," said Tilley. "Just today, I've pulled all the sheets off your body, turned all the lights on, licked the side of your face—I mean, what else do you want me to do?"

"Blergh."

I heard her walk into the bathroom and slam the door. I knew that I wanted to get up—needed to, really—but my brain was oatmeal and I couldn't put anything together. This was why I didn't have a full-time job. This was why I didn't sleep over after first dates, when I went on them in the first place.

More footsteps, then Tilley dumped a full glass of water over my head. My eyes snapped open. I still couldn't move my limbs but I was conscious of them in a way that hadn't been possible before. I lay in a puddle in the middle of the bed and waited for the rest of me to catch up.

"I know I normally use the ironing spray bottle on you, but I figured we might need something more dramatic for our timeline," said Tilley, gently pushing my slick hair back from my forehead. "You'll be good to go in about twenty minutes."

"So emb'rassing," I slurred, as she pulled off my pajama bottoms and shimmied my stretchy leggings up one leg at a time. "I'm sss-orry you have to do this."

Tilley looked at me and cocked an eyebrow. "Sorry enough that you're gonna let me off the hook for this barre class?"

"N-not a chance."

WHEN WE GOT to the beachside fitness studio, Tilley caught a few disapproving looks from the middle-aged women who were already limbering up on the barre. I'm no detective, but it could have been her fuchsia bodysuit or her retro yellow shorts that screamed CALL ME across the ass. She stared back until they glanced down at the smooth wooden floors.

"Barre bitches," Tilley muttered, kicking off her sneakers and straightening her neon green scrunchy.

"To be fair," I said, somewhat recovered from my morning black hole, "you look like a glow-in-the-dark mini-putt course with an attitude problem."

"Why, thank you." She preened and tossed her hair.

At the front of the studio, ladies in perky ponytails slid purple yoga mats out of slim cupboards and arranged them in a checkerboard pattern across the room. The wooden barre ran around the studio in an L-shape, leaving the remaining sides open to the ocean's salty breeze. Overhead, a giant hanging fan circulated air, barely audible above the sound of island beats pumping from concealed speakers. I watched a few early bird tourists pass by the studio on their way to the beach and longed to go lounge alone in the sun like an iguana. Instead, I spotted Misa near the cupboards and decided I might as well go get credit for showing up on time.

As soon as she saw me, she pressed a squishy mat into my hands. I accepted it gingerly, noting the matching periwinkle shades of her gym clothes and her neat French braids. You could tell she was the kind of person who proactively bought athletic wear and wasn't just handed it as a suggestion disguised as a gift.

"I'm glad we get to do this together," Misa said, like participating in morning activities was an everyday occurrence for me. "Suzanne is really going to push us today."

I thought briefly about pushing Suzanne too, like maybe off the edge of a cliff. "Sounds fun."

"Honestly, this class will be so good for resetting your brain," she continued. "And hopefully it'll make Matt feel better too—I can tell he's really worried about you. He was completely out of it after you left last night!"

My heart soared. "Did he say anything?"

An intimidatingly fit woman in a sports bra and matching leggings waved impatiently at us. "Grab some dumbbells, ladies," she sang in a posh British accent. "If you have extra breath to chat, you have extra breath to push!"

The thump of the bass picked up as Suzanne fastened a tiny microphone to her sports-bra strap and proceeded to beat the living shit out of us in the warm-up alone. We jumped, scrambled into lopsided planks, collapsed through push-ups, and then got up again. My muscles screamed every step of the way. I searched for flaws in the clean ripples of Misa's shoulders, wondered how I looked next to her—hips sagging, arms shaking, hair plastered to my sweaty forehead, quetiapine stomach hovering inches away from the floor.

Misa caught me staring at her mid-plank and shot me a quick smile. "You're doing great, Dee. This is going to get your endorphins way up!"

I dropped onto my belly and pressed my cheek into the mat. "So I have to manage my depression in order to exercise, which will then manage my depression? I'm no scientist, but that seems wildly unfair."

"Of course it is," huffed Misa, rotating into a side plank and raising her left arm above her head. "That's why I sleep in my gym clothes. Eliminate obstacles!"

By the time we made it to the barre, my arms were linguine but I had started to fully inhabit my body. I could feel myself pushing against the foggy edges of depression with every militant plié executed under Suzanne's watchful eye. I tried not to track Misa, who was performing better than me for the twelfth time that week.

"Come on, ladies," cheered Suzanne. "Let's firm up those underbutts!"

"Is that a medical term?" quipped Tilley, bending suggestively over the barre. Misa looked annoyed.

"Think about all the wobbly bits that hang out of your bikini!" Suzanne was in full force, walking down the row of sweaty women to straighten our backs as we squatted. "You see them? Now *destroy them!*"

"I haven't heard this much body shaming since *America's Next Top Model* was on the air," hissed Tilley.

"That's funny, coming from you," panted Misa, pulling herself up to stand with the barre.

Tilley narrowed her eyes. "What's that supposed to mean?"

Misa straightened her leggings and gazed at Tilley, workout music still banging in the background. "You don't seem to have a problem making comments about Matt's body," she said, quiet but unwavering. "You'd really get along with my great-aunts."

I was surprised that she would pick a fight with Tilley in the presence of witnesses, but when I caught a second look at her steely glare, I realized this was something she'd been swallowing for a while. My stomach turned over in apprehension.

"Look, Misa," said Tilley. "I get that you're in love or whatever, but Matt and I have an understanding. He fucked over Dee once and now I get to openly hate him for all eternity."

"It's not his fault she was discharged!" Misa hissed, attracting wary eyes from the rest of our class. "Dee doesn't blame him for what happened, so I don't understand why you do."

"Dee would never—" Tilley caught herself.

"Dee would never talk about Matt that way because she knows how hard it is to be on heavy medication," said Misa. "Do you know how many times he's asked doctors for help for something else and has been told to just lose weight? And you're always laughing about him, and the hospital, like it's some sort of joke. I thought maybe you'd rein it in, seeing as it's our wedding, but I've heard you making snide comments since you got here and I'm sick of it."

Tilley glanced at me, and I didn't say anything because I was too busy falling through a trapdoor. I knew the reason Tilley was so hard on Matt was for my benefit, to pull me back from my obsession. But for all the time I had spent pining over Matt and arguing with Tilley about his place in my life, I had rarely called her out for her remarks about the way he looked. And if I was being honest, it's because I harbored some ugly feelings about how my own body had changed on medication. I should have stood up for him ages ago, the way Misa knew how to. No matter how many burpees I survived or weights I lifted, Misa was just better for Matt. She always would be.

I could feel my eyes brimming with sad puppy tears, the kind that made Misa fawn over me and Tilley want to punch a wall. I took off for the exit, searching for my running shoes.

Tilley raced after me and only caught up as I paused to shove my feet into my still-laced sneakers. "Fine, I promise I'll lay off Matt," she said to Misa, who had followed us to the door. "You make some good points. But I still think he owes Dee an apology."

"It's okay, Tilley." I finally found my words. "It's over. I'm fine."

"Yeah, except it's not," she said. She sat down and yanked on her laces, trying to keep pace with my escape. "Because they have jobs and are getting married and you're still living with me, walking dogs, and wondering when things are going to turn around."

It was the truth, but somehow it hurt more coming from outside of my own brain. The tears I had been holding back finally burst through. I backed away from both of them, started walking down the concrete path leading toward the breakfast buffet. "I'm gonna go grab some water."

"Dee, wait up," said Tilley. She finally had her shoes on but couldn't find her gym bag in the heaping pile of belongings beside the door. She called down the path after me as I walked away. "I'm sorry. That came out wrong."

I stalled at the fork in the path, wondering if I should let it go.

"Please, Dee," said Misa, who was trailing behind me. "I didn't mean to upset you. Can we talk?"

That's what came out of her mouth, but our telepathic ward connection told me the real truth. That I was a ticking time bomb, easy to set off. That the people I loved had been walking on eggshells around me forever, and even they couldn't keep up with that kind of emotional calisthenics anymore. I hung a sharp left and took off through the dining area, dodging tables like I did phone bills.

༄

BETWEEN THE OMELETTE station and the poolside bar, I lost Tilley and Misa for good. Eager to avoid the bustling breakfast crowd, I walked past Grace's desk in the lobby and found myself standing by the circular driveway at the front of the resort, my tears subsiding. The breeze seemed fainter than in past days and the sun beat heavily down on my exposed shoulders. I knew I should have grabbed sunscreen, but my pride prevented me from circling back to the hotel room and possibly having to face Tilley. I just wanted to wallow a little bit without her witnessing.

Washington's Land Rover was parked at one side of the loop,

towering over the elegant flowerpots that lined the entrance to the lobby. He leaned up against a white column, laughing open-mouthed at Marco, who was shaking one hand toward the sky as he spoke. Washington noticed me watching them and straightened up, prompting Marco to turn around.

"Hey, Miss Dee," said Marco, beckoning me over. "How was your party last night?"

I shuffled toward them reluctantly, still smarting from my last social interaction. "It was good, thanks."

"If you think *that* was a good time, you should check out Bugaloos in Five Cays," said Marco, ever the salesman. "Find yourself some real island music. Rihanna's been there and you know she knows what's good."

"Marco, were you even born when Bugaloos started up?" Washington shook his head and turned to me, gesturing toward the hotel lobby. "Before all of this was built, this place was my family's church, and Bugaloos was a shack in Blue Hills where my dad went to eat conch. Now it's got wine tables in the ocean just for Instagram." He swiped a bead of sweat from his forehead and gestured at Marco. "This guy goes to university for hospitality and tourism and starts forgetting the way it used to be."

"Come on, Wash—I've lived here my whole life too. I'm the kind of person who should have a say in what's going on," teased Marco, and I realized I hadn't thought once about the kind of training he must have completed to be in his position at Breeze Bay.

I shifted my weight. "I know Misa has been so grateful for your help this week."

"Oh, Marco could run this whole place, no problem," said Washington with a grin. "There's just a lot of 'international talent' that keeps showing up."

Marco laughed. "You're really on your best behavior, aren't you?"

A black taxi pulled into the roundabout, and a party of impossibly tall blonde women clambered out the sliding door, sporting hideous pink bachelorette sashes. "Well, thanks for the vote of confidence, Miss Dee. I appreciate it." Marco consulted his clipboard and took a deep breath. "We'd better get going. Wash, want to help me with the bags?"

Marco and Washington spun to greet the group of girls, whose voices jumped an octave at the sight of the complimentary rum punch arriving from the front desk. I watched the women engulf them—Marco's smile never wavering once—and wondered if Breeze Bay took him for granted too.

I turned and strolled through the lobby, past the check-in desk, through the outdoor dining area, and toward the clear blue infinity pool. The breakfast buffet crowd was finally starting to migrate toward the poolside bar, where a bartender hoisted a silver cocktail shaker in the air and her colleague carefully arranged sliced strawberries for an assembly line of daiquiri glasses. On the opposite ledge, Kei was sitting with their feet dipped into the rippling waters, while Ana swam leisurely laps from one end of the pool to the other. I looked toward the row of alcoholic slushies and back at Kei and Ana, and figured I might as well make one responsible decision on this entire trip.

"Dee, Ana. Ana, Dee," said Kei as I plopped down beside them.

"I do love a name that's also just a letter," said Ana, coming up for air. She ran her fingers through her brown hair, pushing wayward strands away from her round face. "Short for anything?"

"Yeah." I stared at the drain in the bottom of the pool.

"Cool, cool," Ana said. "Leave it a mystery. I'm a fan." She hoisted herself out of the pool and stood dripping over us. "Kei, do you have my towel?"

Kei unzipped a truly enormous backpack with infinite pockets and handed Ana a turquoise towel from the depths of it, along with a tube of ChapStick. Ana slung the towel around her waist and mashed the lip balm enthusiastically against her mouth.

I frowned. "So are you two still doing the space thing?"

"Yeah," said Kei. "Slight time-out, but yeah. We had some time to talk at the party last night."

Ana handed the ChapStick to Kei, who applied it with far less brute strength.

"No further questions," I said, and Kei glared at me.

"Where's your evil twin?" they asked, and I remained tight-lipped. "And did you say anything to Matt yet?"

"Not exactly," I admitted. "Like, he's definitely going through something. But I need more time—and maybe fewer drinks."

"Well, I hate to break it to you, but the wedding's only two days away," said Kei. "And I'm already babysitting half my family, so I kind of need you to handle this one."

On cue, a very small cousin with short spiky hair swam over from across the pool and tugged on Kei's board shorts. "You said you'd play tag with us," he whined. "It's been forever already."

Kei looked pointedly at me. "This is exactly how I feel, except with you. Ana, please take over my guilt trip while I dunk this kid." They scooped up their cousin, who was screaming with glee, and launched him way into the deep end. Ana sat down beside me, dangling her feet in front of the pool's jets.

"So, you were in the hospital with Misa," she said. I nodded slightly, and she steamrolled through the next sentence. "My childhood best friend was in a place like that—she found out later it was the same ward her grandfather had been in years earlier. Isn't that wild? Her parents never told anyone, so she never got to ask him about it."

"How's your friend doing now?" I asked, glad we had skipped all pretense of small talk.

Ana sucked in air. "Oh wow, I did not plan this conversation out well. She's—well, she didn't make it long after she got out. I miss her a lot."

I wanted to tell Ana that there was no need to tiptoe around the truth, that most conversations I had like this ended in one of two ways—either with a miraculous recovery (complete with steady employment) or with an untimely loss. A year after my own discharge, I still wasn't entirely sure where I'd end up on that spectrum.

"That's why I think it's so cool that you still hang out with Matt and Misa," added Ana, noticing my silence. "From what I understand, not everyone gets an epilogue to their hospital friendships."

I thought about Liz, the one person from our floor who I knew for sure hadn't stuck around afterward. The others filtered through my memory so frequently that I couldn't imagine their nonexistence, even though deep down, I always knew it was a possibility. "Yeah, I guess not," I said, then abruptly shifted gears. "So what's the deal with you and Kei? You still seem pretty close."

Ana glanced sideways at Kei, who was busy chasing a rogue cousin around the deep end. "Honestly? It's kind of embarrassing."

"Try me," I said, thinking of that time I broke up with a guy and rode a tandem bicycle with him the next day.

"Okay," said Ana, ready to set the scene. "After Kei graduated, they got their first full-time job and we moved into a new place in Toronto. I had never really dated seriously before but it was kind of nice, you know, getting excited about light fixtures and houseplants."

My stomach crawled with jealousy. "Sounds like it."

"But then three months in, Kei gets this health benefits package. Drugs, dental—the whole deal. And they come home and show me some bureaucratic form they started filling out, this big old pile of paper that calls me their partner."

"Okay," I said, waiting for the climax.

"That's it!" she howled. "I completely freaked out and told them I needed space. And all they were trying to do was take care of my dental hygiene. They know my Sour Patch Kids consumption is disproportionally high."

Across the pool, Kei launched into an unexpected cannonball, causing the crowd of kids who had gathered around them to cheer. Ana looked longingly toward them, then covertly pulled a crisp notebook from her satchel beside us. "I've been working on a letter for them this week—just to help me figure out why I overreacted so badly. Do you ever do stuff like that?"

"I've been asked to journal by a few well-intentioned doctors," I said. "I love the idea of writing for someone else, though." I imagined the kind of stationery I'd use to confess how I felt to Matt. Thick edges, rich texture—maybe sprayed with a bit of my drugstore perfume?

"Well, I'll let you know how mine goes," said Ana, swinging her legs out of the pool and gathering up her damp towel. "I don't know what it is about other people's weddings, but they really get me deep in my feelings."

"What's your dream outcome here?"

She cocked her head to the side. "Dream? We get back together. But if that's not what Kei wants, I'd rather us be honest about our limits than damage ourselves over an unbalanced friendship. I could already fill a brunch table with my friends-slash-exes."

She said it so breezily that it almost felt reasonable, as if she wouldn't be giving up, but letting go. She noticed my tongue-tied expression and gave me a wink. "I guess we'll see what happens after the weekend."

"I respect your hustle," I said, and meant it.

Ana caught the longing in my voice and grinned widely. "I think I might respect yours too."

ⓖⓛⓛ

MISA'S BRIDAL BRUNCH was held at a beachside café on the west side of Long Bay. Since we were actually arriving on time for once, one of Washington's crew members dropped us off in an identical shuttle, with far less chitchat than we had grown accustomed to. The Nagasakas had booked the whole place for the morning and arranged a long sequence of tables stretching out toward the beach, paired with white wooden chairs on either side. Outside the restaurant, a local woman in a jaunty floral jumpsuit alternated between selling conch shells to passing tourists and renting kayaks by the hour. I figured if this get-together was anything like the last one, Tilley and I could always jump in one and paddle our way back toward the Saint Lawrence River.

On my way back to our hotel room, I had picked up one of those strawberry daiquiris for Tilley as a truce—I decided she deserved to be honest at least as often as she put up with me being sad. Instead of using her words, she threw me into a cold shower, then dolled me up in a tea-length linen dress that barely kept my boobs from bursting out. We did our makeup side by side in the bathroom mirror, reconciling over a shared tube of coral lip gloss. We emerged from our hotel room reunited in sisterhood and ready to take on a traditional Scottish breakfast.

Misa was sitting at the head of the table with Elinor and Julie on either side of her. Her dark hair shone like a granite countertop, with not a strand out of place despite the insistent Caribbean breeze. You would have hardly guessed that she had just subjected us to what Tilley had taken to calling "butt seizures" at sunrise. Tilley was still wheezing as we mounted the wooden stairs of the patio.

"If this place doesn't serve Bloody Caesars, I'm leaving," she whispered.

"If you don't make yours a virgin, I'm leaving first," I whispered back. "You're about one burpee away from tossing your cookies as it stands."

"Exactly. I need the alcohol to counteract the exercise."

Misa rose to greet us in a romper that should have looked like Christmas pajamas but was maddeningly classy instead. I could feel Tilley's body deflate as she approached, a rare moment of self-consciousness.

"It's good to see you, Tilley," Misa said in the same kind and discreet way she forgave me after an outburst or kept Matt on track in a difficult conversation. I'd spent a lot of time trying to find Misa's fatal flaw, but I never had any doubt about her superpower. She was always a few moves ahead on life's chessboard and wasn't afraid to help you get into a winning position.

"My butt is less enthused about running into you again," said Tilley, recapturing her nonchalance. "You destroyed us this morning."

Misa winced. "I'm sorry—"

"Never apologize," growled Tilley. "I loved it. Same time to-morrow?"

"Of course." Misa laughed. "Can't wait."

We lingered awkwardly as the remaining few guests trailed in and then chose seats along the artfully splayed palm fronds that bisected the table. Elinor fussed over each person who sat down, waving over waiters for drink orders, while Julie kept a watchful eye on Obachan, who was trying to wobble down toward the water.

A few seats away, a beaming Anila conversed with the waiter about vegetarian options. Elinor swept by and whispered something in her ear, and the two of them giggled away like schoolgirls.

Kei arrived last, wearing a button-up plaid shirt radiant with daybreak hues. No one really wanted to sit beside Tilley after she stuffed a bunch of miniature jams inside her beach bag and, with a gratuitous wink, promised she'd "be making a jam sandwich later," so Kei wound up next to us at the far end of the table.

"I think we're almost done with mandatory bridal events," said Kei. After checking to see if Julie was watching, they pulled their crochet hook and bursting bundle of yarn out of their bag. "Unless there's a wedding piñata no one's informed me of yet."

"We can only hope," I replied, grinning. "But out of all of them, brunch seems to be the most non-threatening."

"I love seated parties because then I can just talk to two people and no one thinks that's weird," said Kei, and my heart exploded in friendship. "Also, if we can stay away from the Nag, that would be great because she's starting to ask about my formal-wear options."

Tilley winked again, her mouth open. "We'll take care of Aunt Julie."

"That sounds like we're going to murder her," I said.

"I don't think I packed enough clothes in my suitcase to accommodate a murder," replied Tilley. She plucked a leaf from the table foliage and pressed it to her cheeks. "Do you think this stuff heals sunburns like aloe?"

Waiters began to emerge from the back room, arms wobbling beneath massive silver platters. They carefully placed them on top of the palm fronds, forming a thick silver train down the length of the table. The heavy smell of grilled meat hovered over us long after the plates were set down. There were piles of streaky bacon, heaping bowls of baked beans, sausages that looked like they had been run over by a Mack truck, and Matt's favorite: black pudding, which vaguely resembled a burnt hockey puck.

"I think this is what a heart attack looks like," breathed Tilley. "Did all the vegetables on this planet shrivel up and die?"

Kei nudged her. "I know this is hard for you, but can you try not to be rude? This is Elinor's family thing."

"Wait, aren't you a vegetarian?" I asked.

"I will be enjoying the potato scones," Kei said with dignity, using tongs to snag what looked like a cross between a pita and a potato chip. "And I am over the moon about it."

As I sawed off the circular crust on my first-ever black pudding, I briefly wondered how Misa's family could have acquired such a specific set of meats for Elinor's party. Then again, this was an island where everything was imported, so a frozen pizza already cost twenty dollars. The only limitation in either situation was money.

By the end of our meal, Elinor had sent the sausages back twice for additional burning, Kei had eaten their weight in potatoes, and the rest of us agreed that black pudding was not really a dessert but additional meat in disguise. Misa had spent most of her time slicing Obachan's meal into tiny pieces. I eyed Misa's plate and spotted the telltale sign of her worrying—food moved around just enough for visual effect. Elinor stood at the head of the table and beamed, holding a fizzing glass of Perrier.

She raised her glass overhead and we all returned the gesture, Tilley spilling a drop of her Caesar onto the white tablecloth.

"Thank you all so much for coming to our little brunch," Elinor said. She looked almost girlish in the spotlight. "You can't imagine how much it means for me to share this Scottish tradition with our new family."

"And your adopted family," added Anila slyly.

Elinor beamed at her. "Of course! It's such a change to have everyone we love in one place. You know, Matt and I have been just the two of us for so long, it's lucky we haven't forgotten how to be with other people." She chuckled slightly, then turned to Misa. "And now that we have you joining our little family, I can't wait for us to keep growing."

The corners of Misa's mouth turned upward, but I could tell her body was tensing. Elinor put her glass down for a moment, then reached into her purse and grabbed a small white cloth bag tied with a thin blue ribbon at the top.

"I wanted to give this to you, as part of our family tradition," continued Elinor. She opened the bag and let Misa peek inside. "These are cones from Scots pine," she said. "In Inverness, we believe if you keep these by your bedside or under your pillow at night, it will help your chances of having children."

Misa's entire face froze, but Elinor didn't seem to notice. "I know it's a little early to start thinking about all that, but, well, now that you're getting married, I hope we'll one day hear that pitter-patter of little feet."

"Oh man," Tilley whispered. "She definitely should have done a shower registry."

Misa's brain finally caught up to speed with the situation. She flashed Elinor a brilliant smile, her teeth glinting sharply in the sunlight. "Thank you, Elinor. This is so kind of you. So kind," she repeated.

I watched her grip tighten around the white bag until I could almost hear the pine cones crunching between her fingers. "Give me a second," I said to Tilley and Kei. "I think Misa's giving herself splinters."

I approached the head of the table with the false confidence of every high school acquaintance who has approached me with a pyramid scheme (five and counting).

"What a lovely tradition," I cooed, pushing past the chairs of close friends and family members until I was at Misa's side. I grabbed her hand, the one crunching pine cones like the Hulk, and lowered my voice so only Misa and Elinor could hear. "It's a shame Misa has a pine allergy. We can't risk a reaction right before the wedding."

Misa pushed the bag into my hand like it was a hot potato and nodded quickly. "This is an incredibly thoughtful gesture. I really do appreciate it. But Dee's right, pine does tend to irritate my skin."

Elinor looked like she was about to suggest that Misa sleep in a hazmat suit for the good of her future spawn, so I decided to evacuate the premises. "We should actually go and wash your hands before you get a rash," I said, pulling Misa out of her chair and toward the bathroom. "Excuse us a moment."

Noticing the other guests exchanging murmurs, Julie swept in to smooth over the situation with Elinor. "Misa will be right back," she said warmly to the table. "And in the meantime, let's toast our wonderful hostess!"

Everyone raised their glasses again as Misa and I hustled past the entire length of the table and around the corner to the back of the restaurant, the ill-advised pine-cone bag still in my hand. The washroom door was locked—single-use only.

"Elinor is going to come after us and apologize," said Misa, the pitch of her voice rising by the second. "I can't be near her right now. I don't want her to see me like this."

I took one look at her wild eyes and scanned our surroundings for a possible escape, spotting the joint conch stand–kayak rental in the process. "This way," I said, leading Misa off the patio steps and toward the woman in the floral jumper. She was rearranging wooden racks stocked with conch shells of varying sizes. The shells boasted intricate spirals blooming into polished pink openings.

"Is it just me, or do you also think this is how boys picture vaginas?" I asked Misa, who was having trouble breathing.

The saleswoman looked unimpressed. She looked pointedly toward the restaurant, her glamorous chunky earrings bouncing off her jawbone. "Would you like to buy a shell?"

"Actually," I said, "we'd like to rent a kayak."

12

଴ଲ

"OCEAN AVENUE"
—YELLOWCARD (3:18)

"I CAN'T JUST kayak away from my own bridal brunch!" Misa whisper-yelled as I waded into the ocean with our bright purple getaway boat. When she realized I wasn't coming back, she peered through the bushes behind us to scout any unexpected movement from the party.

"I feel like this is one of those bridezilla scenarios where you get to howl 'It's my day!' at the moon and everyone just leaves you the fuck alone," I replied, unsuccessfully trying to tie the hemline of my dress into a knot. It quickly unravelled into the water, the linen slick and heavy against my thighs.

"I can't—I can't," Misa heaved, her eyes darting along the coastline. "Elinor did this all for me, and I'm ruining it. I'm bad, Dee. I'm bad and I can't fix this. I can't go back there. I can't—"

"You don't have to," I said calmly. "You can take a break. You're allowed to take a break sometimes."

"They're going to know something is wrong with me," she said, not processing. She stood there, clenching and unclenching her hands. "I can't do this, Dee, but I can't go back."

I sighed and took a few steps back toward the shore, then reached out and put a cold, clammy hand on her arm.

She wrenched her arm out of my grasp, another step in the dance we'd rehearsed for months. "Don't touch me! I don't need your help. I just don't want to go anywhere, okay?"

Behind Misa, beyond the bushes, I spotted sudden activity on the back patio. Someone was about to figure out we weren't camped out in the washroom.

"Misa, you can either have a panic attack in front of everyone or with just me in the middle of the ocean," I said, hoisting myself ungracefully into the back seat and splashing her in the process. "We won't be gone long. You coming?"

Dripping wet, Misa nodded.

WE PADDLED IN silence for about five minutes before Misa was ready to acknowledge our grand escape.

"I think you might have prevented me from having real Christmas trees in my house for all eternity," she said, her breath evening out. I tried to keep time with her methodical strokes, but I kept skimming the top of the water and drenching myself instead.

"You're welcome," I said, then paused. "I haven't seen you like that in a long time."

"It's the wedding," she said automatically. "It's been a lot of work."

"Remind me never to get married," I said, then stopped. "Why are you so worried about them seeing you? You're allowed to have bad days now and then."

Misa shook her head. "I've gotten so good at managing myself that when things slip, it feels like I've lost everything. I don't want people to look at me differently. You know they always do after they've really seen you."

I knew this was often the case, but I also couldn't help but recall that glimpsing the full spectrum of Misa's experience had helped me understand her better. The unrelenting pressure to maintain appearances, her fixation on her individual responsibility for an illness outside of her control—it was easy to focus on the hardness of these habits, instead of the strength and vulnerability that they sheltered.

⋰

In the ward, the recreation room was always locked up when the therapist was off duty. I don't know what dangers they thought an upright piano or decrepit exercise equipment would pose to us—it's not like we could run away on the hospital treadmill. But every so often, they'd open the room and we'd do arts and crafts on a big table. The day after Misa checked herself in to the hospital, we were streaking watercolor paint across printer paper, ignoring the colors running off the sides of our pages.

Wearing a full face of flawless makeup and flickering with a familiar electric undercurrent, Misa filled in the petals of a pink ranunculus and told me why she had come. "My mother had become Medusa," she said earnestly. "And I knew that even when something isn't strictly real, it can be true in other ways. My behavior was starting to raise questions in the community, and she was so, so angry with me."

"Did you tell her that something was happening to you?"

She smiled sadly. "The words I have to explain myself are not the same words that would carry meaning for her.

I didn't even try. I just went to the train station and sat there, waiting for the bell. And once it started ringing, I walked across the tracks."

"Wait," I said, putting my paintbrush down, "when the train was coming right at you?"

"I just wanted to touch the other side of the tracks and come back," she explained. "To prove that I could come back, that I was still in control. Then I called my uncle and asked him to bring me to his hospital."

I whistled lowly. "You're hard core, you know that?"

"I've been told I'm a bit intense," she said lightly. "That's actually the only part of me that feels consistent sometimes. But I'm hoping I can build some better habits in here."

She looked around the room. Jermaine had dropped his craft supplies and was staring out the window at something the rest of us couldn't see. Harsha was drawing a winding portrait of her brain, complete with canal ways and mirrors and roses with thorns. Even Liz, fresh out of the intensive care unit, was contentedly gluing pom-poms to a Popsicle stick. More into the musical side of the arts, Matt picked up the rec room's guitar and played the opening riff of "Give a Little Bit," his favorite Supertramp song.

"Does he ever play with anyone else?" she asked, nodding toward Matt.

"I don't think the rest of us have any musical talent," I said, suddenly uneasy.

"I'd like to try sometime," she replied softly. "It's been a while since I touched the piano. My mother taught me how to play."

She got up from the table and ran her fingers over the worn keys of the upright like she was retracing forgotten steps. Matt put down his guitar and didn't say a word, just watched with a bemused smile as Misa found her place on the wooden bench. As her fingers reached across octaves to play that first chord, I thought again about her determination to "come back" from the darkness, wondering who she might bring with her on the way.

At Misa's request, it hadn't been hard to get Matt to duet, but we hadn't expected him to drag the rest of us into the shenanigans too. He would get everyone organized as Misa took her place at the upright piano, her fingers tracing harmonic scales before the others had even picked up their instruments. Harsha usually waved the tambourine while Jermaine kept a rhythm on whatever was closest to him. Liz just liked to listen, closing her eyes and losing herself in the warmth of the sound. Brandishing the sole guitar on the floor, Matt strummed the Supertramp riff we'd come to recognize anywhere—the deepness of A7 rising into a clean D, over and over again. I'd sit on the sidelines, waiting for the words to kick in.

When Matt sang the chorus of "Give a Little Bit," the gruffness of his voice would melt into the lyrics and he'd close his eyes like he was dreaming. And even though you could hold my own musical aptitude in a thimble, there was something magical about the way our voices assembled to belt it out in a crummy hospital rec room. Almost everyone was able to sing, heavily medicated or not, because there were only a few words that mattered. The song promised us that, even here, we had something to give, and we'd find our way to wherever we needed to be.

Holding us together through the verse, Misa caught Matt's eyes and beamed before they launched into the interlude *together, matching each other's leaps and bounds through the song. Even the grouchiest nurse would stop by the doorway just to listen, her eyes on us without the usual accompaniment of a clipboard and pen. When the chorus came back around again, it was the closest most of us had felt to home in a long, long time.*

IN THE BOAT, we approached a tiny, jagged island covered in weird species of cacti, then veered to its left. Misa paddled furiously while I held my oar in the water, steering us around the rocks. I think it was the first time we'd really functioned as a team since the hospital, which made sense because it involved me sitting still and Misa carrying both of us.

"Do you want to try paddling?" Misa panted after a few minutes.

"But you're doing such a good job without me!" I replied, and she stuck her tongue out in response.

After we cleared the shallow sandbanks and there was nothing in our way, Misa stopped paddling and turned around in her seat. "Can I ask you something personal, Dee? Are you planning on having kids?"

I rested my paddle across my lap and let us drift away with the current, waves lapping against the side of the boat. "Honestly, my doctor asks me that every time I switch medications, and it always seems too far away to matter. I haven't been on a real date in ages anyway." I let out a short laugh, like I thought it was funny instead of sad. Swallowing my usual venom, I ventured out toward connection. "But I think the real question is whether *you* want kids."

Misa wrung salt water out of the bottom of her romper. "I think I took it off the table completely when I was really sick," she said quietly. "Like, so sick I couldn't even feed myself. Now I'm in a different place, but I haven't forgotten what that felt like, and I know having kids is one of the few things that could easily put me back there. And I'm not sure I'm willing to risk it. Is that selfish? Or is that just being responsible? I'm not sure anymore."

As someone who had been called selfish for the past decade, I knew all about that riddle. I said what I had never been able to articulate to anyone, not even Tilley. "It's okay to be scared and take your time with things. But I think there's a difference between not wanting to do something and not believing you're worth the trouble of trying."

As these words left my mouth, I realized that I also could not tell the difference between these two feelings anymore, not in terms of motherhood so much as my entire recovery strategy. I wasn't sure if my bad attitude had gotten me kicked out of the psychiatric system or if the psychiatric system had left me so jaded that I no longer fit inside medical charts and group therapy circles. I tried to think five, ten years ahead, picture where I'd be, and all I could see was the stucco ceiling of my childhood bedroom. Part of me wanted to help Misa, but a bigger, uglier part of me was jealous that she had graduated on to adultier problems than surviving herself, at least on the surface.

"I think it would be easier if Matt and I didn't approach things so differently," she said. "I want to have every possible scenario mapped out beforehand, but he really believes that having a kid will push us in the right direction, whatever that looks like. And Elinor is just so excited for the future that I'm embarrassed to tell her how scared I am. I already feel like a bad mom and nothing has even happened yet."

"I don't know," I replied. "I feel like you'd be great. You already have so much practice taking care of me."

Misa laughed. "I wish it was that easy. I wish I didn't have to weigh all these pros and cons and make a conscious choice to put myself at risk. But as you know, we don't really have that option."

We. It had been a long time since I had considered Misa and me as anything more than frenemies. I had convinced myself that she had changed, but now that we were literally in the same boat, I realized that it was me who had retreated, expecting her to stay the same. As we rocked back and forth in our tiny purple kayak, I knew that this didn't have to be the case forever.

She smiled toward the floor of the kayak. "Wouldn't Matt be the best dad?"

I grinned. "He'd have the worst dad jokes, for sure."

"When I get worked up about it, I try to think about the songs he'd play for our kids," she said. "I just have so much faith in him and none in myself."

It felt like something straight out of my own brain. Misa gripped the back of her seat with one hand and gasped for air, overwhelmed by the endless potential for disaster. "What if I have a kid and they're crying and I can't get out of bed because I'm too depressed and my blankets feel like slabs of concrete?"

I grabbed her hand. "I'll come over with a sledgehammer." The promise rang in my ear, a twinge of hope pressing against the belief that I would screw everything up.

"But what if—" She paused, leaning into me. "What if they grow up going through this *hell*—not wanting to be alive and then being too alive to stay inside their skin—and it's my fault?"

I squeezed, and her breathing slowed. "That doesn't sound like something you can control."

"I know you're right," she said tearfully. "Growing up, my mom was afraid of drowning, so she forced me through swimming lessons until I was good enough to be a lifeguard. That's what you do for your kids, right? You make sure they don't suffer the same way you did. But how is that possible for something like bipolar? What could I possibly give them?"

I tried to look at Misa the way she would have looked at me in group therapy—enveloping her insecurities with my eyeballs and enveloping her with the serenity of an elderly golden retriever.

"If anyone on this planet has the skills to raise a kid like us, it's you," I said. "Plus, you're like the Michael Jordan of bipolar. You have more championship rings than can fit on your damn hand."

She laughed and I felt my heart expand, not the same breakneck explosion that I craved from Matt but exhilarating all the same.

"If you don't want to have kids, then I suggest you chuck these pine cones into the ocean." Letting go of her arm, I reached into the depths of our kayak and handed her the little white bag. "But if you do, the best part is you don't have to do it alone. You have the greatest support system in the world," I said, shoving my jealousy deep down where it could never return.

Misa held the pine cones in her hand and studied them intently. "I don't know that I'm going to decide the future of my uterus in a kayak," she said finally. "But I think when that time comes, I'd like to talk to you about it."

She placed the pine cones in my hand and I looked at her, genuinely touched. "You think I give good advice?"

"Well," she said, ever the diplomat, "I think you give me slightly unhinged advice that helps me figure out what I actually want to do."

"I'm still taking that as a compliment."

She laughed. "As you should."

We sat in silence for a long moment, bobbing with the waves.

"I've barely had time to take in that I'm getting married on

Saturday, and all of these hypotheticals, they're going to become real soon," Misa said finally.

When she said it like that, I realized the truth—that in less than forty-eight hours, whether Matt and Misa ended up together or not, I'd have to take some kind of step forward in my own life or risk sinking completely. And at this point, I still had no idea what "forward" looked like. I packed the pine cones in the corner of the kayak and started steering us toward the shore. "We should head back," I muttered. "You probably have lots to do."

"Thanks for bringing me out here, Dee. I really needed some space," she replied, already paddling. "You know what I always admire about you?"

"What's that?" I said, apprehension weighing down every stroke across the water.

"You always know how to do the right thing, even in the wrong place," Misa said. "Does that make sense? I mean, you're not bogged down by circumstance. I think it's something I need more of."

My brain skipped right over the compliment and fixated on whether or not I should tell Misa about Matt's medication while I had the chance. In the hospital, we had shared responsibility for each other's care, but lately things had become about me and Matt, or Misa and Matt, and now it was just Misa and me, floating toward an uncertain future with a man we both loved.

"I don't know if I'd recommend living like me," I said, thinking about all the people I had the potential to hurt.

"I wouldn't recommend living like me either," Misa said quietly, and I knew that I wouldn't be able to help Matt without her support. It was time to get the psych ward band back together again.

13

"YOU KNOW I'M NO GOOD"
—AMY WINEHOUSE (4:16)

BY THE TIME we paddled back to shore, the bridal brunch gang had mostly cleared out, except for Tilley, Kei, Elinor, and the Nag. They were waiting for us in beachside loungers as we casually kayaked around the bend. Tilley had swiped a cloth napkin from the restaurant and waved it dramatically as we crashed the boat into the sandbank. Kei hopped into the water and helped us heave the kayak to shore, while Julie supervised with pursed lips. Clearly flustered, Elinor hugged Misa—life jacket and all—as soon as she stepped onto dry land.

"Oh, bunny," she said, stepping back and clasping Misa's hands in hers. "Did I make you upset? I really didn't mean to. This week is all about you. Just say the word, and I'll jump right into that ocean there."

Usually I'd expect Misa to graciously sidestep such an overzealous apology, but instead, she looked thoughtfully at Elinor. "Your gift actually helped me figure out a few things that I'd been struggling with—and I think you'd be a good person to talk to about it, if you have the time later."

Elinor's face shifted from worry to sheer delight. "I would like that very much."

"Me too," said Misa warmly. She turned toward Julie and offered a timid smile. "We almost got through all the pre-wedding events without incident, didn't we? I promise tomorrow's dinner will go more smoothly. And luckily we'll all get a much-needed break tonight."

We had checked so many boxes on the itinerary already that I didn't even know what dinner Misa was referring to. Julie, on the other hand, seemed to be mentally mapping out the rest of the wedding like a marathon game of Risk.

After a moment, she nodded slowly and turned to address Elinor, her eyes flitting away from her daughter. "It was a wonderful breakfast regardless of the ending," she said sleekly. "It's very special to get to share these traditions with each other. You'll have to tell me more about Inverness . . ."

Kei motioned for me to pick up the back end of the kayak, and together we carried it back to the conch shell booth. They hoisted one end of the boat in the air and let the water drain out of a tiny hole in the plastic.

"Look, I appreciate a good boat hijack as much as the next descendant of the sea, but I need you to tone it down a bit," said Kei, shaking the kayak for the last few drops of salt water. The woman in the floral jumpsuit was busy selling her wares to a Chinese family with a very small daughter jabbing her finger excitedly at a very large shell.

"It was less of a hijack and more of a runaway-bride-type situation," I said, watching the little girl hoist the shell toward her mom, arms shaking.

"Whatever it was," said Kei, "you really didn't do Misa any favors."

I whipped my head around, surprised at their change in tone. "She didn't want anyone to see her having a panic attack, so I got her the heck out of there. What else was I supposed to do?"

"Did you see the Nag?" said Kei, carefully lowering the boat to the ground. "She's so embarrassed that Misa bailed out, she'll barely even look at her. That's not what we need two days before the wedding."

"It'll all blow over by then," I said. The little girl waddled toward the shoreline, forgetting all about the shiny conch her parents just bought her.

"You say that like our family isn't still harboring deep resentment over the seating plan of our last family reunion," said Kei. They sat on one side of the overturned kayak and waited for me to join them. "The Koyanagis are intricate. We have a lot of layers and a lot of invisible rules. And you're kind of breaking all of them."

I sat down beside them. "I didn't mean to make things harder for everyone."

"It's not your fault. There's just a lot going on," said Kei. "Like, Julie is Sansei. Third generation. And for her, this wedding isn't just about Misa. It's about all the things our family has been through to get to where we are today. It also could be one of the last times our whole extended family will be together with Obachan. There's a lot of expectations and a lot of pride. Pride means she doesn't just get over things."

My face burned as I thought about the countless moments when I had been critical of Misa for the expectations she always seemed to be fulfilling. I had thought about it as a performance, not a necessity to keep her family relationships intact. But I should have learned a long time ago that there were stories behind this careful choreography—stories that I wasn't always privy to.

It had all started with the notebook. Smooth blue leather, monogrammed with her initials. We weren't allowed any electronics in the ward, so it's how Misa was able to keep track of her life, her progress. When the hospital brought a peer worker in to speak to us all, I had never seen her scribble so fast.

"What are you doing?" I whispered.

"I'm taking notes," Misa replied, barely looking up from the page.

The peer worker lived with schizophrenia, rented her aunt's basement, and worked part-time at a local mental health center, running a comedy program. She talked about how mad folks make great comics because we're either completely invisible or dramatically center stage, and that's where all the best observations come from anyway. Misa looked at her like she held the keys to the universe.

Afterward, Obachan came to visit and we reconvened in the common room, sipping from bottles of Calpico that she had lugged all the way to the hospital. She hated everything in the vending machines downstairs.

"I don't know if it's reassuring or depressing to find out that comedy is even more unstable than music," said Matt. "But at any rate, it was definitely an upgrade from chair yoga."

"I feel like I learned a lot more from her than my doctors," said Misa, poring over her notebook. "She had so much good advice. And not out of a textbook either."

"Someone's going to get an A in group therapy today," I half joked, but Obachan picked up on it immediately.

"Misa comes from a long line of learners," she said, not unkindly. She put down her Calpico so I knew it was serious business. "My eldest brother went to university in Vancouver, you know. But after we were sent to the camps, he couldn't finish his program."

"That's terrible," I said, immediately feeling guilty for my wisecrack.

She nodded. "Many decades later, he received an honorary degree, but he always repeated what our mother used to say—that no matter what, they could never take away our education."

Misa put a hand on Obachan's arm, and she turned to smile at her granddaughter. "She was right, you know. There is always something to learn, no matter where you find yourself." She glanced toward Misa's notebook and back again. "I see her in you sometimes. It reminds me that we have so much to hold on to, even after all these years."

It was as if Misa and Obachan were the only people in the room. Misa's eyes welled up with tears, and Obachan reached up the sleeve of her jacket to hand her some covert Kleenex. They didn't hug, but then again, maybe they didn't need to.

Even though Misa didn't volunteer at the cultural center like Julie wanted, even though she had long ago lost the language her obachan grew up with, I knew their shared history had shaped the path that Misa had carved for herself. And sometimes, it was all too easy to forget how that history intersected with our time at the hospital—coming from a

family that had experienced generations of pain, for Misa,
it could feel impossible to acknowledge yet another struggle
they would have to face together.

UNDER THE BEATING sun, I rose from the kayak and dusted myself off. "I think I owe Julie and Misa an apology," I said. "And a big one, at that."

"Okay, I'm going to ask you something and I don't want you to take it the wrong way," said Kei gently. "Do you think that's actually what they would want? Or is that just what would make you feel better?"

"Ah shit," I said. "I'm really bad at this."

"Want my advice?" Kei asked, then didn't wait for my reply at all because, clearly, I needed it. "Be part of the solution. Help smooth things over." Their face broke into a grin. "And hey—I know this isn't your strong suit, but less is more when it comes to my aunt."

We ran into Tilley on our way back to the shoreline. Holding her flip-flops in one hand, she was hightailing it toward the parking lot. "I've served bad Tinder dates less awkward than this family," she huffed. "I'll be waiting by the car."

When we made it back to the beach, Elinor had stepped aside to call Anila and let her know that everything was fine, and the Nag was radiating displeasure as Misa tried to explain why we had left in the first place. Even when Misa described what her panic attack felt like—without naming it, of course—Julie nodded, then deftly swung the conversation back to Misa's obligations as hostess, as if she could put her difficulties in a box for a more convenient occasion. Misa had once told me how Julie had vacuumed, wordlessly, through a one-sided conversation about her going away to school, but I had thought it was an odd anecdote, not an encapsulation of a whole dynamic. This, the way Misa was being asked to hold back her heart, felt painfully recognizable. I thought about my dad and the time I read out all the side effects of the medication I was on, hoping he'd understand why I couldn't work a job that started at six thirty A.M. anymore. At the end of it—me stumbling over fourteen-letter words, him yawning widely—he told me maybe I shouldn't be on medication if I wanted to survive in this world. I locked myself in my room and sobbed into a pillow, because all I had been trying to do, every damn day, was survive.

I stepped forward, unable to watch Misa bear the burden of my mistake. "It was my fault we took off on you," I said. "It was my idea, and it was definitely not a good one."

Misa exhaled slightly as Julie turned her stare toward me. I tried out my ward telepathy on her, projecting my sincerest apologies. To my surprise, she softened her gaze and nodded.

"It must be hard to keep up with so many events," Julie said, her voice suddenly thawing, like, fifteen degrees.

I glanced at Misa, suspicious of the reprieve. She looked unfazed by Julie's change in tone, and in that moment, I realized the origins of Misa's ability to shape-shift in front of an audience. "I mean, I'm not the one planning them," I said. "I think I have it pretty easy in comparison."

"I think many of the best things in life are the result of hard work," Julie replied, and again it was like I was intercepting a secret transmission between Nagasakas. "A wedding, a marriage, a strong family—they're no exception."

Misa nodded mechanically, like she had heard this refrain many times before. To me, it seemed like Julie wanted her daughter to be happy, but the more she tried to control how that happiness unfolded, the farther Misa got from it. As she and the Nag locked eyes, they didn't even notice that Elinor had finished her call and reentered our circle.

"Love can be deceptively easy, though," quipped Elinor, startling the Nagasaka women enough to break the deadlock. "One day you meet someone, and suddenly, you can't imagine your life without them."

Funnily enough, I didn't think of Matt when she said this. In some ways, I had always imagined losing him—to the dark fog of depression, to the walls he had learned to construct in an instant, and, most recently, to Misa. But for the first time, I thought about losing Misa's friendship and the giant gaping hole it would leave in my life. Sure, Matt understood me more than anyone else on the planet, but in many ways, Misa was the one who actually made me a better person. My stomach churned, a mixture of mimosa and contrition.

Julie turned gently toward her daughter, trying to lighten the mood. "I'm glad you've found that, Misa. I just want the rest of the week to come together easily as well." She glanced at her watch and motioned to Elinor. "We should go settle things with the restaurant."

"Yes, you lot should head back first," said Elinor, still looking at Misa with concern. "I think everyone could use some rest."

Since we had missed the scheduled shuttles, Misa hustled Kei, Tilley, and me into the Nagasakas' vacation car. Sensing the family drama, Tilley kept quiet for once, swiping through Instagram filters that would best highlight her ample cleavage. As soon as Julie and Elinor pulled out of the parking lot, Misa put Island FM on blast.

"I'm amazed you survived that one," said Kei from the passenger seat.

"She's biding her time until all the witnesses are gone," replied

Misa. She turned the radio down a notch and turned around in her seat. "Thanks again, Dee. It was nice to get away from things for a while."

"I'm sorry I made things worse with your mom," I said sheepishly.

"Things are always tough with us. We'd do anything in the world for each other except have a real conversation about how we're feeling." She turned back and clenched her hands around the steering wheel. "It's just what it is."

"Whoa," said Kei. "You're going all shikata ga nai on us."

"Who said letting go is a bad thing?" Misa said.

"It's not, unless you're going to carry around the whole weight of it anyway," Kei replied, studying her from the passenger seat. "Don't you think our family's got enough of that already?"

Misa just kept driving down the dusty street like there was nothing left to say. As we pulled up to a crosswalk downtown, we saw another roguish brown puppy walking its human across the street.

"What's the deal with all the dogs here?" asked Tilley, seizing an opportunity to change the subject. "There are tons of them just running around the streets."

"Potcakes," said Misa, stopping to let tourists cross the main road. "Really friendly, usually a mixture of German shepherd and Lab. They came here on European ships ages ago, but now there's so many of them that the island's set up an organization to find them new homes."

"I keep trying to get Misa to take one back with her," Kei added.

"I don't think I could handle the shedding," Misa replied. She looked at me in the rearview mirror. "Dee, if you're missing your dogs at home, you can actually visit and volunteer to walk a puppy."

I wondered how my dogs were doing while I was away, if their owners had picked up the slack or if my pups were lying placid beside swivelling home office chairs and suede couches.

"Maybe tomorrow," I said. "I feel like barre plus kayaking was a lot more exercise than I bargained for already."

She smiled again, and my guilty conscience kicked me in the gut. "Do you have anything planned for your night off tonight? I was actually thinking of you when I budgeted in some recovery time for everyone."

"It's half-price rum punch night at the hotel next door," sang Tilley, returning to her regularly scheduled programming. "And I need someone to come with me so it looks like I'm splitting a pitcher."

"Keep your night open," said Misa, ignoring her. "I might have something else for you to do."

After what we had been through that morning, I figured she wanted to make our renewed friendship official, and honestly, that wouldn't be the worst way I could spend a Thursday night. Something had clicked back into place for us in that kayak—suddenly, it wasn't so hard to remember how important Misa had been to me in the hospital, even if we'd dealt with the aftermath in different ways. What had become more difficult was the knowledge that I had been rooting against someone who had always just wanted the best for me.

⁂

AFTER WE GOT back to the resort and took a power nap, Tilley and I decided to try to get some semblance of a tan before the week was up. Matt was still out golfing with Vik, Misa's dad, and Dr. Koyanagi, so I was off the hook for the big meds intervention for the time being. As I fastened my bikini top, Tilley strutted out of the bathroom in a V-neck one-piece that plunged almost to her belly button.

"Don't you ever worry about tan lines?" I asked, slathering sunscreen onto my shoulders.

"No," she said, tossing her hair. "Why spend time worrying about tan lines when you could be busy giving a shit about climate change?"

"I'm sure you'll be first in line when they start releasing electric Fiats."

We walked out to Grace Bay. The wooden boardwalk was flanked by a towel bar on one side and an outdoor café on the other. Turquoise umbrellas spotted the sand in between, speared into the ground by smiling attendants in pristine white-and-blue uniforms. As we stepped onto the beach, one of them approached us and asked if we needed a place to sit. His metal name tag, reading JEF-FREY, gleamed in the sun as he wiped the edge of his black do-rag.

"Oh, don't worry about us," I said quickly, gesturing toward two empty chairs by a vacant catamaran. "We can just throw some towels over the chairs."

"I will bring you chair covers and umbrellas," Jeffrey replied, just as quickly. "It's a hot day. You should be comfortable."

He grabbed two white bundles and led us over to the loungers, carefully laying fabric against sun-warmed plastic. I realized that trying to avoid his service wasn't actually helpful because he could get in trouble for not providing it. Then I wondered if this whole vacation was an encapsulation of this very problem.

"Thanks, Jeffrey!" said Tilley, as he stabbed blooming umbrellas behind us. She always seemed so comfortable in these situations, maybe because she was used to being on the service side of such exchanges.

"Yes, thank you," I said, plopping into a lounger and leaning back awkwardly. Jeffrey grinned at us and turned back toward the towel bar, where his co-worker was tossing a Frisbee with a small, freckled child. I gazed at the turquoise waters ahead of me and took in the rows of tanning bodies that lined the shore, as if this were the natural shape of the coast.

I don't know how long I was out, but I woke up as soon as Misa poked her head underneath my umbrella. She was wearing a white lace cover-up and clutched a thick graphic novel at her side. I yawned and sat up, catching a brief glimpse of Ana pushing Kei into the ocean, her feet planted widely in the sand.

"I thought I might find you here," Misa said, pretending not to see as I wiped a bit of drool from the side of my mouth. "You better flip or you'll get a burn."

"No one will even believe I went on vacation if I don't come back with a burn," I said. "And people are already skeptical that I have friends who would want me at their wedding."

"Can confirm," mumbled Tilley into her towel.

"Well," said Misa, "we're not the only ones who wanted you to come." She looked around furtively, then perched herself on the edge of my chair and put down her book. "I think Matt must talk about you a lot because Vik was asking us for ages if you'd sent an RSVP."

"Really?" Tilley suddenly sat bolt upright in her lounger.

"Really," Misa said, looking at me intently. "If you're interested, I can set up dinner for the two of you tonight."

My mouth still felt dry from my sun nap and I couldn't figure out why Vik would be into me. He was a fully functional human who ran for fun. I was a psych ward dropout with an occasional drinking problem (if you count the minor drug interaction between booze and quetiapine as an issue, which unfortunately for my doctor, I never did). I had never been good at math, but even I knew that didn't add up.

"Are you talking about a date?" I asked suspiciously. The word felt weird as it fell out of my mouth. It had been ages since I'd even attempted to share an appetizer with a person who wasn't Tilley.

"That's up to you," Misa replied. "But I really do think you'd have a lot to talk about. And of course, you're welcome to borrow from my closet if you want a fresh outfit."

I rolled my eyes. "Uh, I'm not going to fit into your clothes, Misa. Have you met my boobs?"

"I have something that might work," she said. "Stop by my room before you meet Vik and you can try it on."

"So I guess I'm going, then," I said with an uneasy laugh.

Misa smiled and picked up her novel. "Don't you think you deserve a chance to be happy, Dee? Because I think you do."

My skin grew hot, partially from the sun and partially because I wasn't sure anyone else thought that I did.

"Dinner will be at seven," she said firmly. "I'll see you at six."

We watched her stroll back up to the boardwalk before Tilley broke her longest silence in recent memory. "I can't believe I didn't call dibs on him." She sighed. "But you know what? I think you need this one more than I do. Consider this your Christmas gift."

"Thank you for your generosity?"

"You're welcome," said Tilley, bowing deeply from her chair. "Just don't blow it."

The evening sun was fading fast as we trudged back up to our hotel room. I collapsed onto the bed, but Tilley immediately swung open my suitcase and started throwing outfits on top of me.

"Why is your wardrobe so desolate?" she asked, holding up a crumpled beige bra. "This suitcase is like a bankruptcy-era Sears."

"I'm sorry, I didn't realize there were going to be 'dates' on this vacation," I retorted.

"But wasn't this trip all about ruining a wedding? Were you really planning on seducing Matt with granny panties?"

"You know my period is coming."

"All I'm saying is that I'm a big fan of you actually having a good time with Vik instead of making yourself miserable over Matt, who I once saw order vanilla ice cream at a Baskin-Robbins. Like, there's thirty-one flavors! Get a life!"

"But what if Vik finds out I'm a nightmare?"

"Then you gossip with Misa about it afterward and you come home with an actual friendship instead of pining sadly, wildly, destructively, for the Scottish Hamburglar."

"Maybe you're right," I said. "Maybe this date is a good thing. Then I won't hurt anyone or burn down a wedding and I still get to be happy."

"You can choose to not do those things whether or not you have a date," said Tilley, slamming my empty suitcase shut. She stood up and brushed sand off her bronzed thighs. "Now channel your inner Anne Hathaway, because we are glamming you up like it's the goddamn *Princess Diaries* out here."

❧

I KNOCKED ON Misa's door like I had so many times before, except this time, we weren't sharing a bathroom.

"Come in," she yelled. Her room was predictably organized—even in the hospital, Misa was the kind of psychopath who actually used the bureau drawers. Besides, her suite wasn't anything like mine. It was basically a full condo with a guest bedroom and a well-stocked kitchen. Kei had mentioned that quite a few of the rich snowbirds were well known by airport security for trying to sneak coolers of steaks and French cheese onto the island to avoid the import costs of food. I guess even when it was all-inclusive, one could only eat hotel meals for so long.

I sat down at the edge of Misa's bed and then quickly stood up again, remembering that she hated outside clothes touching her covers. She stood me in front of the full-length mirror and appraised my outfit.

"Tilley did your makeup really nicely," Misa said. "But you can't wear that dress again."

"Well, it's either this one or the one I'm wearing for your actual wedding. Not a whole lot of room for surprise dates when you don't pay for a checked bag."

The door opened again, and Kei stepped into the room, still wearing a tank top and board shorts from the beach. "I heard you're going on a date," they said with a smirk. "Didn't want to miss all the action."

"I don't know if there's going to be any action," I said, panicking. "I haven't been on a first date in months. What do I talk about? How do I know if he wants to kiss me? Kei, what do I do with my hands?"

"Why is it," said Kei, "that straight people get like 99 percent of romance plotlines, love songs, and self-help books, but you still ask your queer friends to provide all your relationship advice?"

"Because I saw you and Ana at the beach and you looked happy?"

Kei started to say something, then stopped and studied me carefully. "Hey, didn't you wear that dress yesterday?"

"I told you people would notice," said Misa, turning back to the closet.

"This is clearly a distraction maneuver!" I yelled, and Kei grinned at me.

Misa flicked through hangers. "Do you think you would wear

something like this?" She pulled out a flowing black dress stamped with tiny pink flowers and twirled it in front of me. "It's got a high-low hemline so height doesn't matter so much, and the off-shoulder top is stretchy to accommodate, well, you know."

"My giant boobs."

"Your words, not mine," she said. She threw the dress at me. "Go try it on."

I closed the door of the bathroom and shimmied out of my wrap dress. The cold tile was comforting against my feet. I stepped into Misa's gown, then hiked it over my hips and stomach, feeling the elastic expand as it settled across my chest. I thrust one hip out to the side and admired my shape in the mirror. For a moment, I wished I owned a professional-grade wind machine.

I know for a fact that I'm looked at differently when I do myself up, especially when I'm going into loaded spaces like psychiatrists' offices. Sometimes the greatest joy I'll get in a week is knowing that I don't look like I belong there. If I say I'm well and I'm wearing lipstick, I can almost guarantee my doctor will take my word for it (this, of course, also depends on the neutrality of the color). He doesn't need to know how I got there—spending hours redrawing my lips with liner, lining up shades to see which one looked the most like stability. It's the end product that matters. I look put together, like I could work a nine-to-five or choose vegetables from a supermarket. And when it comes to dates, well—given the bird's nest of problems inside my skull, I might as well make the best first impression possible.

When I stepped out of the bathroom, Kei let out a holler and Misa clasped her hands together in excitement. "It's perfect," she said. "You look incredible."

I actually thought I looked healthy, which was even better than incredible.

The hotel room door swung open and Matt walked in, scratching at the scruff along his jawline. He stopped and stared at me. "Whoa. Who are you and what have you done with Dee Foster?"

I stared right back, parted my lips softly. My heart felt like it was pumping SunnyD instead of blood. I was trying to move on from him, trying to uncomplicate things with Misa, but part of me had always, always wanted him to stare at me like this. Matt coughed and looked back at his fiancée.

"She's going on a date," announced Misa. "With Vik."

"You look . . ." He trailed off, looking for the right adjective. "Different. Good different, I guess."

"Pure poetry," snorted Kei. "You should put that one in a song!"

"I'd better get going," I said, grinding the toe of my sandal into the floor. I was going to enjoy this vacation, starting now, damn it. "Thanks for everything, Misa."

She smiled. "Anytime. Have fun."

I strode past Matt, out the door, and into the hallway. The last thing I saw was him closing the door, still looking at me like he'd never met me before.

14

"WHAT'S MY NAME?"
—RIHANNA FT. DRAKE (4:23)

WHEN I REACHED the end of the boardwalk, Vik was waiting for me, wearing what I suppose was the beach equivalent of business casual—a button-down linen shirt and sage green chinos. The warm wind was ruffling his dark hair as he clutched the handles of a woven picnic basket in his right hand and a glowing lantern in his left.

"It's not a dog," he said, as I approached him.

"Excuse me?"

"You know, in the basket." Vik lifted it slightly and grimaced under the weight. "I always think of Dorothy and Toto when I see wicker baskets, and I didn't want to mislead you. I know you like dogs. Unless you walk them while harboring deep disdain for their existence."

Maybe I wasn't sure about dating, but he was definitely cute. "Okay, what else do you know about me?"

"This one's just a hunch, but despite Misa's efforts to organize us a posh dinner, I got the feeling you might prefer something a bit low-key—hence, the basket."

"You guessed right," I said. "I don't see why you'd ever need more than one fork per person."

"There's a very simple and British explanation for that," he replied. "One for eating, one for stabbing."

"How many forks are in that basket?"

"That," he said, "will remain a surprise." He gestured toward the rolling waves of Grace Bay. "Shall we go find ourselves a spot to eat?"

We walked until the deck chairs clustered along the shoreline became sparse—past the water trampoline at the hotel next door, past the dock where tour boats picked up eager passengers. There wasn't much undeveloped land left along the coast of Grace Bay, but you could certainly tell when you found it. On the beach, abandoned villas were inhabited by dense shrubs and the evidence of roaming potcakes. We marched past seaweed and debris from fallen trees collecting in the spaces where tide and beach came together.

When we finally found the right spot, Vik pulled two rolled-up beach towels from his giant basket and laid them out flat, placing the basket on one corner and our kicked-off shoes on the others. Placing the lantern in the center of the setup, he flipped back the top of the basket and unstacked a mountain of take-out boxes. The first held steamed rice, and the second stored okra and green beans, stir-fried with fragrant spices. The third held neat white squares of what looked like Cream of Wheat, served with a bright green chutney. Baked roti nestled perfectly inside the rounded corners of the last container.

"There aren't as many vegetarian options at the resort, so my mom packed a few essentials for the kitchen in our suite," he said sheepishly. "We used to cook together a lot before I started my bank job and I thought you might like to try some favorites."

"This is perfect," I said, and then pointed at the squares. "What's this called?"

"That's dhokla—made from steamed rice and lentils. I hear you're also rather partial to Fanta," he said, pulling out two obnoxiously orange cans. We cracked them open and clinked them together cheerfully. "Although I'm not sure if you're aware of its rather grim history."

"What do you mean?"

"Well, Fanta was invented by Nazis," Vik said, setting our makeshift picnic blanket with plates and cutlery. He gestured toward the steaming containers. "Help yourself."

"You expect me to be able to eat after you ruined my favorite drink of all time? This stuff got us through the hospital. We ran the vending machine clean out."

"Then you have should have some of this. Khakra is a comfort food," he said, plucking a slim circle from its container and taking a bite. It flaked gently in his hand. "You look like you could use some right now."

While I swirled my dhokla in chutney and heaped veggies and rice onto my plate, Vik told me about some of the races he ran last year in preparation for the London Marathon in April—Brighton, Edinburgh, Yorkshire. I had never been to the UK but it sounded like somewhere I could enjoy once I was better, sitting on a rocky ocean shore staring out at the water without really looking for anything. He told me that even if he didn't want to run, he forced himself to do it for twenty minutes, and then reconsidered his decision after that. Not once, he said, had he ever stopped if he made it that far. I wished I could apply the same theory to living, but I knew my limitations all too well. I wondered if he could sense it too—the insurmountable gap between his potential and mine. The easy comfort I had sunk into whittled itself away in an instant. Vik noticed the uncomfortable silence and gently placed a hand on my shoulder.

"Are you okay?" he asked, the flickering light illuminating the edge of his jaw.

"Yeah," I said, gazing out toward the crashing waves. "It's just, you know—hard to keep up sometimes. I don't go on a lot of dates."

Vik put his hand on the picnic blanket and leaned his weight back into his wrists, his long legs outstretched. His aftershave smelled like a waterfall.

"That surprises me," he said. "I find you to be excellent company."

"Yeah, but this is different," I said, fiddling with the edge of the blue towel. "Usually, when I go on a date, I spend half the time worrying about when I should tell the guy about my bipolar. Do I tell him right away so he knows what he's getting into? Do I let him get to know me first? Am I lying during that awkward space in between?"

"Are you aware," said Vik, "that you're making it sound like you're an axe murderer or something?"

"I don't think you understand the kind of things people say when I tell them." I picked up the last of the khakra and started breaking it into small slivers. "Someone once told me that the number of doctors' appointments on my calendar was a red flag. Can you believe that?"

Vik exhaled. "I'm sorry, Dee. That's really awful."

I didn't look up, just barrelled on and heard my voice getting higher pitched with every word. "Or how about the time I was about to spend the night and the guy looks at me and goes, 'So will you be the same person when you wake up in the morning?' The point is, you can't really know how someone will react until you tell them. So no, I don't go on a lot of dates, and I'm sorry I'm kind of yelling but my head feels really hot and—do you mind if we walk for a bit?"

"Of course not," said Vik, leaping to his feet. He held out a hand to pull me up. "We can come back."

We hugged the shore with our footsteps until I couldn't resist the pull of the current. I hiked Misa's beautiful black dress up to my thighs and waded into the Caribbean waters, squishing my toes into the sand and feeling the tension in my body flit away. I turned around to face Vik, who was standing on the shore, watching me curiously.

"Does water help you?" he asked. "When your head gets too hot, that is?"

"Sometimes," I called above the waves. The water swallowed up my doubts, buoyed me toward honesty. "When I'm worked up, I like sensory activities—swimming, being wrapped in blankets. Sometimes Tilley rubs the pressure points in my hands and wrists. I know that sounds weird, but it gets me out of my head and lets me focus on my body instead."

"That's not weird at all—it sounds like she really cares about you. Not everyone has the kind of support." Vik paused. He rolled up the bottoms of his pants and I tried not to stare at his butt. "I don't date much either, if it makes you feel any better," he said as he waded into the water.

"Is that because everyone recognizes you from reality TV?" I asked.

Vik broke into a grin. "That's really how I should be marketing it, I suppose. I did go on a date a few months ago with a woman who found me online. Didn't turn out so well, I have to say."

"What happened?" I walked toward him, the waves licking at my calves.

"Oh, the usual," he said. "We got to the end of the date and she asked to move in, and when I politely declined, she went, 'Oh, so you can marry a stranger but you can't move in with one?'"

I laughed, and we trudged out of the water, toward the bright lights of a lit-up patio in the distance. Our fingers grazed briefly, then refracted. Silently, I exhaled. "You have to tell me more about that whole thing. What did your mom say when you told her you were marrying someone you'd never met before?"

Well," he replied, "my family is Gujarati, and my grandparents had an arranged marriage. The issue was less about marrying someone I hadn't met than it was about marrying someone whose family she didn't meet beforehand. That is the most important thing for my mom, especially—that our families are compatible and share the same values. It made it very hard for her to trust the relationship."

"What made you sign up for the show in the first place?" I asked. I thought about my family, who weren't even compatible with each other.

"You might laugh at me now, but I really did believe in the science of finding the right partner," he explained, kicking at the sand. "I'm a numbers person, and the behavioral analysis and very thorough questioning I underwent seemed reasonable at the time. Of course, in hindsight, I suppose I could have gone by the science of the one hundred percent divorce rate from Season One."

"Yikes."

"At least it was a beautiful ceremony," he mused, slowing his pace. "I gave my mother as much control as possible to make up for my overall break with tradition. And even with the film crews and live Twitter feed, it really felt like the first day of a new life. I remember looking at Amira when the antarpat between us was lowered and thinking, 'Thank goodness I did this.'" He stopped abruptly and glanced toward the fading glow of our abandoned picnic site. "Should we head back?"

By the time we returned, one of the blankets had blown down the beach and was caught on a low-lying shrub. Vik removed it carefully and placed it in the bottom of his basket before packing up everything else.

"I don't think I told you this," he said, condensing the boxes and making extra room for the dimming lantern. "But I run for Mind. They're a big mental health charity in the UK."

"Good for you," I said neutrally.

"Perhaps." He looked at me carefully. "But I think I was once like those people you went on dates with."

"I find that hard to believe," I said, and meant it. I still didn't really know if we were on a date, but I definitely knew that we had come to an understanding. We were both trying to start over.

"You say that now, but when Matt was in the hospital, I wasn't much help. I didn't know how to talk to him about it—sometimes, I'm still not sure I do." His jaw muscles clenched as he spoke. "I mean, I'm running all these races, but I can't even get my best friend to open up to me."

"It's not just you," I said. "I'm not convinced he's telling me everything either."

"But I don't have the same understanding that you and Matt seem to have," Vik said. "In my community, no one talks about mental illness because no one wants to reflect poorly on their families. It's hard not to worry about what other people will think. It's something that held me back when Matt was in the hospital. I'm just so glad he had you."

"But you don't think like that anymore," I replied.

"Of course not. But it's hard to forgive myself for the all the times I let him down." Vik picked up the heavy basket once more. "How do you make up for that?"

I thought about all the people I'd lost over the course of my illness, the awkward silences that cropped up when I ran into old friends in my neighborhood. In my head, the world was divided into two groups of people—the ones who got it and those who didn't, maybe couldn't. I had spent years trying to bring friends and family over to my side, but after a while, I was exhausted. I had to protect myself. I left the bodies where they fell. But I'd be kidding myself if I said I didn't lie awake some nights dreaming of someone from my past reaching out with a simple message: *I miss you. I'm thinking about you. I'm sorry I didn't know what to say back then but I'm here now.*

"I think the only thing you can do is let them know you're there," I said slowly, picking up my shoes and moving back toward the resort. "And make it easy for them to ask for what they need. Especially for Matt, you're going to have more opportunities to create space for him. It's not like you only get one shot with something like bipolar. It's the Arnold Schwarzenegger of mental illness."

"You could write Hallmark cards for this," he said, switching the basket from his right hand to his left.

"Sympathy notes for wait lists. Edible arrangements for med changes," I said, my face splitting into a grin. "Let's commercialize psychiatric setbacks!"

"You're incredible," he said with a laugh. "I can see why Matt's so fond of you."

"He doesn't like me that much," I said, and felt my entire body go rigid.

Vik threw me a look. "What's that supposed to mean?"

"I don't know," I said. "It doesn't mean anything. That's all."

We walked in silence past paddleboards stacked on wooden racks, the population of white deck chairs growing once more. "When Matt first mentioned you," Vik said after a moment, "I thought you were going to be the one he wound up with."

My heart skipped a beat. "Why'd you think that?"

"Because you seemed to reach him in a way that none of us were able to anymore," he said thoughtfully. "I'd call him at the hospital and he'd sound down, so I'd make a list of things we had to look forward to, and they'd all bounce right off him. And then he'd tell me about your elaborate scheme to find out who was taking single bites out of some bloke's chocolate bar stash and his voice would change. He'd sound hopeful about the smallest, pettiest mystery."

"It was Dennis Rodman," I interjected. "Or at least a guy who looked like Dennis Rodman. We didn't rat him out because we didn't want him to get sent to intensive care. But he had to buy Jermaine a new chocolate bar from the vending machine. Matt was the lead detective on that one. He borrowed his roommate's housecoat to channel his inner Sherlock Holmes."

I glanced over at Vik, and he smiled. "I can see this date isn't going as Misa hoped it would."

I stopped in my tracks. "What do you mean?"

"Well," he said, looking at me apologetically, "I really like you, Dee. It's hard not to. But even though I may not understand mental health very well, it's clear that you're carrying some lingering feelings for Matt."

I shimmied my feet until I was standing in two cool holes in the sand. It felt like I could grow skinny roots out of my heels and plant myself there forever.

Vik gestured at me helplessly. "I didn't mean to upset you," he said. "It's just—I don't want to be party to any more divorces. They're really not as fun as they look on TV."

I didn't say anything, just curled my toes deeper into the ground.

"Dee? Are you planning to tell him before the wedding?" Vik took a few steps toward me, put down the basket, and grabbed my hand. I didn't want him to touch me. I just wanted to go home. "I don't want anyone to get hurt."

I felt hot and spiky again, but this time, I basked in the feeling. It repelled his handsome face, my hurt pride, the wind rippling through hanging palm fronds. "What would you tell Matt to do, if he had feelings for me?"

Vik looked uncomfortable and let go of my hand. "It's difficult to say, without knowing his exact words."

"You think I'm unreliable. You don't think I could marry anyone, do you?"

"Dee," he said, "I never said that. I would never say something like that."

"That's what everyone thinks of me, though, isn't it?" My voice was shrill above the waves. I saw Vik shake his head, say something else deflective, but all I could hear was a steady drumbeat in my head telling me that I would never recover, never escape, never be happy.

"Is that what you think of yourself?" he said finally, and I said nothing for a long, long time, tears streaming down my face, ruining Tilley's bang-up paint job.

"I just want to be good," I sobbed, and Vik wrapped his arms around my deflating body.

"You are good," he breathed out, pressing his face into my tangled hair.

I sobbed into his linen shirt until there was no noise left in me, and then we walked toward the lights of my last-resort resort. Even though I had ruined yet another date and cracked open the well of insecurities I'd been burying all week, I felt grateful for a sense of release as I leaned into Vik, feeling the stability of his arm beneath mine.

15

"EVERYWHERE" —MICHELLE BRANCH (3:36)

WHEN I GOT back to the hotel, Matt was half-asleep on a lounge chair along the concrete pathway to my room. All the pool lights were off, but you could see the glimmer of the outdoor chandelier reflected in the water. There were six Turk's Head bottles lined up beside him and he was rewatching *Game of Thrones* on his phone, clearly waiting for me. My heart dropped. Especially after unravelling in front of Vik, I knew I needed to talk to Matt before the wedding—about his meds, and my heart, and all the crazy in between—but I hadn't really imagined a late-night, half-in-the-bag conversation. I tried to sneak past him and escape into my room, but the robotic whir of the room key gave me away.

"Hey! Dee!" yelled Matt, rolling over.

I shushed him and quietly closed my door. "What are you doing here?"

"I had to tell you something," he said, eyes glassy. He pulled up a mass of text on his phone and waved it at me. "I had a breakthrough with my vows tonight, and it's all thanks to you."

"Oh," I said, watching a tiny lizard scuttle out from underneath the manicured bushes. "Good."

"Do you remember when we were in the ward? And Liz's mom died? And then she got a day pass to go to the funeral?"

"Of course," I said, trying not to fall into the pit of sadness that always opened up at the mention of her name.

Liz was one of my favorite ward regulars, a tiny, gray-haired lady with big glasses and a foul mouth. She ran like a short-circuiting microwave, alternating between comforting warmth and striking heat without warning. Something about her unpredictability made me feel right at home.

It was strange to think of someone as old as Liz having a mother still, but when she got the news, she had been surprisingly jovial. "To my mother," she said over lunch, and we all raised our juice boxes in unison. "She tried her damn best, didn't she?" Liz sucked the whole thing dry and slammed the empty shell onto the table.

Jermaine watched her from the next table over. "There's no seconds at lunchtime," he wheezed.

Misa rolled her eyes at him, then turned back to Liz. "I think I have a dress that would look lovely on you, if you haven't decided what to wear yet," she said softly. We all knew Liz's closet was empty.

Since so many of us didn't get to wear our own clothes anyway, it was easy to forget that some people in the ward didn't have families to bring them food from the outside, a change of clothes, or a book to pass the time. Even Matt didn't have any visitors, on account of him refusing to let his mom see him in this situation.

"What do you think about this one?" said Misa once we were in her room, pulling a black cotton dress from the bottom drawer and handing it to Liz.

Liz eyed it uneasily. "I'd need to wear a bra with that," she said. Without skipping a beat, Misa reached into the top drawer and yanked out a shiny black bra, sending Liz to our bathroom with that and the dress slung over her arm. I thought about the intimacy of it all and was repulsed by my own discomfort. Matt always said we were different from the others—that we'd get out and stay out. I always pushed back, partly because it wasn't kind, but partly because I could see myself years down the line, still pressed against the same revolving door.

After she changed, Liz pushed open the wide bathroom door and stood before us, arms hanging loosely by her sides. The dress was a little big on her, but after Misa tightened the belt and pulled the fabric down a bit, you could see the gentle curves of her body. She looked like she belonged in that dress—no, that wasn't quite right. She looked like she *felt* she could belong anywhere at all. And I knew how precious and fleeting that feeling could be.

Liz smiled broadly. "My mother's ghost is going to love this!" she sang, and this is the way that I choose to remember her now. Misa laughed so hard that Matt—double tapping on the doorframe—poked his head in from the hallway, caught up in her glow. His jaw dropped, and I realized that I had never seen her laugh like that before—head thrown back, guard down, heart open.

It turned out it was the first time Matt had seen it too.

"Earlier tonight, when I saw you in Misa's dress," he said, knocking over an empty beer bottle, "it just brought me back to the hospital, and the moment I fell in love with Misa."

My stomach clenched, and I gripped my room key so hard the edges bit into my skin.

"I've been wracking my brain for some grand sweeping gesture that sums up the way we feel about each other," he continued. "But that's not what Misa's about."

I nodded, hoping the right words could crawl out the back of my throat.

"It's the small, thoughtful actions that she always makes time for. The kind where you don't even realize how important they are until they're in the rearview mirror." He was looking past me, through me, toward the future he'd been waiting for this whole time. "That's what I love about her. And I think that is something that's gotten lost in this big expensive wedding."

I waited, but there was nothing else. Matt just looked at the placid pool like it could fill in the overwhelming silence between us.

I didn't know why it felt like this was the end of everything—I mean, Matt being in love with the person he was marrying was hardly a plot twist. It was the reality that everyone had been hammering into me. I had thought I was smarter than them, that I could see something no one else could. Maybe the only thing I couldn't see was that waiting for Matt had kept me spinning in place for an entire year.

"That's great," I finally managed. "You know why you love her."

He shook his head slowly, still watching the gentle ripples of the pool. "If I've finally got it all figured out, then why do I still feel so terrible?"

I collapsed beside him on the sagging lounger, wishing I could secure that answer for myself. Trying to drown out the bad thoughts, I tore at the skin along the edge of my thumbnail. Matt snapped out of his reverie and yanked my hand out of my mouth.

"You'll just make it worse."

"Sometimes, I don't think it can get any worse."

Matt held on to my hand, swallowed me up with his hazel eyes. "Do you ever think that you and I should just run away from all this?" he said, his voice breaking over the last few words.

A few months ago, this would have been a fantasy that kept

me warm at night, that gave me something to hold on to during the times when I was overcome by my own self-loathing. But there was something in that easy phrase that tore at my heart just a little too much.

"Is that an actual offer?" I asked, unable to keep a tinge of bitterness out of my voice.

"You know, sometimes I think it is," he said, letting go of my hand and missing my tone completely.

I wanted to tell him how I'd always felt about him, but the record player in my head screeched and wound slowly, started replaying a familiar sensation I just couldn't place. I tried to focus on the way he looked at me—the way he saw me like no one else ever had—but all I could conjure was the familiar sensation of his fingers slipping through mine, the voice in my head that pleaded, *Don't let me down, not again.*

The night before I got kicked out of the hospital, I couldn't sleep. I stared up at gridlocked ceiling tiles, dimly lit by the eerie glow of the hallway, then decided to take a walk to kill some time. I almost didn't hear him as I shuffled down the corridor in Tilley's old slippers.

"Dee? Can you come here for a sec?"

Matt stood in his doorway and beckoned me inside, gently closed the door behind me. We tiptoed past his roommate, fast asleep thanks to a nightly tranquilizer. I'd never seen him leave the room, not even for meals. Matt slumped onto his stiff white hospital bed, and I gingerly perched myself beside him, feet just skimming the ground. His face glowed in the moonlight, and I could see tear tracks brushed into stubble. I pressed my hand against his, locked fingers.

"What's going on?" I whispered.

He exhaled deeply. "I don't know, the usual, I guess."

"I hear ya."

We fell silent as slow, steady footsteps echoed outside the door. Jermaine was making his nightly rounds, walking laps around the nurses' station with his shoulder pressed against the outer wall. It was only a matter of time before they took him back to his room.

"Can I ask you something?" said Matt, once the coast was clear.

"Anything," I replied.

"What's the first thing you're gonna do when you get out of here?"

I thought for a moment. "Honestly? I want to do something really mundane, all by myself. Like, get a non-life-changing haircut where I endure small talk for half an hour but get a great scalp massage to make up for it. Something low pressure." I squeezed his hand. "How about you?"

He mumbled something into his chest.

"What?"

"I can't see it," he said, a bit louder. "I'm scared because I can't picture myself past this place, and everyone else can. I'm scared that everyone thinks this is my rock bottom, but they're wrong. I think it could get so much worse, Dee—I'm on medication now but I'm feeling heavier every day. I'm sinking and I don't know how to ask for anything more than this. I don't know how to ask."

He leaned into me, breathing hard. I wanted to absorb all his bad, wanted to give him the last few untouched parts of myself. Instead, I asked if he had told his doctor how he was feeling.

"It's not really something you can cover in a fifteen-minute morning check-in," he said flatly. "And I'm tired of being studied like I'm an extreme weather pattern. I don't want more drugs to keep numbing myself. I want to get better, but I still want to be me, you know?"

He nestled his head into my shoulder and a familiar warmth flooded through me. "Maybe they could bottle the way I feel when I'm with you," he said, eyes closed. "That sounds pretty okay to me."

"Ultimate same," I whispered into the top of his head, feeling safe in my body for the first time in years.

When they found us, we were lying side by side in his hospital bed. I was pushed into the railing, my body curled around Matt to fill any cracks I could find. I knew we had broken the rules, but I didn't regret it for a second. I held on to him as long as I could, unwilling to let go of the fleeting comfort we had found together. The nurses screamed at me, told me this was a hospital, not a dating pool. Matt froze, white-faced and silent. They ripped me from the sheets and dragged me back to my room, forced a chalky white pill under my tongue. I screamed back, told them maybe things would be different if they tried talking instead of tranquilizing. My voice was hoarse and exhausted from the effort of being heard. My pillow, wet with futile tears. "He just wanted to talk to someone," I said, over and over again until the words meant nothing to me. The last thing I remember before I fell into the darkness was the overnight doctor standing over my bed and hissing at me. "Don't tell me how to do my job."

SITTING BY THE pool, old spikes of resentment prickled beneath my skin. My knees were shaking, my body tense. How could anyone have witnessed that night and not known that I had loved him more than myself? Matt never told the nurses why I broke curfew. He didn't say anything after I was kicked out without day treatment, not even after he got better and I stayed stagnant, waiting for him. I had spent the past year thinking my life was secondary to Misa's, but maybe the truth was that it had always been secondary to Matt's.

He was still gazing at me like I had all the answers. He was so handsome and drunk and hopeless that my heart hurt, even now. But the longing that I had felt was slowly morphing into something sharper, more recognizable—straight-up rage.

"Why did you bring me here?" I said finally.

Matt frowned. "What do you mean?"

I fixated on a string of lights hanging just above his head. "When you asked me to come, you said you were counting on me. For what? To drive the getaway car from your own bad decisions?"

He stared at me like I was from another planet. "I was counting on you to be my best friend, Dee. The way you've always been."

"I think that's part of the problem, though," I said. "I'm always there for you to the point where it feels like I'm being consumed. Like at the end of this week, there will be nothing left of me for myself or for anyone else."

He ran his fingers through his beard. "Jeez, I didn't think that I was asking for that much—"

"You were asking for everything," I said, my voice boiling over.

"What does that even mean? You're talking in riddles."

"It means that anything good I ever had, I gave to you," I said, barely holding back tears. "And I've had nothing to hold on to myself for so long, and you never even realized."

"I'm not a mind reader, Dee!" he said, shaking his head in disbelief. "How was I supposed to know that you were feeling that way?"

"That's the other thing," I said. An unfamiliar flatness crept into my voice, removed any chance of turning back. "The one thing I'd always wanted, you were never going to give me. You were happy to pretend it never existed in the first place."

He redirected his gaze toward the path, and I stood in front of him, my whole body shaking. "Can you honestly tell me you never considered that I might want more?"

The words I'd been swallowing for months echoed out into the cool night air. I'd never imagined framing them with a question mark, as a demand for the compassion I deserved.

Matt exhaled hard, and I already knew the answer before he opened his mouth. I couldn't look at him anymore, couldn't spend another moment sacrificing myself for his comfort. "Dee," he said, grabbing my hand. "Please, just let me explain."

But I knew there was nothing he could say that could give me back the past year of my life. I had spent months thinking that Matt needed me because he loved me, but I had just been a crutch. Only now could I see that every ounce of support I had given him had sunk me deeper into the ground.

In an instant, the sparks that used to bind me to Matt converted into a hostile jolt of electricity. I jerked my arm hard, and he rolled out of his lounge chair and crashed onto the concrete path.

"Goddammit," he said, clutching the back of his head. "Was that really necessary?"

"That," I said, wiping my sweaty palms on Misa's beautiful dress, "was for getting me kicked out of the hospital. And this"—I kicked over the nearest bottle of Turk's Head so that beer pooled around his limp body—"this is for this entire fucked-up week."

I turned and stomped all the way back to my hotel room, slamming the door just loud enough to wake Tilley up so I'd have company when I cried. My dramatic flair proved unnecessary since she was already crouching behind the window curtain, waiting for my return.

"Did I just see you Humpty-Dumpty Matt off a lounge chair?" she screeched.

I flung myself onto our bed and burst into tears. Tilley clambered over top of me and covered as much of my body as her stringy limbs could handle. "Welcome to my new side hustle as a substitute weighted blanket," she mumbled into my shoulder blade. "I'm so fucking proud of you, Dee."

"Is there something wrong with me?" I asked between sobs. "I just rolled him like a giant cheese wheel and left."

"Not at all," said Tilley, pushing sopping strands of hair out of my face. "You're just tired of being an unpaid therapist."

Tilley crooked her body into the curve of my back and wrapped her arms around me until my breathing slowed and I fell asleep. But when the morning arrived, I couldn't shake the feeling that I had returned to the wholly unlovable state that I had found myself in before the hospital. I wanted to nudge my sister awake for a six A.M. pep talk, but I figured there was no point in asking her to repeat something that I wasn't ready to accept. I gently rolled away from a snoring Tilley, crept into the bathroom to change and wash yesterday's makeup off my face, and slipped out the front door.

16

"UNFOOLISH" —ASHANTI (3:14)

IT WAS EARLY enough that all the cabanas were empty, and as I tiptoed across the wooden boardwalk, I wondered if I could one day become a morning person—and not just because I accidentally fell asleep without my meds and had to wait until my next dose. I wasn't confident about attending the wedding tomorrow with the foamlike buffer of my antipsychotic routine disrupted. It felt like everything was oversaturated—the sun, the blue of the ocean, the turquoise towels folded neatly on white chairs. I headed toward the coral reef, relishing the imprint of each step in the freshly raked sand. I was so concentrated on the sensation that I barely heard Kei calling after me, hitting the end of a barefoot morning run.

"You're up early," they said, once they had caught up. "Are they busting out the fancy waffle bar today?"

"That would be very convenient," I replied.

"So," said Kei slyly. "How was the rest of your night?"

It felt like ages had passed since Vik and I had linked arms and returned to the resort, but only moments since I'd toppled Matt off his deck chair. My heart felt so heavy that it was tough to tell if I had done something meaningful or completely self-destructive.

"Have you ever waited for something you thought would change your life, but it ended up just being another goddamn obstacle instead?"

Kei smirked. "Do you ever ask questions just to hear your own answer?"

"I know, I'm the worst."

"Second worst, since Tilley exists," they said, stopping to roll their sweatpants up to the top of their calves. "Want to walk in the water?"

The waves crashed against our shins, and the hemline of my sundress dipped dangerously close to the fray. "One summer when we were in undergrad," Kei said eventually, "Misa and I finally went to visit Popoff."

"Where's that?"

"Interior British Columbia, in Slocan Valley," they said, and it still didn't ring a bell. Kei glanced at me briefly. "It's the internment camp where Obachan lived during the war."

I felt bad for not recognizing the name, but it also felt like that chapter of history had opened and shut so long ago. It was strange to imagine a woman I had eaten breakfast with just yesterday reliving those memories in the same way I wound through footage from my childhood, characterized by Kraft Dinner and hot dog lunches and *The Princess Bride* on repeat.

"She doesn't like to talk about it," Kei said. "And my dad never seemed that interested either. But for Misa and me, Popoff always felt like the answer key to our whole family dynamic—the ultimate secret to all the secrets. I thought if I experienced it, I could fill the gaps between me and my dad and Obachan."

I found my tongue again. "And did it?"

"Well, I had imagined a Hallmark movie ending to a long history of intergenerational trauma, so . . . no?"

A wave rose to splash me in the stomach. "Oh. Right."

"When I got there, I realized everything was gone," said Kei, barely audible above the water. "Popoff is just an abandoned field now. We walked along where the railroad tracks used to run, and we arrived at nothing, and all I could feel was this strange emptiness."

"Wow," I said, grateful that our conversation had veered away from my own paltry feelings. I had spent so much time obsessing over what I had lost that I never stopped to consider the emotional weight already shouldered by the people who kept picking me off the ground. "Do you regret going?"

"When we came home, I was kicking myself for not feeling more connected. Like that trip was my only chance to find the point of everything my family had been through, and I had failed, again," said Kei, then stopped walking to look at me. "But then I realized that was part of our shared experience—I finally understood that in some ways, when my family communicates with each other, we're still grieving the empty spaces in between. I guess sometimes when you don't find what you were looking for, you've got to search a little harder on the inside."

I thought about Matt holding my hand beside the hotel pool and the creeping wave of disappointment that had washed over me. I thought about sharing a kayak with Misa and feeling more like myself than I had in ages. My relationships with both of them had been deeply formed in the trenches of the hospital—in some ways, I was still learning how to navigate them in the real world. Trauma and recovery were so intertwined with the trajectory of our friendships that maybe I had mistaken boundaries for abandonment, dependence for love, growth for distance. These thought spirals had become familiar over time. But at some point, I had stopped recognizing how these patterns trapped me in place, especially when it came to the ones I loved.

"I get it," I said. "I mean, it's not the same, but ever since the hospital, I feel like I've been chasing some sort of grand epiphany that would make it all worth it. But I can't undo what happened to us, even if I tell the most amazing story imaginable."

"Some things just are hard," said Kei. "There's no point in pretending that it didn't happen, or that it didn't leave some scars. The only thing you can do is accept it and let it shape the kind of future you want to be a part of."

A school of grouper scuttled by their calves, and I retreated toward the sand. Kei laughed at me under their breath. "I mean, you're a bit of a flight risk, but I think you're already taking a few steps in the right direction. Don't you?"

"I don't know," I said. "I think the hospital made me afraid of other people's growth, like I'd be left behind or something. And I've been that way—you know, terribly selfish—with Misa especially."

"A year ago, there's no way you'd have been able to put that together," replied Kei. "That's already huge. I think when you go through a hard time with someone, your relationship takes on a rhythm to counteract the change. You get used to your roles. I mean, even since I've spent time apart from Ana, I've seen sides of her that I didn't necessarily support. And now I have to think about whether that could change if we got back together. I wouldn't want to stop her from growing either."

"I guess that's how you know you really love someone," I said, wondering if I could find the capacity to offer that kind of unselfish care.

Kei's eyes caught mine. "I guess so," they said.

We passed an overturned sand bucket in silence, and I decided that if I was going to start somewhere, it might as well be here.

"You should write Ana a letter," I said. "I heard that's the thing to do these days."

"Maybe," said Kei, "if I could add some wicked illustrations."

We headed back toward the resort, wading through the shallowest part of the water. I found my balance in the sand, taking careful steps behind Kei. When we passed a landmark catamaran, Kei turned around and waited for me to catch up.

"I think you should talk to Misa," they said. "You're changing as much as she is, even if you don't feel it. Leaning back into that friendship doesn't mean you can't both move forward."

"I don't want to be the only one who doesn't get better," I said, avoiding eye contact by picking a piece of seaweed off my ankle.

"Come on. It's your life. Who are you competing with?"

"I don't know." Without the spectre of Matt hovering in front of me, I could see my life for more than what it was—for everything it could be. I was finally free to move at my own pace. "No one, I guess," I said, then frowned. "Ah, shit. I wish I didn't drop two grand on a destination wedding to figure that out."

"Well," said Kei, "we better make up for it by eating our weight in waffles."

BACK AT BREEZE Bay, Elinor was herding bodies into a car bound for tourist central. The relentless itinerary continued, whether or not I had gotten a good night's sleep. She spotted Kei and me as we moved past the front desk, headed toward the wafting smells of the breakfast buffet.

"Well, good morning," she said brightly. "Where are you two off to in such a hurry?"

"Waffles," said Kei, beaming at Elinor while walking toward the breakfast bar at the other side of the room.

Elinor watched Kei heap waffle mix into a steaming iron. "Some of the guests are going shopping," she said, turning to me. "But I was hoping to walk a wee pup at Potcake Place. Would you like to join me?"

Ana materialized from behind a thick column, throwing a surprise fistful of chocolate chips into Kei's waffle pan. They laughed together and I could feel their warmth from across the patio. I was about to make a weak excuse and go join them, but then I spotted Matt beside them, plucking a fresh croissant from a bread basket. "Sure," I said quickly, and climbed into the back seat of the Land Rover. Washington was just about to slam the door shut when I heard a pair of flip-flops smacking against the pavement.

"Wait for me!" screeched Tilley. She threw herself onto my lap dramatically, and Elinor laughed from the passenger seat.

We pulled up outside a small café in the downtown area and piled out of the van. Suddenly leaning up against his car with all the suaveness of a *GQ* model, Washington waved over-casually at a waitress who seemed to be wiping the same table over and over again just to stay in his sight line.

"Is that your girlfriend?" teased Tilley as Elinor directed the rest of the passengers toward the shopping area.

"I'll let you know as soon as I do," he said with a wink, then headed toward the café patio.

We walked across the street to the dog shelter and there was already a line of tourists clinging to the meager shade of the red awning. Children shielded their eyes from the sun to peer inside the windows while parents wiped sweat from their brows. An entire litter of brown spotted puppies climbed over each other in a pink basket, and two bigger dogs slept peacefully in the corner of a gated area. Everyone in the line eyed each other suspiciously and tried to calculate the puppy-to-human ratio. There was a collective sigh of relief when a short, cheery woman stepped out the front door, a heaping pile of clipboards in hand.

"Your dog is Goose," she said, once it was our turn. "She's a bit younger so she can only stay out for three hours. We'll provide you with snacks and water, but try to stay out of the sun when you can. She loves the ocean, this one."

We followed her into the shop, Elinor scribbling down emergency phone numbers while Tilley and I gazed adoringly at our pup. Goose was short-haired and tan, with flopped-over ears and a chocolate-dipped tail tucked between her legs. Her nose was dark too, like she had been caught digging in the garden. I bent down and let her sniff my hand as the coordinator gently gathered her in a harness and handed Tilley a tote bag and the end of the leash.

"You might need to carry her out of here," she added. "She's a tad shy."

After spending fifteen minutes trying to coax her out from underneath a park bench, I ended up slinging Goose over my shoulder and lugging her all the way to the beach, where she promptly leapt out of my arms and beelined for the water.

"She's a bad bitch," whispered Tilley. "Can we take her home with us?" She took off down the beach after Goose.

Elinor and I laid down beach towels and watched Tilley hoist Goose up above her head like Simba on Pride Rock. She spun circles in the shallow water, then waded in deeper so Goose could doggy-paddle freely. She laughed gleefully into the breeze, oblivious to everyone else on the beach.

"Your sister," said Elinor, adjusting her massive floppy beach hat. "She reminds me a bit of myself when I was younger. Always the loudest voice in the room, isn't she?"

"Without fail," I replied, stretching my legs out in the sun. "It comes in handy, though—my doctors are terrified of her. She's the best advocate on the planet, unless she's hungry. Then she's just a nightmare."

"She takes good care of you," she said softly. "And I'm sure you'd do the same for her."

I snorted. "The only thing Tilley's ever needed help with is holding her hair back after one too many espresso martinis. But even then, the girl never leaves the house without an elastic around her wrist." A bit too late, I realized I was being less than delicate and backtracked quickly. "Anyway, Tilley is great. I'm lucky to have her."

Digging through the tote bag that the shelter had provided us, I pulled out two bottles of water and handed one to Elinor. "You know, I'm actually glad to get some time alone with you. I was wondering if I could ask your advice on something."

Elinor lit up immediately. "Of course, sweet girl. Anything you need."

"I think I might be at a turning point of sorts," I began, unscrewing the lid of my water and taking a long sip. "Like, I've spent most of the last year being a walking disaster. I've hurt people around me and I've hurt myself. But I feel like I'm finally ready for things to be different, you know?"

She nodded, lips pursed. "But something's holding you back?"

"I think I'm just inherently suspicious of my own big epiphanies," I admitted. "And for good reason too. The last time I thought I had finally figured things out, I ended up somewhere I really didn't want to be."

⸪

It was September of last year when Misa posted the proposal picture in our post-hospital group chat. I had been hanging out in my bedroom just minding my own business—finishing an online quiz to find out which Muppet matched my personality—when all of a sudden, my world caved in. I rolled myself into a blanket burrito to shield myself from the impact and zoomed in on the photo. Matt was dressed in a suit and down on one knee, like he'd followed a Nicholas Sparks manual. Misa's hands were clutching her face in happy disbelief. They had all the promise of a brilliant future when I could barely imagine tomorrow. My phone dinged, over and over again, as Kei responded with a series of increasingly excited emojis. Heart eyes. Applause. Confetti. My phone slipped out of my hands, clattered to the floor, and I barely noticed. It was like I was outside of my body, watching the conversation unfold.

A knock at the door pulled me back in, if only briefly. "Don't come in," I said automatically. Tilley barged in anyway, carrying a heaping pile of lingerie.

"I think my underwear drawer is cursed," she said, dumping corsets and bralettes and bodysuits with strategic holes onto the empty space on my bed where my duvet probably should have been. "Like, maybe all this stringy fabric is holding on to the bad energy of the dudes I wore it for."

I nodded silently, and Tilley's eyes narrowed, taking in the swell of blankets that surrounded me. "Okay, what's wrong?"

"Nothing."

She didn't believe me for a second. She scanned my room and spotted my discarded phone on the floor. In an instant, it was in her hands and she was scrolling through my worst nightmare.

"Ah, shit," she said, once she was finished. "I'm really sorry, Dee."

I laughed, a sudden sharpness catching at the back of my throat. "What difference does it make? The hospital didn't work out and neither did the meds—why would this be any different?"

"You need ice cream, stat," said Tilley. "Wait here a second."

As soon as she had left the room, I gathered the entire orchestra of medication I kept on my nightstand and dumped it into the toilet, emptying one bottle at a time. I was hit with an unexpected clarity—if this proposal wasn't a sign that my life wasn't working, I didn't know what was. I watched the pills swirl, then disappear. I felt nothing at all.

I put on a light jacket, threw my phone in the left pocket, and snuck past my sister as she scraped the bottom of a mint chocolate chip tub. I walked down the empty suburban streets without a real sense of purpose, wound up on the overpass bridge that crossed the main highway in Scarborough. Hordes of cars—punctuated with the occasional truck—surged below me, and I watched them vacantly.

Logistically speaking, it wasn't difficult to get closer to the blissful roar of traffic. The exit signs for the highway were supported by a thin sheet of metal grating only a few meters below me. I didn't want to jump, really. I wouldn't let myself get that far. But I did want to dive into the heart of the noise, let it overcome all the insistent buzzing inside my head. I placed my hands on the railing, preparing to hoist myself over the edge. Cars started slowing down, but I didn't care. No one could stop me from getting to where I was meant to be, not even the screech of tires on the road behind me. My sneaker scraped against concrete, and it was the most satisfying sound on the planet. One step toward the inevitable, I thought. That's when the music started.

The opening of "I Want It That Way" blasted across the lonely highway overpass, yanking me out of my fog. "Track one," yelled Tilley from the driver's seat of her fire-red Fiat, parked at the side of the bridge. "In case you forgot that I need you around. Two worlds apart, my ass."

I took a wobbly step back from the railing. "What are you doing?"

"Tracking your location, as always," she sang. "Plus I'm making this sweet new playlist to help you get through this. I want to call it Not Today, Bitch—what do you think?"

It was so much more than I deserved. The numbness I had been basking in suddenly disappeared. "I can't, Tilley," I sobbed. "I can't start over again on my own."

"Of course not," she said, leaving the keys in the ignition and jumping out of the car. "That's why I'm here."

Tilley ran over and wrapped her lanky arms around me until I could barely breathe. She squeezed me so tight that it drowned out all the bad thoughts in my brain, the stares from passing cars, even the approaching wail of police sirens. As I leaned into her and the cops came toward us, I

couldn't stop thinking about how lucky I was to have some-
one like her to hold on to.

ELINOR PLACED HER hand on mine, and I wondered how I could explain that my brain couldn't always be trusted, that I had learned to second-guess every instinct.

"It's hard to learn how to trust yourself again," she said, and I realized she might share my knack for mad telepathy. "Really, I've been there."

"I know," I said, and we settled into a comfortable silence. When Elinor spoke again, I could tell she was choosing her words with care.

"You can't expect yourself to always have the right answer or make the right call," she said thoughtfully. "But I'd say it's a lot easier to make better choices when you stop hating yourself."

"But what about the people I've hurt?"

"Not everyone will forgive you, and that's okay," she said, a twinge of pain passing across her face. "You have to love them for knowing their own boundaries and focus on what you can control. That's all you can do."

I sucked in my cheeks. "Sometimes it feels like no matter how much I change, I'll never make up for the mess I've made."

"Do you think that's true for me?" asked Elinor wryly.

"Of course not!" I said, my face reddening in the sun. "I hope I turn out like you."

"Trust me, you're part of a long lineage of women who have had to learn how to forgive themselves," she replied. "And if you ask me, the world is a better place for us. You're doing just fine, Dee."

She paused a moment, flicking a strand of hair away from her face. "Although I did just scare my future daughter-in-law into an escape boat yesterday."

"I think Misa would really appreciate this conversation," I said. "Pine cones or not."

Elinor's face split into a grin. "Then there's still hope for us yet."

Just then, Goose bounded back over to us, dragging Tilley behind her. "This dog thinks she's on *Baywatch* and I'm so here for it," she huffed. "Dee, you're up."

Tilley handed me the wet leash and I held on tight, let myself be pulled into the noise of the ocean. This time, I didn't go to the water searching for an escape. I followed Goose into the fray and let the waves crash into me, searching for the next step toward finding my new normal. I wanted to picture myself ten years down the road, giving some other mad girl fresh out of the ward the words she needed to hold on just a little bit longer. If I could get there, it didn't matter if I was married or divorced or surrounded by a pack of wild dogs. I'd know that the next time I was sinking, I could keep myself afloat. But the first step toward that kind of future was making sure I held it together in the present—which meant I had less than twenty-four hours to make things right with Matt and Misa.

17

"FAMILY AFFAIR" —MARY J. BLIGE (4:25)

TILLEY DECIDED TO honor my newfound resolution to be a Good Person™ with a poolside bottle of rosé, generously arranged by Marco despite some warranted confusion on his end.

"Tell me again—what exactly are we celebrating?" he asked as he uncorked the bottle before neatly pouring two pale glasses.

"The end of an era," crowed Tilley. "A terrible era where Dee made increasingly bad decisions for the sake of a man."

I covered my face with a beach towel. "Don't remind me."

He handed us a glass each. "So this has nothing to do with the wedding?"

"Not anymore," replied Tilley gleefully.

Marco laughed as he carefully placed the half-full bottle into a gleaming silver ice bucket. "Maybe it's best that you don't tell me the rest of this story. Enjoy your drinks, ladies."

As he walked back toward the lobby, Tilley raised her glass high in the air. "To rolling your former infatuation off a lounge chair." She took a long sip without breaking eye contact with me. "And now, it's time to detach from the whole situation and enjoy the wedding as you were always meant to—slightly bored, more than a little tipsy, and in a dress that makes your tits look amazing."

"I am detached, romantically speaking," I said, then paused to test out my rosé. As always, Marco's taste was impeccable. "But I was supposed to make sure that Matt came clean to Misa about his medication days ago."

Tilley rolled her eyes so hard I thought they would fall out of their sockets. "So first it was your moral obligation to break them up, and now it's your moral obligation to get them happily down the aisle? I'm getting whiplash from this entire vacation."

"I know how it sounds—"

"It sounds like this is just another ruse to get Matt alone." She drained her glass and reached over to pour another one.

"I promise I'm not making the same mistake," I said softly, and Tilley immediately glanced toward the poolside bar.

"Fine. Then seal the deal with a pinky-swear shot," she replied. "I'm not letting this ruin our bonding time, and besides, it's in the spirit of exchanging lifelong vows."

"Fine," I said, matching her tone. "Just one, though."

"Your rule, not mine."

A little while later, clad in oversized T-shirts and bikini bottoms still damp from the pool, we made a sisterly commitment to take over the kids' water trampoline at the hotel next door. We traded lazy swigs of the remaining rosé as we stumbled past the vacant pool, over the boardwalk, and onto the sand. In the distance, we could see the water trampoline bobbing easily with the waves, waiting for our unruly bodies. Eyes on the prize, Tilley handed me her open bottle of wine so she could barrel-roll past any onlookers.

I cocked it like a machine gun, rattling off invisible rounds to cover her path. We were so focused on the sound effects and our choreography that we didn't even notice the candlelit rehearsal dinner taking place on the beach a few steps to our left.

"Uh, Dee?"

Kei's voice broke through our rosé haze, and I looked over my shoulder to see Matt's and Misa's families watching us, mouths agape. Vik shook his head slowly, eyes wide, while Ana clutched Kei's arm in melodramatic delight. Elinor was trying to keep a straight face as Julie took a long, regal sip of her wine. Misa's normally unflappable obachan put down her fork for two seconds to stare at us, then kept eating. It was the ultimate measure of our disruption.

We had staggered into a magazine-ready setup—a long, minimalist wooden table on the beach, flanked by white leather benches and encircled by pillar candles and an overall aura of excess. Bodies were swathed in lace and linen, and the heavy scent of disapproval hung in the air. I tried to hide the open bottle of wine behind my back but only managed to whack myself in the thigh with it, sloshing liquid down my bare legs. Tilley didn't even attempt to get up from the ground. She just flattened into a starfish and lay motionless, as if to evade detection.

Leaving Matt to continue looking anywhere but in our direction, Misa rose from her seat at the head of the table and walked over to greet us.

"Hello, Dee," she said evenly, as though everyone had friends who were occasionally drunk ninjas. "Would you like a glass of water?"

"Are you having a party without us?" I said, perhaps with more indignation than was warranted.

"It's just for family and the wedding party," explained Misa.

She was wearing a white crochet maxi dress, see-through from the knees down. I pulled at the bottom of my T-shirt in despair. "No need for you to sit through an itinerary of speeches on top of every-thing else."

Matt kept his gaze focused on a full glass of red wine while I willed it to explode into his face. He was wearing an off-white, shark-print dress shirt that he might have gotten away with at the age of twelve. Still missing last night's medication, I could feel re-sidual spikes protruding down my spine. It was the closest I was ever going to get to my favorite dinosaur—the stegosaurus—if we're not counting that time I got stoned and climbed over the rope barriers at the museum.

"Who's giving a speech?" yelled Tilley from the ground, sud-denly keen to be involved. "Can I give a speech?"

"I don't believe that will be necessary," interjected Vik, trying to keep the peace.

Elinor stood up and walked over to Misa and me, arms out-stretched. "They've come with a gift for the table," she said, beam-ing, and for a second, I didn't realize she was referring to the backwashed wine in my hands. "How lovely! Perhaps they can join us for dessert, Misa?"

"Of course," said Misa, glancing toward her parents. Julie looked me over suspiciously—which I guess was fair after the kayak incident—before offering a slight nod.

"It's *really* not necessary," I said through gritted teeth, but Eli-nor was already waving Matt over.

"What kind of host are you?" she scolded. "Go fetch the girls some chairs."

Matt sighed and stood up. "I'll grab some from the bar," he said, throwing his napkin onto the table and glancing toward the boardwalk. "Dee, wanna help me?"

"She doesn't have to anymore," said Tilley, finally pushing herself to a standing position so she could better glare at Matt. "That part of her life has gone the way of . . . honestly, so many reality TV shows have been cancelled that I can't even pick a singular example right now."

As my sister lost her train of thought for the second time, Matt nodded toward the bar and we inched away slowly. "But there she goes again," said Tilley, like she was delivering live commentary for ESPN. "Off to destroy yet another brief moment of personal growth."

Vik walked over to my sister and gently escorted her toward his seat on the bench. "Do you like breadsticks, Tilley? I have a whole basket I can share with you," he said kindly, then shot me a curious look over his shoulder as I followed Matt away from the party.

Don't worry, I mouthed, and Vik smiled like he almost believed me.

෩

THE SOUNDS OF the dinner party faded away as we walked across the boardwalk, toward the patio, uneasily mounting two towering stools pulled up at the vacant bar. My damp bathing suit bottom dragged across the seat in protest as Matt reached over the bar and pulled out a half-empty bottle of Johnnie Walker Black.

I shook my head, even though I could use the familiar anesthesia. "We're not doing it like this," I said, grateful that I had not matched Tilley's pace by the pool.

He sighed and put it away. "Dee, I don't even know where to start."

"You're off your meds," I said. "Let's start there."

He chuckled lowly. "I should have known I couldn't put one past you."

I sat cross-legged on my lofty chair as Matt told me that he found out his dad died two months ago. He said it as flat as anything, but the clenching of his brows gave him away. I hadn't expected Matt's dad to be at the wedding because I knew they didn't talk much, but it never occurred to me that he might be gone. I could only imagine what it was like to harbor resentment for that long and then suddenly lose any chance at ever resolving it. No wonder Matt was struggling. And I had been so busy avoiding him before the wedding—then obsessing over him and Misa all week—that I guess he never had a chance to tell me.

"I used to think that when he passed, I'd stop feeling so weighed down. So when I didn't feel anything at all, I started thinking, did the meds take that away from me?" He pressed his forehead into his hands. "I had spent so much time trying not to be like him that as soon as he wasn't around anymore, I think I forgot who I wanted to be at all."

"That's so hard, Matt," I said.

"Ever since it happened, I've just been screwing up," he said. "Keeping things from my family, barely functioning at work, losing the words to my music. Sounds familiar, right?"

"I might have heard this one before." I grinned, but he didn't smile back.

"It feels different this time," he said, his voice low. "Misa is counting on me to be the guy she committed to six months ago. And that guy feels like a total stranger to me now. I went off my meds to try and find a way back."

"I totally get that," I said, then paused. "But you know being on or off your meds doesn't change who you really are. What changed is that you didn't tell Misa about your decision."

"How could I? She was already balancing so much with her family and this wedding. The least I could do was try and take care of myself for once." He paused, his eyes shining beneath the bar lights. "And look where that got me. I've made such a mess of everything, Dee. I'm so sorry about last night, and everything that led up to it. I haven't been fair to you."

I shook my head. "You put yourself under so much pressure that it always ends in some kind of personal explosion that hurts everyone around you." Realizing there was some obvious crossover with my own experience, I softened my voice a touch. "And it doesn't have to be that way. Especially now, you can build an actual support network. You can do things differently."

"This is my problem," he repeated. "I can handle it myself."

"You clearly can't!" I said, months of frustration edging past my empathy. "You were so busy shielding Misa from how you were really feeling that you didn't even notice that you were putting that weight on me. And it was all too easy to overlook my feelings when you needed the support."

Matt looked around, embarrassed at my volume. "I never realized—"

I shook my head vehemently. "You saw what you wanted to see, you gave what was convenient for you, and you didn't care how that affected me."

He exhaled deeply. "Even if things were difficult sometimes, I really thought we were helping each other get through it," he said, his eyes widening. "Or maybe I just needed to believe that. But the hospital, the overpass—I should have realized that being there for me damn near killed you."

I didn't say anything, because as far as SparkNotes versions of the past year went, it was pretty freaking accurate. He gazed at me with a mixture of admiration and earnest regret. "You're my best friend, Dee," he said finally. "You really are."

It was a phrase I'd heard him say many times before, but this time, it felt like a black hole absorbing all the gravity around us. Matt sat motionless, staring into the jumble of bottles in front of us. And I was finally too exhausted to pretend this was enough.

"Then let me tell you one more thing," I said, figuring that if I had nothing left to lose, I might as well be honest about the only way our friendship could continue. "If you really cared about me or Misa, you would have gotten actual help—even if it meant you had to ask for it—instead of closing yourself off and leaning entirely on two women who love you so much, we're willing to dig ourselves into a hole to build you up."

When I finally stopped to take a breath, Matt pressed his face into his hands and exhaled into his palms. I watched his shoulders rise and slump and I wanted to hold him one more time, tell him my pain had been worth it all along. But the impulse was hollow.

He reached over and clasped my hand so tight I thought my bones would collapse in on themselves. "You and Misa are the last people I ever wanted to hurt," he said hoarsely, and for the first time since the hospital, I watched him cry.

He sobbed into the sleeve of his dress shirt and I just sat there and looked on. I fought my instinct to tell him everything was okay, because it definitely wasn't, and we both needed to sit with that knowledge. I don't know if he cried for the way he treated me, or Misa, or if he was still thinking about his dad, but it felt like this was the way it always should have been—his unburdening without me overloading, grounded by the fact that I didn't have to stay but could choose to.

In that moment, I knew whatever mutation of love had been

drawing me to Matt wasn't compelling anymore. It wasn't even him I had been in love with. It was the promise of a quick and easy recovery, a shortcut that came in the form of a teddy bear human with a complete encyclopedia of my trauma. Someone who had known and cared for me at my worst, so I'd never feel the pressure to grow. But in desperately clinging to what was comfortable and safe, I had almost missed out on the person I could be if I did push myself to keep growing, took a chance on myself, asked for what I truly needed. And I suppose, in some ways, he had made the exact same mistake.

When Matt's breathing slowed, I handed him a pile of cocktail napkins from behind the bar. "Thanks," he said, blowing into a thin layer of tissue. "I don't know how I'm ever going to make this up to you."

I thought about Elinor's advice. "I don't think I should be the first person on your list," I said. "You need to talk to Misa about your meds."

"She's going to be so mad at me."

"I think she'll understand why you wanted to try," I said. "It's hard not to search for the parts of yourself that get lost between medication cocktails."

He laughed bitterly. "I went off them because I wanted to believe I didn't need rebalancing to live in this world. Isn't that just the craziest thing you've ever heard?"

I knew people from the ward who felt themselves shrinking on medication, others who took seven pills a day and were grateful for even the dimmest of morning sunlight. I had friends who kept their illness in check through running and meditation alone (and I hate them a little bit). Beautiful souls I knew went through shock therapy and regained ground, and others lost more than I could ever understand. Liz, Harsha, Jermaine, the chorus on the tenth floor of a concrete hospital. My friends.

"You know, Misa will support you through this, no judgment at all," I said softly. "Care plans are meant to be rewritten every so often."

"And you?" he asked, leaving only the evening air between us.

My friends and I have tried cutting out sugar and just plain cutting, magnet stimulation, talking to empty chairs, herbal remedies, pulling out our hair on the bathroom floor, every therapy in the alphabet, and we still feel like we don't deserve to live. I had friends, like Liz, who believed that so fully that now I can't hold them anymore. We're all just trying to make the best decisions we can, trying to drown out the loudest internal scream you could imagine. The craziest thing I've ever heard is when people tell us we're not trying hard enough.

"We can't go back to the way things were. Something's gotta change, for both of us," I said, and it felt like I was finally pushing my way out of the hospital's revolving door. I slid my elbow across the bar to touch his, then bumped it softly. "But if you can find a way forward—for you and Misa—you can bet that I'll still be cheering you on."

His face broke into a tentative smile and he bumped me back, hard enough that my stool rocked against the wooden deck. I laughed and clutched the bar with both hands.

"Dee," he said, wiping his eyes one last time. "I couldn't imagine my life without you."

We heard metal scraping against the deck behind us and turned to see Kei hoisting two patio chairs over their shoulders.

"Hello, friends," they said, politely pretending not to notice the last traces of Matt's tears. "Just wanted to give you a heads-up that despite Vik's best efforts, Tilley seems to have reached a whole new level of alcohol-fueled assholery. Figured it might be a good idea for you to hustle back and help wrangle her before Julie commits a felony."

I glanced at Matt, then bolted from the bar and scrambled down the boardwalk, terrified that just as I had managed not to ruin Matt and Misa's wedding, Tilley would do it for me.

18

"WHAT'S MY AGE AGAIN?"
—BLINK-182 (2:26)

BY THE TIME I returned to the beachside dinner, an inebriated Tilley was pacing up and down the length of the table, muttering expletives under her breath. Vik caught my eye and shrugged help-lessly, because there was only so much on this good earth that free breadsticks could take care of. When my sister caught sight of me, and Matt trailing close behind, she seemed to lose the last string of civility she had.

"Are you two done?" she snapped at me. Not waiting for an answer, she marched over to Vik and swiped his champagne flute, raising it high in the air. She tapped it twice politely with his but-ter knife, and then when no one paid attention to her, hit it so hard she smashed the glass to pieces in her hand.

"Excuse me, everyone," Tilley said, holding shards of glass in her palm. "I'd like to make a toast."

"How should we tackle this one?" muttered Matt behind me. Kei shrugged and set down the extra chairs at one end of the table, eager to escape association with us.

"You sit down and pretend this is entirely normal," I replied under my breath. "I'll handle Hurricane Tilley."

Matt shot me a grateful look before circling the table to take his seat beside the horrified bride-to-be, putting a comforting hand over hers. Misa's hostess smile was frozen across her face, and Vik handed Tilley a cloth napkin to contain the blood. "You do know this is just the rehearsal dinner, right?" he said quietly.

"Oh, I know," Tilley said, beaming and bleeding at the same time. "I'm just practicing so I do a really good job tomorrow."

"Somehow I don't think we're invited anymore," I said, still looking at Misa. Everyone else was captivated by Tilley, who wiped a bloody hand on her bare thigh.

"From the beginning of time," she began, ignoring me completely, "weddings have been kind of bullshit. Take this one, for example—the lovely couple made everyone use their vacation time to get sunburnt at a six-day affair, plus we still had to buy them shit from Williams-Sonoma. Haven't you ever heard of Walmart?"

Julie looked around for assistance—perhaps a bouncer of sorts—but it was just us and the ocean witnessing the toast from hell. Meanwhile, Tilley paused to take a sip of champagne, then realized her flute was basically a bar-fight weapon. Vik offered her a glass of water instead and she shooed it away like she was Marie Antoinette. "When Matt and Misa first asked me to give this speech—"

"No one asked for this," said Vik conversationally to Misa's grandmother. "Not even a little bit." She smiled politely and swallowed another bite of lava cake.

"I told them, 'How could I ever capture your whole love story in just an hour?'" Tilley dramatically raised one hand above her head like she was delivering a *Hamlet* monologue.

Kei's eyes nearly popped out of their head. "This girl will be lucky to live another hour once Julie gets ahold of her."

Right on cue, the Nag rose from her seat—but so did Misa. "It's fine," said Misa quietly, and Julie sank back down, watching Tilley like a lit fuse.

Misa took a few steps toward Tilley, still wearing a gracious smile but also wielding a full decanter of water. I wasn't sure if she was planning to pour it down Tilley's throat or dump it over her head. "Tilley, can I speak with you a minute?" she asked.

"Of course," said Tilley, then abruptly continued giving her unwanted speech. She took a casual stroll in the other direction, coming toward me instead. "I've given it a lot of thought, and I understand why so many relationships break down—"

I started walking toward her, hoping to catch her before Misa did. Tilley's gaze met mine and she kept pace, refusing to back down. "Love," she said, her eyes boring into me, "can make you selfish."

I stopped in my tracks, unnerved by her tone. I replayed her words, searching for that signature sarcasm—the tiniest hint that we would we be okay, as always—but came up empty. Taking advantage of my brief hesitation, Tilley pushed by me, smacking me on top of the head like we were playing Duck, Duck, Goose. "Love reveals your real priorities, even if they suck."

At the other end of the table, Misa inched closer, ready to cut her off.

Tilley barrelled toward Matt. "Love can even make you crazy," she said, flicking him in the head before looking slightly abashed. "Huh. Maybe not the best choice of words for this crowd."

I watched Misa's entire body go rigid, even though no one else picked up on the detour.

"Get. Over. Here." I hissed at my sister.

Pretending not to hear me, Tilley walked toward Vik and dragged her hand across his back before grabbing the top of his head with her viper nails. He recoiled. "You don't get to choose who you fall in love with," she purred, letting go and turning to face Misa. "But you do get to choose who you put the work in for. And if you're willing to make that choice again and again, and build something that makes you want to get out of bed every day, I think that's worth choosing one more time."

Misa barely reacted. She was Hulk-gripping the decanter's curves, beads of condensation trickling onto her white dress. I glanced over at Matt for help, but he was staring at Misa like he was waking up for the first time all week. She didn't look back at him, just watched as Tilley slammed her bleeding hand down on the table for dramatic effect.

"I object to this wedding," she said, wincing a little on impact, "not just because it's super fucking extra, but because I don't think any of this is about you. You and Matt built your whole relationship on a shared understanding that most of the people here will never get. You don't have to re-create that feeling in front of an audience for it to be real. We know it's real! Why else do you think Dee can't get her shit together about Matt?"

The decanter slipped out of Misa's grip, knocking against the wooden arm of an extra chair and smashing to pieces on the ground. My mouth dropped open and I snapped it shut, but not before Misa whipped her head around to look at me. Her eyes pierced through the last of my emotional buffer, leaving me vulnerable to the whispers, stares, and laughs that my brain began to conjure. I sank my nails deep into the flesh of my palms and started counting my breaths slowly.

Tilley staggered sideways, and Vik leapt out of his seat to herd her away. "Misa," she yelled, fighting him. "Do you honestly think this will be the best week of your life? Or are we setting the bar low enough that you two will find joy in every day afterward?"

"Getting philosophical, are we?" muttered Vik, dragging her away from the table. My feet stayed sunken in the sand, heavy with what I had done to my best friends' wedding.

"Weddings are giant money pits and vow renewals are just a way to sell more wedding stuff to people who are already married!" Tilley wasn't quite done yet. "No one is going to remember if your napkin rings were goddamn gold-plated, and you know why? True love has no price range." She finally pried herself from Vik's grip and bellowed across the beach, arms outstretched. "TRUE LOVE IS ALL-INCLUSIVE!"

There was only a brief moment of shocked silence before Ana put her hands together and led the table in an off-beat slow clap that never quite accelerated the way it does in the movies. Misa looked overwhelmed by the sound, her eyes searching for an escape route but her body immobilized.

"I think that's enough for tonight," said Julie sharply, and even Tilley fell quiet. Julie made her way over to where her daughter was still standing, motionless. "Let me walk you back to your room," she said with a worried look on her face, and Misa nodded gratefully.

Matt rose from his seat, looking a little shaky. He grabbed Misa's hand just as she was about to leave. "I'm going to get you some tea and a bag of Doritos, okay?" he said, trying to summon his usual spirit. "We can still turn the night around. I know it's been a long one, but I've got plenty of spoons for cheering you up, always."

"I think I just want to talk to my mom," she said simply.

Out of nowhere, Marco swept in sporting a baby blue dress shirt and his signature grin. "How are you folks doing tonight? Enjoying your special dinner?"

He stopped and took in Tilley's bloody hands, Misa's sopping dress, and my look of utter mortification. "I think maybe we could all use a drink on the house," he said finally, bewilderment etched across his face.

⟡

WHILE MARCO SHEPHERDED everyone else to the poolside bar, Vik and I rinsed Tilley off in the outdoor shower to (a) sober her up, (b) avoid tracking blood into the hotel, and (c) buy time to think about how I was going to deal with Misa, who now understood the real reason I had come to this wedding. Vik held Tilley still while I doused her with cold water and she shivered in the brisk night air.

"You look like *Art Attack: Murder Edition*," I said, turning the metal faucet while trying to avoid the stream.

"So do you," she said, her eyes refocusing under the spray. I glanced down at my shirt. There was a giant bloody handprint over my left boob and haphazard smears down my arms. "Get in here with me."

"I don't want to be wet," I said, spiky as ever. "I just want this night to be over. I was finally getting my shit together, and you blew it all up like it was nothing, because as usual, you needed to be the center of attention."

"Come on, Dee," she said, stepping away from the shower and wringing out her hair with one hand. "I'm sorry. We're both really tired. And super drunk. And we didn't even get to jump on a trampoline."

She dramatically presented her mangled hand to Vik, who dabbed it dry with a beach towel. He pulled a roll of gauze out of his back pocket, a helpful gift courtesy of Marco.

"Wrap it up, soldier," she said with a wink. Vik looked despairingly toward the sky.

"Misa is never going to speak to me again," I said. "And you don't even care."

"All I care about is that you get some fucking space from this toxic three-way you have going with them," she said. "Also, let's not forget that up until yesterday, you were fully trying to steal her fiancé! Were you really that concerned about staying on good terms?"

"It's not that simple!" I yelled.

Vik wound the gauze around her hand patiently. "I know this isn't how anyone would have wanted things to go, Dee," he said, "but in some ways, isn't it best to get it out in the open so you can all move on?"

"Exactly," said Tilley, redirecting her gaze toward me. "Look, can you please just rinse off so we can go to bed? It'll take five seconds. I'll get your pills together and everything. Drunk Tilley still knows the routine."

"No," I said bluntly, familiar rage swelling between the ligaments in my fingers. I flexed them over and over again, searching for release. "I don't need to shower. I don't need you to get my pills. Stop doing things for me like I'm a fucking child, okay? I don't need you."

Tilley jerked her hand away from Vik and the roll of gauze tumbled down the wooden boardwalk. Vik chased after it, probably relieved to get away from us.

"Dee," said Tilley, "I am literally on a weeklong babysitting mission. And I'm sorry if I embarrassed you tonight. But for the last few years of my life, I have functioned as your human fire extinguisher. Doesn't that count for anything? Do you really think you don't need me?"

"Need you? You just threw me under the bus!"

"I was trying to help you move on," she said. "Maybe it wasn't the most elegant way of doing it, but some things you have to set on fire. Like cigarettes and parking tickets."

"I need Matt and Misa," I said under my breath. "They're the only ones who understand."

"You have me," she said, grabbing onto my hand. "You'll always have me."

"You don't get it," I yelled, pulling away. "You'll never understand what it's like to feel like this."

"How can you say I don't understand?" howled Tilley as Vik cautiously walked back toward us, trying not to get caught in the crossfire. "I've sat through every single doctor's appointment you've had since your breakdown. I drag your comatose ass out of bed, I drive you to the hospital, I talk to the doctor after you flip out on him, and then I go home and spend all my free time making sure you don't kill yourself. Every. Fucking. Day."

"Maybe I should save you some time and just kill myself, then," I yelled, and Tilley shook her head so wildly I thought it might fall off.

"Don't you *dare* use your illness as a weapon right now," she said. "I understand that you're sick, and I understand that you're hurting, but you have to take some fucking responsibility for yourself, Dee. I'm exhausted." Her voice broke slightly, and I stared at the ground. "How can I ever live my own life if I'm always wrapped up in yours?"

Deep down, I knew she was right. Tilley had been the only thing keeping me grounded since the hospital, and if anyone deserved to be cut some slack, it was her. But that's the thing about mental illness. Whatever you lean on the most is in the greatest danger of disintegrating beneath you. And after a week of disrupted routines and poor sleeping schedules, high stress and major heartbreak, the part of me that loved her more than anything else just wasn't strong enough to drown out the part of me that told me I was worthless and didn't deserve anyone, not even my sister. The spikes burst through my skin and punctured the last person holding on to me.

"There's no such thing as secondhand bipolar," I said sharply, and Tilley flinched. I balled up my fists. "Maybe I'm not the only one who belongs in therapy."

"You know what?" said Tilley quietly. "I started going to therapy months ago. Do you know why?"

I released my hands and looked up at her. "Is it because of me?"

Tilley shook her head slowly. "No, Dee," she said. "It was actually because of me. But you would never think of that, would you?"

She pushed past Vik and headed down the boardwalk, out toward the rhythmic waves of the Atlantic Ocean. I watched her walk into the night, and all the destructive energy that had been pulsing through my body drained out of me. I felt tired and husklike, as if I could tumble away with the next gust of wind swaying the trees.

"I thought I was finally doing the right thing," I said mechanically. "I let him go. I stopped carrying around all this regret and jealousy. And somehow, I still managed to fuck it up."

"I wouldn't call this a successful rehearsal dinner by any stretch of the imagination," said Vik kindly, "but it's not the end of the road for you. Tomorrow, Tilley will still be your sister. You'll get a chance to do better by her, and I have no doubt that you will."

"But the wedding—"

"I have a feeling you've been told this before," he interrupted, "but this is not your wedding. If Matt and Misa need to work some things out, they will. All the rest of us can do is show up for them when they ask. I think you told me something similar about the hospital."

I couldn't decide what I hated more—that he had used my own words against me to prove a damn good point, or that he was being so hot and so reasonable at the same time.

Vik nodded toward the shower. "I'll go after Tilley. You should get in there and maybe give yourself some time to think." He followed her path down the boardwalk, disappearing into the darkness that surrounded the shore.

Before I towel-dried my hair and fell asleep in our empty hotel room, I counted four pills into the palm of my hand, all by myself. I snapped a banana from our stash and swallowed mournful bites until I was sure I could hold down the medication. In the last moment before the chalky tablets slid down my throat, I thought about how many times Tilley had prepared this nightly ritual for me, rubbed my hands when I felt nauseated, held my hair back when the banana wasn't enough.

But when my stomach clenched and I found myself gripping white porcelain fifteen minutes later, I knew it wasn't just the meds this time. It was the knowledge that I had told the only person who had always been there that she wasn't enough. I had said it so many times that she had finally believed me.

19

"YOU GET WHAT YOU GIVE"
—NEW RADICALS (5:00)

ON THE DAY of Matt and Misa's wedding, I woke up to Tilley embedding her fang-like nails in my forearm at seven in the morning. It was a welcome distraction from my pounding headache, courtesy of last night's rosé.

"Dee," she said, curled up on the ground, one arm outstretched. I could smell a haze of booze seeping out of her pores. "I did a bad thing."

I flashed back to our argument and knew that nothing could be worse than how I'd treated her last night. I wondered if I should offer an apology up front but decided to venture into our uneasy truce the only way I knew how. "The last time you said that, you let a line cook give you a haircut based on directions from a Magic 8 Ball."

She sniffed. "I looked like Robert Downey Jr."

I pushed myself off the bed and sat on the floor beside her. "All right, lay it on me."

Tilley leaned in and breathed into my ear like a sea cow. "Dee, we lost Misa's wedding ring last night."

"Who's *we*?" I asked, mildly jealous that Tilley could accomplish bad things without me.

"After you were a total jerk, Vik chased me down to see if I was okay, and then we grabbed some drinks at a hotel bar a few resorts over, and then we found these really cute feral cats on our way home so we took them to the spa at the hotel next door—"

"Great, so now you have rabies," I said, forever amazed at Tilley's natural ability to get even the most levelheaded of men drunk enough to make bad decisions.

Tilley clapped a hand to the side of her face. "It doesn't matter what I have because Misa is going to kill me!"

My heart dropped. In addition to the news of my betrayal, Misa was also going to drop-kick Tilley to the moon once she found out about the missing band. It wasn't like we could just run out and replace it—knowing Misa, it was probably made from sustainable metals and engraved with their fingerprints.

"Okay," I said, taking a deep breath. "When did you lose the ring?"

"Ideally it's either at the hotel bar or in the spa," she said. "Or worst-case scenario, it's been swallowed up by the stretch of sand in between those two places. I don't think we went swimming so it's probably not a *Titanic* necklace situation. Although to be fair, I will end up at the bottom of the ocean if Misa finds out. Please join my search party? Vik has to pretend everything is normal and do best man stuff with Matt right now so it's kind of up to me."

"I'd be honored," I said, standing up and holding my hands out to Tilley. She grabbed them and I pulled her to her feet. "About last night—"

She sighed. "It's whatever, you weren't feeling like yourself—"

"You know, you're really, really good at making excuses for me," I said.

"I never know how to be mad at you because you've already got so much going on," she replied, and again, there was no wisecrack lurking behind her words. Only care and a little exhaustion. "I just want you to be okay."

"I totally get that," I said. "And I'm so grateful that I had you to lean on when I first got sick. But it's been years now, and I think I might have to face the fact that my 'okay' may never look the way it used to. Which also means that I need to learn how to be accountable for my own bullshit—I'm just sorry it's taken me so long to figure that out."

Tilley slung her arms around me. "It wasn't all on you," she mumbled into my shoulder. "As much as I've enjoyed being a meat shield for your mistakes, I think part of the reason I started going to therapy was that it was easier to focus on taking care of you than it was to acknowledge that I wasn't taking care of myself."

"I worry about you too, you know," I said, hugging her back.

"As you should," she retorted. She let go of me and plopped down on the cushy bed. "It took all of three sessions to realize that I have some real bad coping strategies. Like, former-child-star-level hang-ups. I've basically come to the conclusion that the only time I really like myself is when I'm with you."

"Good thing we hang out so much, then," I said, putting my hand over hers.

Tilley shook her head. "I actually think I've been holding you back too. If I'm always there to clean up your mess, and you're always there to justify mine, how can either of us get anywhere?"

We sat like that for a moment, letting her words sink in.

"Damn," I said. "We're lousy enablers."

"The absolute worst," she said with a grin.

I bit my lip. "So what do we do now?"

Tilley glanced at the clock on our nightstand. "Find the missing wedding ring and figure this one out on the flight home?"

"Deal."

"Excellent," said Tilley. She stood up abruptly, suddenly all business. "Now go fix yourself up, and you can search the spa while I search the bar. I think we tried to bathe the cats in the last cabin on the left, if you can get in there."

"I want you to repeat that last sentence back to yourself."

"Don't fuck this up," she said, peering out the front door for any signs of Misa. "Only one of us is allowed to be in crisis at a time. And you owe me, like, twenty crises."

She slammed the door behind her, and I couldn't help but grin.

THE SUN WAS up but most of the tourists weren't. To get into the spa next door, I snuck past hedges with crisp haircuts and a vacant reception desk decorated with crystals that boasted the same empty promises as my old therapists. After sweeping the area for potential witnesses, I slipped into the women's change room and swiped an extra robe from an open locker. Safely camouflaged, I walked out the back door and stood squinting in the sun.

This resort was on a whole other level of relaxation. In front of me, two bubbling fountains fed into a T-shaped pool, the water lined with private cabins and palm trees. Underneath a massive white pergola, a sunburnt couple lay in lounge chairs, occasionally rousing themselves to take a sip of fruit-infused water. They were mastering a level of chill that I had thought was only possible through sedatives or an industrial-sized tub of mint chocolate chip. Actually, based on the clientele of this beach, I wasn't ruling out the sedatives just yet. I tiptoed past white cabins labelled SUN,

EARTH, WIND, FIRE, tossing a look behind me before pushing through the last set of curtains on the left.

Everything smelled like lavender oil. The room had a colossal clawed bathtub on one side filled with floating shreds of seaweed, and a massage table with fresh sheets on the other. I knelt down and lifted the massage table's trailing linens, hoping to find the missing ring and redeem myself for the previous night. But as impatient footsteps approached the cabin, I ducked underneath the table completely, hoping to avoid detection.

"Dee? I know you're in there."

In one furious movement, the white curtains were swept aside and Misa stormed into my stolen spa haven. I jumped and whacked my head on the underside of the table.

"Dee," she said quietly, which was somehow ten times worse than if she was yelling. "If you took the ring, you can tell me."

"Excuse me?" I rubbed the back of my head and swore under my breath, then crawled out of my hiding place.

"I know the ring is gone and I think Tilley is covering for you. You're three days away from a total breakdown," she said, trying to keep a lid on things. She perched her butt on the edge of the massage table and offered me a tight smile. "But you don't have to go through this alone. You're not well right now. If you took the ring, I'll forgive you."

"Are you seriously making this about my illness and not about my unrequited love for your fiancé?" I asked. I stood up and tried to look like a halfway reasonable person. "Why can't you just respect my ulterior motives?"

"You're sick, Dee," she repeated gently, and I wanted to punch her.

"Yeah sure, but I was also in love with Matt! I'm a really bad friend who wanted your wedding to be called off!" I walked over to the seaweed bath, dipped my fingers in, and flicked water at Misa. "Why are you still trying to take care of me? You should drown me in this bathtub right now—seriously, just take your shot and we'll both feel a lot better."

Misa wiped a droplet from her cheek. "I suppose *you* would."

We stared each other down for a moment before I broke away and opened the back window for some air. "I don't have the ring," I said into the breeze. "I'm not proud of much this week but I wouldn't lie about that."

"You used past tense," she replied. "You said you *were* in love with him. You aren't anymore?"

I shifted uncomfortably. "I don't know how to talk to you about this."

"But isn't this what you've always wanted?" Her eyes flashed and she spat the words out like sunflower seeds. "For me to stop pretending that everything is fine? How dare you look down on me for wanting to keep parts of my life private, and then turn around and hide something like this for so long." She looked me square in the eyes, and I wanted to melt into the floor. "So, this is your chance. Let's talk, Dee. Tell me about how you pretended to care about me just to get closer to Matt."

"It wasn't like that," I said, but I knew it wasn't enough.

My words echoed dully through the wooden hut, and Misa's shoulders hunched in toward her chest. "Maybe you were pretending this whole time," she said, "but I wasn't. I thought that when it came down to it, we had something special too."

※

After my dishonorable discharge from the hospital, I had been floating around without day treatment or medication that made any sense. My morning routine included a new narcolepsy drug to combat the effects of my night drugs, which Tilley said was like hiring a hit man to neutralize another hit man ("ideally, both characters played by Gerard Butler"). When Misa got discharged from the hospital two weeks before Matt and two weeks after me, she called me up and asked if I wanted to come visit her at Obachan's house. I was overjoyed to have somewhere to go.

Obachan lived in a tiny bungalow off Kennedy Road, with a driveway so long you could get winded walking to her side door. Misa told me guests used the front door and family used the side, and I felt honored to be in such good company. After Misa let me in, Obachan shuffled over to the top of the hallway stairs in fluffy pink slippers and handed me a pair of my own. I kicked off my shoes and stepped into padded warmth. Misa gently picked up my beat-up Converse and placed them on the stairs, toes pointed out toward the door.

Misa was staying there to avoid telling her parents about day treatment, and to make sure Obachan had stopped driving (she hadn't, license or no license). She took me on a quick tour of the house—the living room with every possible surface coated in clear plastic, the basement where Obachan kept an Armageddon's worth of toilet paper, her grandfather's TV room that sat exactly how he had left it, with the noted addition of framed photographs, his gold watch, and a marble box filled with his ashes.

We settled with Obachan in the gleaming white kitchen. Her slippers slid along the floor as she made us a pot of green tea and placed small bowls of senbei—one of our favorite Obachan-approved snacks—on the table. She waved Misa off as she lifted the heavy teapot from the kitchen counter.

Her fridge was covered in magnets from places her grand-children had travelled: Paris, Morocco, Mexico, Costa Rica, Japan. I asked Obachan if she had ever been to Japan. She wrinkled her nose and said, "Japan! Who wants to go there?"

Misa told me we were making onigiri, and I nodded eagerly before escaping to the bathroom to google what that was—Japanese rice balls, as it turned out. We sipped tea as we waited for Obachan's pot of steamed rice to cool slightly.

"Misa," she said in her careful voice, "you know the Toronto Star? I cut this out for you. You should read it."

She plucked a clipping from the top of an endless pile of grocery store coupons and editions of Nikkei Voice and slid it across the table to Misa. I craned my neck to read the headline: "Outbreak of E. Coli Tainted Romaine Lettuce Claims First Death in US."

"You better not eat salad this week," she continued, and Misa and I stifled smiles. "Only wakame."

"Okay, Obachan," said Misa, but she was already pushing a second article across the table.

"This one too," she said solemnly, and I watched Misa's face change as she absorbed the headline: "How to Talk About Mental Health in the Workplace."

"Thank you, Obachan," she said, reaching over to squeeze her grandmother's arthritic hand. Obachan gave her a wide smile and squeezed back, and my own fingers flexed with phantom jealousy.

Once the rice had cooled enough, Obachan cut nori sheets into thirds with her kitchen scissors while Misa and I wet our hands at the sink. We dipped our fingers into a bowl of salt and rubbed the tiny grains across our palms. Obachan stood over us and spooned out rice from a wooden bowl. I imitated Misa as she cupped the warm rice firmly between her hands to make a little triangle, leaving space to press a dried-up purple fruit into the middle. "Umeboshi," said Obachan, by way of explanation. After she buried the salted plum, Misa took a slim nori sheet and wrapped it around her rice ball like a cape, then handed it to Obachan for inspection. She nodded and gestured toward the sink for another round. As Misa rose, Obachan's attention turned to my rice ball, which looked more like a very sad snowball.

I gave it one more valiant squish and turned to Misa. "I think maybe I should have come in the front door."

Obachan laughed about that one on her way downstairs to find an extra package of sesame seeds in her stockroom. In her absence, Misa lined up rice balls in a clean row inside Obachan's spotless Tupperware.

"I'm glad you decided to come," she said.

"Me too," I said, adding my rice ball to the procession. "I don't exactly have a packed social schedule these days. Although some guy I hooked up with once in a parking lot heard about the pool incident and messaged me to see if I 'needed a hug'—with an accompanying winky face, of course."

"He sounds questionable."

"I mean—so am I, right?" I choked on a half-hearted laugh, and Misa cocked her head to the side.

"Do you really believe that?" she asked, suddenly serious.

I scooped out another spoonful of rice while I thought about her question. This was the kind of thing Tilley asked me when we were drunk and falling off the living room couch, and somehow that always seemed to make it feel low stakes. But in the daylight of Obachan's kitchen, in the middle of a rice ball assemblage that felt vaguely ceremonial, I decided to be honest. After all, what did I have to lose?

"I don't think I've felt like I deserved happiness for a long time," I said, ignoring the clenching of my stomach. "Or if I ever got a brief handle on it, I kept waiting for it to be taken away. You know, as punishment for the way I've dealt with everything."

Misa nodded. "I know how that feels. I keep waiting to fix everything before I let myself open up to other people, like we don't deserve love while we're sick."

I had never heard Misa talk about sickness in this way, like a weight we could never put down. I suddenly felt protective over her, maybe because I knew this kind of conversation wasn't as commonplace for her as it was for me, maybe because I wanted her to find comfort in who she was so I could learn to do the same.

She wrapped a cooling rice ball in stiff nori. "I've been thinking lately that I'm ready to take a step forward, but I'm scared that I'll lose all the progress I've made. I'm just getting used to taking care of myself again—what if I get swallowed up by the pressure of caring for someone else too?"

"I don't know," I said slowly. "Hypothetically, I think being in a good relationship means you don't lose yourself to the other person. You just learn the best ways to care for each other."

"What I like about this person is that I feel both independent and supported when I'm with him. He makes me feel comfortable in any room we walk into together." She laughed lightly. "That might sound silly, but as a fairly anxious person, that's pretty special to me. And you can tell he cares about the people around him, even if he doesn't always find the right words to tell them. That's something I can certainly relate to in my family."

Of course, I knew she was talking about Matt. But somehow, her description didn't sound anything like mine would. It was like she could already see him outside of his diagnosis, beyond the sentimentality of the run-down recreation room where they met. She just saw Matt for who he was, and everything he could be.

"I don't think we can wait to be perfect versions of ourselves before we allow a little space for happiness," she said as she reached back into Obachan's Tupperware. Her eyes met mine as she offered me a chunky triangle of onigiri, and we both smiled. "I'm glad to have friendships that remind me of that."

It's funny that I've never thought about that afternoon as the moment I knew for sure that Misa was my romantic rival. Maybe it's because even though we both cared so much for Matt, we weren't in love with the same person at all. What felt more recognizable was finding out that she too struggled to imagine a future post-hospital where she was loved. I felt so close to her, and I never could have had this conversation with Matt. But as time passed and Matt got out of the ward, I stopped reaching out to her and fixated on his presence. Conversations like this one became a footnote to my obsession. I demanded the louder kind of love I received from Matt and Tilley and didn't know how to respond to Misa's

understated care. I forgot to see those small, quiet moments
as leaps in the trajectory of our friendship.

I WATCHED MISA shrink into herself and wished I knew how to make things right without leaning on empty words. Despite all the grand promises Matt and I had made to each other, it was Misa who kept reaching out to prevent me from drifting away. I had rejected her support time and time again because it felt like it was driven by duty, not love. But who was I to say that duty wasn't a form of love? As I had learned in the hospital, often just showing up was the greatest gift that you could give someone—and finally, it was my turn to balance the scales.

My eyes darted around the room and landed on the massive porcelain tub in the corner, which looked like it was straight out of *Architectural Digest*. It was surrounded by a sculpted rack of fluffy folded towels and tiers of potted plants, and seemed like a pretty good place to work through our problems. "Do you want to take a bath?" I asked.

Misa looked at me like I had just asked for a second helping of hospital potpie. "Is this how you avoid all your problems?"

"Maybe." I threw my robe over the massage table but left my clothes on, gingerly testing the water with my hand. "It's nice and warm. Come sit with me."

I turned on the faucet to add some extra heat, then stepped inside one foot at a time. Misa shook her head as I lowered my butt to the bottom of the porcelain and leaned back with a sigh. "You're actually crazy," she said. "And you know I hate that word."

"So are you," I replied, wiggling my warm toes. "We did meet in a psych ward."

"I was voluntary!"

"I'm sorry," I said. "Do you want a crown for that?"

Misa frowned, kicked off her shoes, and stepped into the tub with me, cringing as seaweed hugged her calves. She sat down with a splash and stared at me defiantly, her T-shirt clinging to her skin. "Okay, now what?"

I took a deep breath. "Not appreciating your friendship is one of the greatest regrets of my adult life, along with that time I let Tilley drag me to a Train concert. Every time I hear 'Hey, Soul Sister,' I have to spend an extra half hour in therapy."

She cracked a smile. "Glad to know that I rank so high."

"You always have," I said. "But I convinced myself that you were ashamed of being anything like me. It was easier to be hard on you than to admit that's how I really felt about myself."

We sat cross-legged in the bathtub, feeling the water lap against our chests. My breathing slowed, and I leaned my shoulders back against the lip of the tub.

"I used to think that I was in love with Matt," I said. "And I'm sorry I kept that from you. But really, I think I just wanted what you had. Love. Recovery. Kitchen appliances. I didn't know how to say out loud that I was scared of being left behind. That your happiness felt like a threat, even though it shouldn't have."

"I've never once felt ahead of you," Misa offered, her arm squeaking against the porcelain as she shifted closer to me. "We just have different skill sets. I tend to struggle with emotions that I don't see as productive, but I've always admired the way you're able to talk about the hard stuff. It helps me appreciate my own bad feelings for what they are."

"That's just a nice way of saying I talk too much."

Misa's eyes sparkled. "You do, but I like it. Drowns out whatever's swirling in my head."

"Oh god, am I your Tilley?"

"You're my friend, Dee," she said. "Even when you're trying not to be."

I watched as she cupped her hands together and let the water drain between her palms. "You and Tilley actually did me a favor last night. After everything blew up, I finally told my mom about the hospital."

"Wow," I said. "How did she take it?"

"I mean, at first, she was really scared. I think that's pretty standard for families like mine—there aren't as many opportunities to talk about mental illness, and a lot of the resources that are out there don't apply as neatly," she said softly. "But, I don't know, we spent a long time talking and I realized that what she cares about and what I care about are more aligned than I thought. A lot of people in our community are struggling with their mental health—even if they don't have an exact diagnosis—and it's hard to separate that from the history that my mom is working with."

"Oh man," I said, unable to keep the pride out of my voice, "if you and your mom start running mental health events together, the world will never be the same."

She laughed. "We'll see about that. But while we're being honest, I should probably tell you that even before the wedding, I found myself in a low place more often than you'd think. Or maybe more often than I was willing to admit."

After all the jealousy, the self-hatred, and the wishful thinking, knowing Misa struggled as much as me didn't bring me any satisfaction. It only brought me closer to her.

"So," I said. "Where are you right now? On a scale of one to miserable."

She smiled without her eyes. "Well, I'm hiding out in a bathtub and might need to call off my wedding."

"When you put it like that, I guess it doesn't sound super on-brand for you," I said. I thought about the way I'd want to call one off, with fireworks and a loose tarantula. Then I realized people who have ideal wedding-ruining scenarios should probably not attend anyone else's wedding, let alone have their own. "Wait, is it because of me?"

Misa put a hand on my arm. "No, it really isn't. I mean, your situation didn't help, but it's because Matt lied to me about going off his medication. He finally told me last night."

Amidst all the turmoil, it was nice to think that my tough-love conversation had prompted at least one good decision on this trip. Although I suppose I couldn't celebrate too hard, because I had also caused an objection speech, a lost wedding ring, and a prenuptial scandal in a matter of twenty-four hours.

"You already knew," she said, watching my neutral expression.

"He needed to tell you himself," I said softly.

She nodded. "But he needed to tell me months ago."

I didn't say anything, because of course, she was right.

"Ever since we started planning the wedding, it's felt like he's been shutting down. And I completely understand that we're all going to struggle sometimes. That's part of who we are," she said, her voice tight. "But when those moments come, that's when we need to be honest with each other. I'm heartbroken that he chose not to trust me after all we've been through together. All I've ever wanted is for us to be a team." She looked up at me, eyes glistening.

"I know," I said, grabbing her hand.

She held on to me tight. "If I had known that this wedding would put what we had in jeopardy, I never would have wanted it. Maybe it was more pressure than we could handle."

I shook my head. "This sounds like a conversation you needed to have, no matter what brought it on. If you want to figure this out before you take that next step with Matt, that's totally valid."

"I'll be letting everyone down," she whispered.

"It's okay to ask for what you need. Especially from someone who loves you as much as Matt does." Misa still looked unsure, so I gave her a little nudge. "This is your chance to do the right thing in the wrong place. Who cares about an expensive destination wedding? Let's not get bogged down by circumstance here."

Misa laughed despite the tears streaming down her face—that same musical laugh that had drawn Matt in at the hospital, the one that I now knew was hard-earned and worth every inch of effort in our tumultuous friendship. She wiped her eyes and looked at me, heart wide open. "Wedding or not, after everything that's happened, do you think we can make it through this?"

I'd asked myself if all of us would make it countless times. The odds of my survival in this world were tied to the gravitational pull of our unlikely friendship, and for that, I was so grateful. It wasn't just our defiant comradery within the medical system that kept me grounded—it was the way Matt and Misa demonstrated how people like us could love and be loved equally, as imperfect as we are. If I believed in anything, it was the fact that they both deserved all the best things in the world and had found just that, set to the soundtrack of a psych ward recreation room in the heart of Scarborough.

I slid across the white porcelain and draped my body across Misa's, hoping I could absorb all the pain that Matt and I had caused her. "If anyone is going to make it, it's gonna be you," I muttered into her shoulder. The bathwater cooled around us, and I felt Misa's breathing align with my own, rising slow and steady above the trickling fountain outside. I wanted to offer her *Cosmopolitan* advice and maybe another kayak for escaping, but I knew that wasn't what she needed. In a rare moment of reserve, I gave her what she asked for. Friendship, and a little more silence than I was used to.

All of a sudden, Matt burst through the curtains. He stood over the bathtub with a fresh face and a neatly trimmed beard and looked down at us like we were taking a joint bath in our clothes, which is exactly what we were doing.

"Are you both nuts?" he said.

"Yes, actually," said Misa, finally lifting her head. She caught my eye and smiled before pushing up to stand, her skirt dripping all over me.

Matt helped her out of the tub, and then reached out a hand to me. I decided to maintain independence and climbed awkwardly over the side, almost tripping on my way out. I grabbed a towel off the pile and threw it at Misa, who caught it and started drying herself off.

"I'm glad I caught you here," he said, the light from the open window catching the red in his hair. "Because I want to say something that I don't think we could really cover in our vows—you know, if we ever did anything the traditional way."

"Don't mind me," I said, speed-drying my legs in a panic. "I'll be out of here in two seconds."

"If you don't mind, I'd actually like you to stay," said Matt. "For one thing, I know you'll keep me honest. But also, if we're making promises we need to keep, I think you'd be the perfect witness."

Misa nodded. "You should stay, Dee."

I was touched by the gesture, but also deeply worried that I would find a brand-new way to mess things up. Taking a deep breath, I perched myself on the edge of the bathtub and channeled my inner Kei. "Okay."

"Misa, I am so sorry for not being honest with you about my

medication," he began earnestly. "Finding out like this must have hurt so bad, especially given how much you've opened up to me over the past year. I know it's not always easy for you either."

Misa didn't say anything. She just folded her towel, and then another one, sporting the same stubborn look that I had come to recognize on the Nag. He was going to have to do a lot better than that.

"Even after everything we'd been through, my brain convinced me that you would leave if I couldn't keep it together," Matt said, regret ringing through his voice. "It was the scariest thing I could imagine. So I made a rash decision. Then I started self-sabotaging and, even worse, dragged Dee into my self-sabotaging." He gestured toward me sheepishly. "Again, I'm really sorry about that one too."

"Uh, yeah. I prefer heartfelt confessions as a spectator sport," I said, giving him an awkward salute. "But we're good. Don't lose steam now."

"Right," he said, turning back to Misa, who folded her arms across her chest. He took a few cautious steps toward her. "It's hard to explain, but I used to think the only kind of love that mattered was completely unconditional. I was looking for you to love me in ways that I couldn't love myself, partly so I'd never have to deal with my own problems."

"And what do you think about it now?" asked Misa, some warmth returning to her voice.

"Well," he said, "this might not sound the most romantic, but I think the kind of love we need requires conditions. It should be built on mutual honesty and respect, kindness and empathy—and without those needs being met, and each of us growing on our own *and* together, it's not really love. It's dependency."

Coming out of the hospital, we had all clung to our distorted ideas of what love needed to be to make us feel whole. These ideas had warped our real-life relationships. But maybe there was a chance for us to learn from each other's mistakes, to hold on a little longer.

"What I'm saying is that you deserve to marry a guy who's as willing to work on himself as he's willing to work on his marriage," he finished. "And this time, I know I can be that for you."

Misa glanced at me, and I tried to send her telepathic courage. It was time to be inconveniently honest. "There's so much to talk about and so much that needs to change between us," she said to Matt, a hint of wistfulness in her voice. "But if I'm being truthful, I don't think we can get married today."

"You're right," he said instantly. "We can't get distracted by what everybody else wants from us right now. We've only got so many spoons, and I'd rather use them to make things right between us and ensure we get another chance in the future. But like, not too far away, because I'm pretty excited for the part where you move out of Obachan's house and we get to spend Sunday mornings together playing Waffle Jenga."

A smile crept across Misa's face. "I don't know how I'm supposed to argue against that kind of logic," she said, and Matt took both her hands in his.

"In the hospital, we built our own support system because no one else was ever going to show up for us," he said gruffly. "But I'm starting to realize that being part of what we have together also means a responsibility to work through my own issues before they spill over and affect you."

"Every time you shut me out, I feel like I'm failing you," Misa said quietly. "And it's not fair. Even if everything around us is falling apart, we have to come through for each other. Otherwise, what else can we depend on to keep us going?"

In this world, all we had to hold on to was mad love. Mad friendship. Mad joy. The music that kept us moving, even if no one else could hear it.

"I promise that I'm finally ready to make the changes I should have made ages ago," said Matt earnestly. "Especially if I'm considering staying off medication, I think it might help if I had a wider network to lean on. A more balanced kind of care plan. So this morning, Vik helped me email a couple men's support groups back home—you know, to make up for losing your ring. Small steps, you know?"

"I guess that's a start," Misa said with a laugh, and Matt's face broke into a boyish grin.

He tucked a loose strand of Misa's hair behind her ear and adopted a more serious tone. She didn't take her eyes off him, not for a second. "And since there will probably be a wait list to deal with, I was thinking in the meantime, maybe I could volunteer at the hospital with you."

Her eyes lit up, and he continued, encouraged. "I could even teach music in the ward, you know, as a way of honoring everything that brought us together. I never want to forget how lucky we've been."

"It's perfect," she said, looking him up and down like he had just proposed all over again. "You know I'm a sucker for a good plan."

Matt brushed Misa's hands gently against his lips. "I want things to be different for our future together. I want to give you all of my best days, even though we can't always predict when they'll be."

"All my best days are with you," she said. "That's what I signed up for. And if you're ready to make a commitment, not just to me, but to yourself, then I'm here for it."

Emboldened, he got down on one knee, and the corners of her

mouth curved upward. It wasn't the most elegant kneel in the world, but the way he looked at Misa, I knew he'd stay there forever if he had to.

"Misa, I promise to sit with you under your sad lamp on winter mornings. I promise to keep track of my own moods as intensely as I keep track of your prescriptions. You will never have to use the emergency med stash in your tea jar," he said, and her eyes shone underneath the ceiling lights.

"And I promise to listen to you play the same dozen songs on your guitar over and over again," she quipped. "But know I'll never get tired of 'Give a Little Bit.' Not now, not ever."

Matt laughed deeply. "You say that now, but wait until we're back on the ward together. That's my go-to, you know." His hazel eyes grew serious, and he gazed up at her in adoration. "I want to spend the rest of my life with you, if you'll still have me," he said. "But I don't expect you to take me as I am today."

"I would like that too," she said. I watched over them with a wide smile, grateful to have witnessed the only ceremony that counted this week.

"Misa Nagasaka," said Matt, "will you consider marrying me again a year from now?"

Misa kissed him so hard that he nearly toppled into the rack of perfectly folded towels beside them. Laughing, she helped him to his feet before throwing her arms back around him, a rogue tear or two smudging into the pressed fabric of his dress shirt. He beamed into her shoulder, holding on tight.

"I hope for your sake that you guys elope next time," I said, wiping back a few tears of my own—so sue me, it wasn't every day that you got to watch your two best friends fall in love a second time.

"That's an easy promise to make," replied Misa as Matt took a step back and bowed deeply in front of her.

"Excuse me, miss," he said suavely. "You look like you might have participated in recreational figure skating for at least ten years. May I have the honor of this dance?"

"That's my cue," I said with a grin, pushing myself away from the bathtub's ledge with a slight groan and heading toward the exit.

The last thing I saw before I closed the door was Matt's arm wrapped around Misa's waist, his cheek pressed against hers. There was no sound at all except for the steady trickle of the fountain outside the window. Their fingers found familiar grooves as they retraced their steps, moving toward a future they could both embrace. It was like there was nothing else that mattered, and for that, I was grateful.

20

"ALWAYS BE MY BABY"
—MARIAH CAREY (4:18)

WEDDING OR NO wedding, the party was spectacular.

When Matt and Misa broke the news, Marco reacted quite well for someone whose breakout event had disintegrated into a week of casual backstabbing and emotional confessions. He rummaged around the hotel's event storage room and added pops of color to break up the white decorations. He busted out beach games, channelling the enthusiasm of a soccer mom at the end of a winless season. He donated the wedding cake to a local church and arranged a s'mores station instead.

"I'm so sorry about all of your plans," I whispered as Marco stopped for a brief glass of water at the outdoor bar. "Are you going to be okay?"

He beamed at me. "Miss Dee, there is always another party, but we only have one life. I am glad your friends are doing what's right for them." He began to push a trolley full of elaborate floral arrangements toward the tent, then turned over his shoulder. "And me? I will try to do the same." Washington later told me that Marco got promoted before the end of the night.

Ken and Julie had been surprisingly calm about the ceremony's change of plans, partially because Obachan very stubbornly insisted on extravagantly tipping all the resort staff to make up for the inconvenience. She had reached into the depths of her fanny pack and pulled out stacks of straight hundos, waving them around like racing flags. As usual, she was Misa's biggest fan.

Although the rings were no longer needed for this particular occasion, Tilley managed to redeem herself by finding Misa's missing band as we were getting changed for the event—it turns out that it had been safely tucked away in the padding of her bikini top the whole time. "Honestly, given my track record, that was the first place I should have looked," she grumbled. "I once lost a whole digital camera in this rack."

As much as Vik was relieved to be let off the hook, he seemed a little scarred by his night out with Tilley. He spent the entire evening toasting Matt and Misa with the same glass of lukewarm champagne, even as he challenged me to a friendly game of cornhole after dinner.

"Thanks for helping Matt get his head straight," I said, collecting the scattered beanbags. "I can't believe you thought you'd be bad at this mental health stuff. You were our ringer."

"I was well prepared after our chat on the beach," he said graciously. "Plus, it helped that Matt was finally ready to talk to me."

He tossed a blue bag past the wooden platform on my side and onto the sand. "So will you come visit me in London the next time you're out that way?" he asked. "You know, now that you're no longer otherwise occupied."

I blushed, but luckily I was so sunburnt that he probably couldn't tell. "I'd love to, but I think this trip has blown my travel budget for the foreseeable future."

Vik looked disappointed as I took my shot, sinking a red bag straight through the hole on his end.

"Because of my job, I hardly ever take vacation myself," he said quietly. "It would really be a blessing to use my airline points to bring you over."

"Why do all you financially stable people have so many airline points just lying around?" I said, trying not to roll my eyes.

Vik broke into a broad smile. "To impress people we want a second date with, I suppose."

"But our first date was a disaster!"

"I know," he said kindly. "That's why I think we need another one."

AT ELINOR'S REQUEST, we replaced the ceremony with a ceilidh. Standing in two lines along the beach, we watched Matt and Misa link arms and spin each other in a dizzy ring before circling each of us in turn—Vik and Misa an uncoordinated mismatch of height, Tilley trying to hurl Matt across the room, me just wanting to hold all of them at once. We drank sake until we were the only ones left on the beach, Ken patiently showing me how to pour with two hands before tucking a sprig of white jasmine behind Julie's ear. While Matt sat Elinor down to tell her everything, Misa and I watched Ana stuff a crumpled letter into Kei's most formal backpack before they slow danced and made out to "Time After Time."

"At least this wedding was good for something," Misa hollered, clinking my cup. "Kanpai!"

"Kanpai," I replied, stealing a moment to absorb the scene

before downing my drink. "I can't believe we all survived this week."

"That's certainly the right verb for this," said Misa.

I glanced toward the fire pit, where Julie was roasting a stack of marshmallows for Obachan's s'mores. "Somehow I think you'll be okay," I said. "But we're flying out tomorrow and I didn't even get you a non-wedding present yet!"

Misa thought for a moment and gave me a playful nudge. "If you really want to, you can get me the blowtorch off my registry. That feels about right."

"Deal."

Handing the marshmallow skewer to Obachan, Julie caught Misa's eye and made her way toward us. "You're lucky, you know," said Julie gently. "My mother would have reacted very differently had I postponed my wedding. She loves you very much."

Misa nodded, unsure how to respond.

"Sometimes, I see you together and I wonder what I've missed out on, with both of you." She put a hand to her mouth for a moment, then reached into her satin clutch and pulled out Obachan's pearls. "But it's not too late for me to find out."

"You don't have to—" began Misa. She stopped, searching for the right words. "We can wait until next time."

"I think I've waited too long already," said Julie simply. She draped the necklace across Misa's chest with a warm smile. "Even though you didn't get married today, I think you started your new family, and I'm proud of you."

Julie fastened the tiny latch around her daughter's neck, then pulled her into an embrace, patting her hard on the back. Touched, Misa burst into tears for the third time that day, impressive for someone who had made it through the opening of *Up* without cracking once.

"You mean everything to us," murmured Julie into the top of her head. I made an excuse under my breath and slid away from their conversation, happy to see Misa finally enjoying a family vacation.

LATER THAT NIGHT, Matt and Misa sang Supertramp around the roaring bonfire and we threw fistfuls of M&M's in the air to celebrate their new life together. Julie swayed along to the music with her eyes half-closed, and I wondered if she was picturing the song's origins the same way I was, if Misa would one day take her to see the place we'd all come from. After Matt let the final chords of the song ring through, Kei walked over to me with a plate loaded with candy-colored wagashi.

"Take your pick."

I plucked a skewer of dango and took a chewy bite from the top. "Thanks."

"So are you going to disappear on me again as soon as we get back to Toronto?" they asked.

"No," I said through a mouthful of dumpling. "Haven't you heard? I'm turning over a new leaf."

Obachan, having spotted the sky-high pile of sweets, waddled over to us and plopped down next to me on a sea-worn log. She plucked a manju bun from Kei's plate and pulled a napkin out of her sleeve, ready to catch any crumbs.

Kei raised an eyebrow. "Are you just saying that because I'm holding all the dessert? Or are you actually going to let me meet all these dogs you walk?"

"It's a promise," I said, and this time I believed it. I might have missed New Year's by a few months, but my newfound resolution was to put time back into all the people who had supported me through a year of absolute chaos and still wanted more.

"Good," said Kei, "because we're kind of Misa's A-team over here. I mean, it's great that we don't have to talk in code around the Nag anymore, but I think she's going to need us all the same."

I grinned widely. "Count me in."

Kei high-fived me, then Obachan, who even put down her dessert for it. It was good to feel like part of a team again.

A few logs down, Elinor had Misa wrapped in her arms like she had been lost at sea for seven years. "It's not just you and Matt that get a second chance now," she said over the roar of the party. "You've given us more time too."

"I think we have lots to talk about," said Misa warmly, and hugged her back just as hard. "Time is all we need."

As I looked at Elinor's ecstatic face squished against Misa's shoulder, I realized I had never met anyone so thrilled about a wedding being postponed.

"Now, you absolutely *have* to tell me," said Elinor breathlessly, "are you really thinking of eloping? I swear I won't be bothered—I think it's terribly romantic. Have you thought about Scotland? How do you feel about castles?"

Misa swallowed a laugh and tried her best to navigate the hailstorm of questions about her future wedding, while surviving her current one. Like Matt said, it was all about the small steps. I had no doubt she and Elinor would find their footing too.

As the evening was winding down, Matt, Misa, and I took selfies in the vintage photo booth on the beach, our faces glowing with an unadulterated joy that only one short year ago, none of us thought we'd ever have again. My head, leaning into Misa's shoulder. Her hand, gripping mine. Matt's arms around the both of us, holding us together. Our smiles as wide as the shoreline. I wished we could have had a photo of the night we first met. But the way I choose to remember that place, and who I used to be, was something the flashes of a camera couldn't capture. I just had to close my eyes for long enough, and I'd be there.

I DIDN'T GET a chance to talk to Matt again until our suitcases were packed and waiting for Washington's pickup in the lobby. I spotted him saying goodbye to Elinor, who had decided to adopt Goose after finding out she'd have to wait at least another year for the possibility of grandchildren. Once her shuttle had pulled away, I tapped Matt on the shoulder of his floral T-shirt.

"Got a minute?" I asked.

"Of course," he said, as we walked to the half-empty parking lot. "The only thing in my calendar is a reminder that throwing a weeklong wedding greatly reduces your chances of actually making it down the aisle. But you know what? I think it all worked out the way it needed to."

"I'm really happy for you," I said, trying to look right at him but squinting in the sun. "And I'm not pretending anymore. I think you're doing the right thing for you and for Misa."

"I hope so," he said, then paused. "Do you ever wonder how we'll know when we actually get better?"

I sat down on the curb and thought about it. "I used to think I'd never get there because I was bad, but now I think I'll never get there because it's not a real place. It's just the feeling that there's more steps in front of you than you've taken yet. That's all I have room to think about most days."

"Damn, Dee. Hit me right in the gut, why don't you." Matt eased himself onto the curb beside me and clapped me on the back. "So are you going to let me make it up to you? The next year's worth of Frostys are on me."

I let the vibrations of his touch ring through me one last time, then steadied myself. "I think I might need more time," I said, glancing at him.

Matt sighed. "I was worried you might say that. I just don't want to lose you."

"And I don't want to lose you either. That's why I have to set some boundaries." I paused, furrowing my brow. "Wow, I guess I learned one, single helpful thing in therapy."

Matt grinned. "I can get behind that."

"All in the name of future Frosty runs," I said, and meant it.

"Can I leave you with a song for the road?" he asked, a playful glint in his eyes.

I held out my arm. He grabbed it and immediately started drumming a steady rhythm that I just couldn't place.

I frowned and he kept tapping to the beat. "Wait for the call-and-response," he promised. "It's the pride of Scotland."

My eyes lit up. "Are you telling me that '500 Miles' is our new post-hospital anthem?"

"It would seem that I have an awful lot of steps to take in the near future," he said, deadpan. "It couldn't hurt to have a theme song for them."

We both smiled just enough that I knew we'd be all right, maybe not right away, but possibly by the time Misa talked the hospital into throwing us a reunion or something. And who knew what kind of potpies they'd be serving by then—maybe swordfish, maybe Wagyu beef? Maybe I could bring my own, potluck style. Anything's possible for a mentally ill girl with big dreams and a box of frozen pie crust stashed at the back of her freezer.

We almost missed our flight because Tilley was trying on designer sunglasses in the duty-free store. "Is this look giving classic Jackie O. or early 2000s Nicole Richie? Actually, who cares—they're both fabulous," she drawled as I yanked her toward the gate. We'd barely taken our seats on the plane before my sister picked a fight with the woman in the aisle seat beside me, who was knitting with her elbows stuck out aggressively. Tilley made us all get up so she and I could switch spots, then slid the armrest between her and the offending knitter with a pointed look.

"Thanks, Til," I said, nudging her.

"I bet she has like four cabin bags too," muttered Tilley. "I'm gonna run her over with my suitcase on the moving sidewalk."

"I love you, you know that? You're my best friend in the whole world."

"Don't get soft on me, Dee," she said. "Remember that time you cried during a car commercial? Made me respect you less."

"You respect me?"

"This is the kind of shit I'm talking about."

When I got up to use the washroom later, I hailed a flight attendant and used the final wiggle room on my credit card to order Tilley a chilled glass of champagne. Unfortunately, they didn't have any Fanta to go with it.

"What's this for?" she asked, balancing the glass carefully as I slid back into my seat.

"Everything," I said, then paused. "Well, maybe to celebrate a little too."

She took a gulp of the drink. "I'm down. What are we celebrating? The end of your low-ponytail era?"

"I think I'm finally going to sign up for some courses when we get home," I said, ignoring the customary jab. "Maybe learn some legitimate dog-training skills, make my side hustle into a real job, get some sweet business cards printed—"

"Hold up," interrupted Tilley. She placed her champagne glass on her fold-down tray table. "Why are you suddenly in a rush to girl-boss your recovery gig? You went through a heck of a lot this week—don't you want to take a few seconds to recalibrate?"

"But I need to move forward so I don't drag you down," I said.

"Yeah, but you don't have to do it all at once," she replied, lifting an eyebrow at me. "And you don't have to get all your big ideas from emotional breakdowns. What if we both got home and made a single manageable change?"

I swallowed the lump in my throat. "Do you want me to get my own place?"

"I said *manageable*!" she shrieked, then tapped a manicured finger against her lips. "Although I suppose you could start paying some rent. And maybe you could take one course to see if school still makes you shrivel up like a teenage vampire in the light."

"Deal."

Tilley looked down at her half-finished glass of champagne, stuck out her tongue, and pushed it toward me. "Besides, I need you around to make sure I stick to my new change too. So on that note—want to finish this for me?"

"Sure thing," I said, down for whatever her new normal might look like.

Tilley leaned back and closed her eyes like she was meditating. "One nice thing is that now that you've released yourself from the hospital vortex and have more than just me behind you, I think I can be more honest about how I'm doing too."

"I'll always be behind you," I said, finishing her drink and handing it to a passing flight attendant. "Except when it comes to aging."

"Maybe not," she snorted. "I think you've taken at least ten years off my life this week alone. But don't worry, I'll let you make it up to me."

We grinned at each other before I lay back in my seat and dreamt of my last-resort resort. This time, I didn't need Michelin star cooking or rich people sports to convince me to stay tethered to this earth. I had no use for "wellness" separated from the beautiful messiness of my own life. I knew I could find exactly what I needed at home, surrounded by the people I loved. There were options out there for a mad girl with a solid support network. I could put my name down for a new doctor who might listen a little closer. Maybe I could check out the community health center sandwiched between the loan shark and the best jerk chicken place in the east end. I could see myself stopping by between dog walks with Kei and movie marathons with Tilley, on the way home from visiting Obachan's house with Misa. I could even imagine a future Wendy's run or a visit to London if I was feeling brave. The location was less important than the feeling—that I had been lucky to have the love that I did and wouldn't forget it again.

As Tilley turned on a *Real Housewives* rerun, I peered out the tiny window of the plane, taking in the sea of white clouds beneath us. I caught a glimpse of my reflection—hair still slightly curled from last night's celebrations, Tilley's favorite tinted lip balm swiped across my lips and cheeks, a hint of a smile creeping across my sunburnt face even though I was headed back to a life I had once thought was going nowhere. In the hospital, I had been so focused on just getting to tomorrow, over and over again, that I forgot how to imagine what the years to come could stretch into. Sure, there was a long road ahead, but for once that felt almost like a gift—more time to laugh, to cry, to make mistakes (for sure), but also to finally get things right. I wondered if another year from now, the people and places I leaned on would be the same. If anything, maybe I'd be the one to change, to be a better support for those who had held me up for so long—for Tilley, especially, and for myself. Now that was something worth growing for.

ACKNOWLEDGMENTS

Throughout its journey from a lonely hospital room, to a lovably chaotic MFA thesis, to the kind of story that I wish I'd gotten to read ten years ago, this novel has been held with such care by so many people.

The original version of this manuscript emerged with the support of my wonderful cohort at the University of Guelph's MFA program, and the dedicated mentorship of Kyo Maclear, who is everything I hope to be one day as a writer and a teacher. I also owe infinite thanks to Catherine Bush, Michael Winter, Mona Awad, Blake Morrison, Carrianne Leung, Amy Jones, Farzana Doctor, and Greg Rhyno for offering so much kindness and encouragement while I prepared to release my slow and steady book into the publishing world.

Before I was ready to write through my own hospitalization, I was also lucky enough to have a safe space to share my deepest secrets (and worst jokes) at UTSC's undergraduate creative writing program, guided by the incredible Daniel Scott Tysdal and Andrew Westoll. To my whole Scarborough support system—and especially Chelsea La Vecchia, Oubah Osman, Téa Mutonji, and Natasha Ramoutar, who read the original short story in our writing group years ago—thank you for always giving me a place to write home. To Sheryl Stevenson, who told me I would pen a rom-com long before it crossed my mind—thank you for reigniting my love of literature and walking this path with me for so many years.

There is no question that this book wouldn't exist without my team at Bell Canada, who not only supported my decision to work part-time and chase my biggest dream but also helped carve a path for stories like mine through the Bell Let's Talk mental health campaign. To Mary Deacon, Clara Hughes, Michael Landsberg, and the entire community investment and corporate communications teams, past and present, thank you for offering me the space I needed to grow. And a special shout-out to my forever work wife, Miri Makin, whose side commentary truly elevated my manuscript-editing experience.

Of course, *Never Been Better* wouldn't have made it this far without all the amazing people who took a chance on a weird and wonderful story. To my agent, Jackie Kaiser, who kept in touch with me for years after a suicide attempt derailed my first manuscript— I can't believe how lucky I am to have you, Meg Wheeler, and Westwood Creative Artists on my side. I am equally grateful to my HarperCollins Canada superteam of Iris Tupholme, Julia Mc-Dowell, and Mikaela Roasa, who worked so closely (and patiently!) with me to make these characters the best versions of themselves, and artist Zeena Baybayan for designing the original cover. And of course, a huge thanks to my editors Kate Dresser and Tarini Sipahimalani, cover artist Christopher Lin, and the entire Putnam Books team, whose positive energy and keen editorial eye have made me fall in love with this book all over again. To my amazing marketing and publicity teams at HarperCollins (Cindy, Neil, and

Kristina) and Putnam (Emily, Kristen, and Jess), launching a book wouldn't be half as fun without your support.

I also owe a big thank you to my colleagues, classmates, and students at the University of Toronto, who make the writing life far more fun than I could have ever imagined. To my students from Trinity College's BIPOC Writing Circle—it's your turn next! Thank you especially to Sidrah Rana for sharing her immense knowledge of the book world and for supporting *Never Been Better* at such a crucial time. And a huge nod to Abbie, my doctoral supervisor at OISE, for helping me balance teaching, research, and a novel while trying to be a somewhat reasonable person.

It's important to note that I would not be here (but actually) without the medical team that has supported me since my hospitalization in 2013—Dr. Sinyor, Dr. Hershkop, Natalie, and Karen, plus my OG diagnosis team from the Shoniker Clinic in Scarborough. I am lucky to be living a life that I never thought was in reach.

A few personal notes—to Rob, for being my best friend in the worst place. To Brad, for giving me all my best Scarborough stories. To Bing, for the heart-to-hearts, and Rianne, for our post-revision *Bachelor* nights. To Sen, Nico, Joy, Michael, and my Mata Ashita writers, for helping me find the JC community I've always longed for. To Adam, for being a fantastic running mate and reality TV expert. To Meg and Rohan, for sharing the best picnic ever and giving Vik the abs I'll never have. To James, for always checking in. To Oubah again, for the constant laughter. To Gabs and Hails, for being the absolute best bonus sisters.

To Dr. Lauren Dwyer (!!!), who has read this story more times than anyone else on the planet—I don't know how I could ever thank you enough for all the panicked phone calls, blurry snapshots of Microsoft Word, and playlist decisions that have shaped the past few years of our friendship. Near or far, I know that we'll always find a way back to each other. You are always the loudest voice in my head, and for that, I am eternally grateful.

A massive thank you to my family for supporting me through my most difficult years. To my grandparents and Auntie Marianne, who often appear in my work when I need something to hold on to. To Kelly and Maclin, for practicing self-control and not stealing my dog while I finished this book. To Tom and Catherine, for always dropping everything to help me achieve my goals and casually providing the most beautiful writing spaces ever. To Mom and Dad, for arguing over who got to read new chapters first, always keeping cold Fanta in the fridge, and being my safe place for so many important years. I hope this book makes you proud.

And last, but not least, to my husband, Graeme, who has opened up possibilities for a beautiful life that I never could have imagined when I started writing this book. I wake up every morning and feel so lucky to have the kind of love that perseveres through the good days and the bad, to live in a home with a squishy little dog named Gracie who always makes me feel supported, and now, to be so excited to start our next adventure with baby Niko. I love you and can't wait to continue this journey—traffic or not, when we're together, we're always where we're meant to be.

ABOUT THE AUTHOR

Photograph of the author © 2023 Nick Wong

LEANNE TOSHIKO SIMPSON is a mixed-race Yonsei writer who lives with bipolar disorder. Named Scarborough's Emerging Writer in 2016 and nominated for the Journey Prize in 2019, she co-founded a reflective writing program at Canada's largest mental health hospital and teaches at the University of Toronto. Since her hospitalization, Simpson has connected with students, cultural centers, companies, and media outlets about the power of storytelling in shaping recovery. *Never Been Better* is her debut novel.

VISIT LEANNE TOSHIKO SIMPSON ONLINE

LeanneToshikoSimpson.com

LeanneToshiko